BILLY VERITÉ

BILLY VERITÉ

RICK HARSCH

STEERFORTH PRESS
SOUTH ROYALTON, VERMONT

For information about permission to reproduce
selections from this book, write to:
Steerforth Press L.C., P.O. Box 70, South Royalton, Vermont 05068

Library of Congress Cataloging-in-Publication Data
Harsch, Rick, 1959–
Billy Verité / Rich Harsch. — 1st ed.
p.   cm.
ISBN 1-883642-92-2 (alk. paper)
I. Title.
PS3558.A67557B55   1998
813'.54—dc21   98–21800
CIP

The characters in this book are inventions, though it would be a simple
matter to find real people equally impervious to insult.

— R. H.

Maps by Tim Jones

Manufactured in the United States of America

FIRST EDITION

To Tom Kneifl, and to the memory of Robert D. Bott, who during World War II survived a New Guinea shore leave genital disease incident that claimed sixty-five percent casualties, and who that same year was captured while hiding in a gun turret and was forced to box a Diamond Belt Champion from a rival ship, and who triumphed in a fair fight.

CONTENTS

[x]

N
W E
S

La Crosse,
Wisonsin

Mississippi River

Lake Onalaska

Red
Oak
Ridge
Island

French
Island

MINNESOTA

La Crosse

Mississippi River

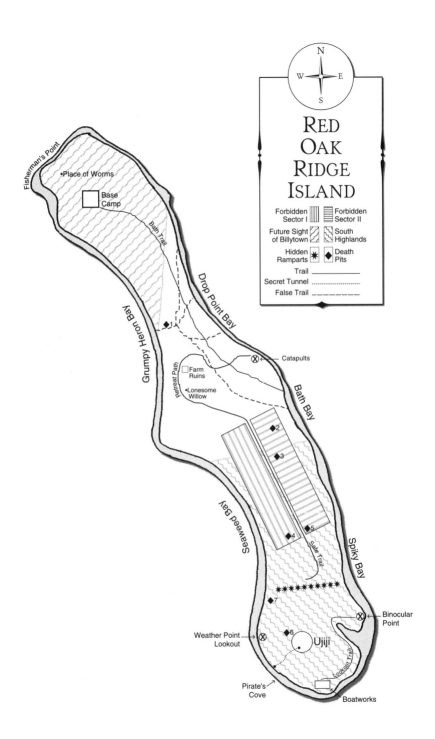

\

LOLA WAS A SLAVE TO HER PASSIONS

"Lola is just a slave to her passions — she's a wild filly, but they can be broken."
Gerard told me that a few weeks before his death — let that serve as foreshadowing: Gerard's a goner — though even now I see nothing of prophecy in his comment. At most his words were a rather sportive link in the same desultory chain that got him killed. Anyway, a conversation in a tavern always resembles a man's final days, especially in a place like the Wonder Bar, a place groomed by years of squalid patronage for bad luck. I left Gerard there for some dubious pursuit of my own, bumping into Lola in the doorway. Before long the anti-Othello of Gerard's demise showed up, and Lola never got to drink her whisky.

Lola was a lousy artist and was proving it on a napkin when Gerard saw the black undercover cop enter the bar. He didn't yet know how fast things were happening. He looked down at the napkin Lola was trying not to shred with the pencil and did not know what he saw: the napkin was torn only at the point where form was most desperate for continuity, where what perhaps could have been a torso disengaged itself from a grotesquely avian profile.

"What is it?" Gerard asked Lola.

"I'll give you a hint," she promised, and then became distracted by her thigh. Gerard looked down, expecting that some kind of bug would be there. As far as he could see there was just the naked thigh. He didn't care about the drawing on the napkin; nor, for that matter, did he care about the thigh — though he liked it; it was big, and what men call luscious — but he wondered how far away his question had gotten, if it had escaped, or would be found clinging like nylon to that thigh they continued gazing at as if it were just another log cruising bland the hysterical river; the two of them, Gerard and Lola, on the banks of a summer's eve, just watching that river, watching that log.

Gerard broke the spell first, lifting his eyes to his beer, then taking a drink. He set the bottle down next to the wet ring it had left on the bar and used the napkin to wipe up the ring. Lola was running a finger under the hem of her skirt, snapping absently at her underpants. Gerard could hear the sound, faint like the slapping of two turbid thoughts against each other.

Gerard squeezed the napkin in his hand; moisture ran out between his fingers. He didn't think the black undercover cop would recognize him — he'd shaved off his beard since his affair with the cop's old lady.

"Huh?" Lola asked.

Gerard tried to place the question. Lola was still looking down at her thigh. Now she had two fingers run up under her skirt, which she had pushed as far as it could horizontally go.

As a mammal, Lola easily fell prey to habit.

Returning to the subject of her drawing, Gerard figured, would be a little like capturing the insect that wasn't on her thigh. He looked across the horseshoe bar at the black undercover cop, who was disguised as a man ordering a beer from a bartender in a dive where nobody had the specific lethargy required to play the jukebox on a sunny afternoon.

"Want to know who the most slimy narc in the city is?" Gerard asked.

"Oh," Lola said, assuming it was she who misplaced the sequence. "Sure." And as if struggling to regain a momentum present like a night breeze beyond closed windows, she lifted her drawing hand, holding the pencil poised over the bartop.

Gerard, a man long used to spending time alone, persisted. "See across the bar? The guy in the hat that says 'Black Velvet,' the black guy?"

Lola was with him now. She focused on the black undercover cop, who transformed himself from the object of Gerard's directive into the man Lola thought she knew him to be.

The pencil snapped. Lola was a big-boned gal.

She hunched her shoulder and nuzzled her snout into her armpit, snarling to Gerard, "Did you say narc?" A revolt in her abdomen recalled innumerable past encounters with the bluster of her own lies.

"He's an undercover cop," Gerard explained, "Llewellyn Torgeson. He likes to bust — "

"Oh my god," Lola interrupted, "I've got to get out of here."

"Why? What — "

"I've been giving him head for two weeks . . . fuck me — he knows everything, I've got to — " and she swiveled away from the bar to eat the rest of her words.

Gerard slapped his hand down on her thigh, right where the bug should have been. The napkin hit the floor and didn't bounce.

"Hold on — you'll attract his attention. I don't know if he's noticed you yet."

Lola held on. Gerard had the thick, strong fingers of a lathe operator.

"He's not paying any attention to you," Gerard barwhispered, and as soon as he said it, realized he had it all wrong. If Torgeson had been under Lola's covers for two weeks, not paying attention to Lola was precisely what he was doing in the bar. That being the case, he would be paying particular not-attention to Lola's associates, the only one present being Gerard. And since cops have good eyes for faces, like those of clean-shaven suspects who once slept with their wives, it was likely he had already "made" Gerard. In fact, he was certain that Torgeson had

[3]

him very much in his mind. The resulting discomfort was entirely a practical matter. He felt no guilt — the affair was brief, honest, and loveless — and he knew anyway that moral considerations were void in times of action and crisis, especially when the jealousy of a crooked cop was involved.

Gerard's hand amorally squeezed Lola's amoral thigh. Torgeson averted his amoral eyes. Some dullard fed the jukebox an amoral coin.

"What do I do?" Lola demanded in suppressed panic.

Gerard had to think fast. If Lola had been attending to Torgeson for two weeks, Torgeson had no intention of arresting her. He was using her to gather evidence against virtually everyone she knew so he could bust them all for petty drug violations. But if she discovered his true occupation the investigation was done for, in which case arresting Lola would be his best option.

"What does he have on you, possession?"

Lola's eyes widened as Gerard's question opened for her new vistas of clarified disaster. "Dealing. He's got me on dealing. I sold him a little coke. It was all I could do to get my hands on it for him."

Sometimes irony is too explicable to be consumed. A desperate woman in a bar, hoping to remain undetected, whispers furtive and frantic enough that the row of slouching indifferent loners glowering into their beers can't help recall moments in their lives when curiosity played a negligible role, just as the jukebox surrenders its slovenly forgettable song that only breaks the muddy silence in the retrospect of the attention this blowsy, if beautiful, brunette has brought down on herself, and the context is lost to the instinctual focus on the woman's outburst and the vague hope that somehow, somewhere quite near, mayhem is in the offing.

At the moment of extremest tension before the point of no return, as the docile familiar yielded before the demands of her new chaos, Lola looked with diffuse beseechment to Gerard, who felt her fear traveling up his arm like blood poisoning and knew it was time to act.

"I think the thing to do is take flight," he said.

2

BILLY VERITÉ IN THE VAN

While Gerard's hand gripped Lola's thigh in the Wonder Bar, Billy Verité was crouched in the back of his Surveillance Van, parked in an alley two-and-a-half blocks away waiting for his Voice Activated Listening Device to reveal the secrets that could conceivably get Detective Stratton, Torgeson's partner, off his back, as well as earn him a McKinley or whoever it was had his face on the thousand dollar bill.

Billy had been at this private detective business for more than a year and this promised to be his most lucrative case: an easy grand if he could find out who the new president of B.A.D. was going to be. Through his deft handling of advanced technological snooping mechanisms he'd already found out it was going to be an outsider, handpicked by Earl Strafe, Vizier Grande of the worldwide organization Guns Over Zion. All he needed now was a name and Stratton would have to pay up.

It probably would have done Billy some good to consider Stratton's motives. Why would anyone pay a thousand dollars for a name? But Billy didn't think past the reels of stale lines he ran through his mind: 'A job's a job' and 'Being a copper's a dirty business' and 'If you want me to do your dirty work it's going to cost you.' Only later would Billy realize his mistake.

Since the demise of Deke Dobson B.A.D. had been in a state of chaos. The rival motorcycle gang, the Outlaws, was threatening to corner the local drug trade. The deviance of the Outlaws was incorruptible and that was bad news for politicos like Strafe, whose interest in hinterland fundraising was implacable, silent and mysterious, and even worse news for a vice cop like Stratton, whose interest was a thing as common as graft. B.A.D. could be bought. The Outlaws were too explosively violent, too wild, too casually antisocial either to acknowledge their place in a larger systemic scheme of things or to actually, as it turned out, coexist with a larger systemic scheme of things. As Darryl Skinner, the Outlaws president, put it to Detective Stratton just before blackening one of Stratton's eyes, "That's why we call ourselves outlaws."

Stratton realized he was left to work with the shambles that remained of B.A.D. "To be the head of a motorcycle gang," Deke Dobson once told him, "you have to be a little bit of a philosopher. Now take me: I'm not the biggest, the strongest, the fastest, the best aim, the loudest, the quietest, maybe not even the best smelling; but I'm the smartest, and beyond that I'm a thinker. There's a difference, meaning I take the time to reflect, philosophize, like all great leaders of the past. I keep diaries, man. By doing all this thinking, all this reflecting, by turning things over and over in my mind, I'm able to understand the implications, long term and short, of my decisions. That's why I'm constantly haunted by the accumulating consequences of every single minute petty goddamn single fucking thing I do. And that's why I'm willing to buy you off to the tune of one grand a month. And that's why I know that it would be worth it to have you killed if you one day decided a grand wasn't enough given the vicissiments of inflationary factors."

Stratton never forgot that lecture. He had it in mind when he dropped in on Oneball, the gargantuan redhead who emerged at the top of the heap as leader of B.A.D. after Dobson was killed, and it helped him put Oneball's response into perspective. "Go scratch your ass," Oneball told him, which indicated to Stratton he hadn't the philosophy to realize how much help a vice cop could be to a criminal operation.

Stratton was not a philosopher either, though. His consequent strategy of biding his time was the result of indecision. Rival motorcycle gangs were engaged in a drug war and neither side wanted his help. His income had dropped a thousand dollars a month and there was nothing he could do about it besides rousting more petty violators of petty laws, taking what money they had and letting them go. So Stratton bided his time until one of his snitches, The Fag With No Eyebrows, came to him with the news of a shipment received by B.A.D. that included camouflage and automatic weapons. To Stratton the news was both good and bad. His old friends appeared to be gaining the upper hand — bikers in camouflage marked an historic shift. Clearly they were under new management and the transition had taken place right under his nose. Had he been more of a philosopher he would have felt that history was passing him by, perhaps become morose and taken refuge in erudite reflection. Instead he felt confused and resentful, and wanted nothing more than to punish annoying people less powerful than himself. Opportunities to do so were frequent, yet none so charmed by Stratton's relish as on the night while driving on West Avenue when he spotted Billy Verité's Surveillance Van parked in the gravel lot of Al's Body Shop, conspicuous between a fractured Volvo and a bedless pickup truck. He turned sharply, bouncing his unmarked yellow sedan into the lot, braking in time to slam the bumper of Billy's van without doing any body damage to either vehicle. Jostled in the belch of premature satisfaction, Stratton imagined Billy leaping from the van skinny and ungainly as a marionette, and he thought, roughly: 'skinny fucker in that goddamn white linen suit, who the fuck does he think he looks like, thinks he's goddamn somebody, some fucking goddamn body,' imagining with striking clarity Billy running up to his car all pissed off, then seeing it's him and suddenly scared, for good reason, because he gets out of his car, knocks Billy down, rubs, no — grinds, his face into the gravel,

thinking precisely: 'for no good reason, that's the good part —
because I can.'

Because he could.

But Billy Verité didn't come out of the van. Billy wasn't in
the van. The realization arrived at the same slow rate as the atrophy of Stratton's meanness, at the same rate of onset as Stratton's fog of pathos. "Goddamnit," he said out loud as he got
out of his car.

"I'll kill that fucker," he mumbled without conviction,
unable to censor the niggling self-regulatory voice that managed with exquisite contempt to say 'as if it's his fault he's not
in the van.'

Stratton reached down to pick up one of the rocks at his feet,
and felt a resurgence of unreasoned anger. That rock could've
been lodged in Billy Verité's face, right under the eye socket,
above the cheekbone, which would actually *be* the eye socket so
that it forced the eye to bulge a little, maybe even pop out, dangle
down his jaw swinging from a strand that looked like drooled
blood, the weight of the eye stretching the strand like gum and
the eye swinging back and forth as it descended all the way to the
ground so that Billy, stumbling forward, inadvertently stomped it
and it burst like a grape.

Stratton threw the rock into some bushes lining the yard
next to the body shop.

The rock nearly hit Billy Verité.

Stratton threw up his arms and whirled streetward. He
watched the traffic on West Avenue awhile.

Stratton was a cop, and he could be standing anywhere he
wanted.

He could chuckle, too, and say "I'll be damned," when he
experienced suddenly what might be considered a "directed
epiphany"; that is, when the world arranged itself in such a way
as to deliver a very personally tailored hint, one that meant
nothing to anyone but Stratton, speaking to his simple need for
a couple of very practical answers, answers readily available to
the innumerable passersby who weren't seeking them, and yet
could so easily have been missed by Stratton had he not in the
first place spotted Billy's van, and stopped in the ugliest of

moods, and then in his confusion over what should follow the maelstrom of ingravid emotion — despair, self-loathing, anger, embarrassment, multifaceted torment, the ennui that follows on the failure to whip the self to rage — he taunted himself with, taken a thoughtless moment to scan vaguely a bleak, low horizon-of-sorts virtually dominated by a billboard that might easily have been erected for his sole benefit.

Lit from underneath by a row of spotlights was the billboard Stratton must have passed a dozen times since it had been there, probably not giving it any thought because the figure of Adolf Hitler was familiar enough already and only becoming more so as one century was sweeping itself under the rug of the next one that didn't have a Hitler yet and apparently would be making do with the old one until it did. And as far as Stratton knew, the bold red L'CHAIM that accompanied Adolf's by now quaint salute may well have been just another way of saying Sieg Heil, even if the translation — TO LIFE — slanted neon greenly just beneath. The slogan, "Guns For Your Life," in less histrionic lettering, meant nothing to Stratton — he always got to carry a gun, what did he care? — nor did the explanation, "Every Totalitarian Movement In History Was Preceded By Gun Control Laws." What cosmologically delivered a meaning of specific interest to Stratton was the encoded message in the lower right-hand corner: "Sponsored by *Bikers Against Drinking and Guns Over Zion.*"

"Detective Stratton," said Billy Verité as he slipped between the Volvo and his Surveillance Van.

Stratton turned to see Billy Verité dressed in a black T-shirt and skintight black jeans pulled up far too high. He forced himself to look Billy in the face so he wouldn't have to exist through the night with the image of Billy's bunched genitalia lumped like a tumor in his mind.

"You look like a fucking beatnik," Stratton said.

"I'm on a night job, see — so I got to dress in black."

"What the fuck do you mean, night work? You spying on some guy just trying to grab a piece on the side? Some poor bastard who gets a little horny and figures banging a waitress on the side doesn't have to jeopardize his marital situation? Figures there's no great harm done cause he's just a normal guy who gets a little bored with his old lady like everybody else, figures what the hell, he treats her okay, never beats her, maybe he can have a good time once in a while without his whole life going down the shitter? You want to fuck up that guy's life for a couple of lousy C-notes? Then maybe pass judgment on top of it? Is that it? You creeping around here at night in your black tights passing judgment? Huh? You passing judgment?"

Billy just stood there wondering what this was all about. As Stratton was winding down he fidgeted, gingerly kicking gravel with his toe.

He answered quietly, with his head down. "No, it's nothing like that. It's an *in*surance job. Guy had an accident, got a bad back. The *in*surance company pays me if I can catch this guy chopping wood or something. They think it might be an *insurance* framus."

"A what?"

"*In*surance framus, a grift."

"Christ . . . Well, what did you find out?"

"Nothing, the guy's just laying on the couch watching the TV."

"You figured he might be out chopping wood. What is it, 10:30? Odd to find somebody on the couch in front of the TV at 10:30. Next thing you know the sneaky bastard'll be going to bed."

"No, that's the thing. He used to be a janitor so he stays up nights. I got to watch him all night, see what he does."

"Right. See if he chops wood. Fuck that. Where's he live? That house?"

Stratton strode into the janitor's yard, swelled with the potency of a man who'd just been spoken to by what would have to pass for God. He could see the rapid shifts of TV light behind a sheer yellow curtain as he passed a window; and he felt a sudden draft of dolor at the thought of a world where people like Billy Verité crouched outside the windows of such shabby little stories. My wife's probably watching the same show, Stratton thought with disgust. He banged with authority on the front door.

"Police," he shouted, "open up."

He heard a feeble, "Come in," as if the guy hadn't heard the part about police.

The couch faced away from the door. A tuft of gray hair poked up from it.

"I'm a police officer," Stratton said. "Get up."

Stratton figured the janitor must've been expecting someone or he'd've said "Huh?" and leaped up holding his back with both hands.

It's tough to read people. The janitor was a short, wiry fellow with a face not unlike Humphrey Bogart's, only he looked like he was either in a lot of pain, or *wanted* to look like he was in a lot of pain. It took him a long time to stand up and turn to face Stratton. When he had, he said, "What is this?"

"This is a routine checkup," Stratton said, looking about for something to toss. On top of a hutch to his right he spotted a pig made of glass or crystal. He sidled over and picked it up.

"This thing valuable?"

Before the janitor could answer the pig was aloft, headed his way. His hands flew from his back, flung in concert by instinct, each arriving beside a hip before coming to a sudden halt as a sound like the shredding of weasels slashed at the speed of light from his back to his ears, a sound only he could hear, unlike his scream and the shattering of the pig that shortly followed.

"You pass," Stratton said, and walked out.

Coming upon Billy Verité sitting on the hood of his yellow sedan, Stratton said, "Get your ass off my car."

"What'd you do?" Billy asked.

"Make your report. The guy's telling the truth. Make your report and meet me tomorrow morning at nine, Joie de Gas parking lot. I got a job for you."

So while Gerard's hand gripped Lola's thigh in the Wonder Bar, Billy Verité was in the back of his Surveillance Van thinking the one thing he didn't figure was how hot it could get when he couldn't run the air conditioner, especially in his white linen suit when he had the jacket on, because you have to look really good even when you're alone because *you* know what you look like even if nobody else does.

But a little suffering is worth it if you can get the goods, and just as Gerard lifted his hand from Lola's thigh, the Voice Activated Listening Device picked up Oneball's voice, speaking into the telephone:

— His name's what?

Here's the payoff, Billy thought.

— Skunk Lane Forhension?

3

SKUNK IN KENTUCKY

"Biliary dyskinesia, that'd be my guess."

"I'll be darned — you a doctor?"

"Now do I look like a doctor to you?"

"No, no, I'd guess I'd have to say you don't."

"That's right, I don't. And if you know your history, what I do look like is Lee Harvey Oswald. Only he looked older than he was and I'm not. That make sense? I mean to say, I look about thirty and I *am* thirty. Skunk Lane Forhension, that's my name. And you? You're a bartender suffering from biliary dyskinesia, and right about now you're wondering what in the fuck I am and what I'm doing in your little bar in your little Kentucky town."

"No," the bartender said, a wry grin suppressing itself near the corners of his mouth as he decided to guess this Skunk fella was just a lonely traveler who couldn't help running like a festering wound at the mouth and was not some kind of troublemaker. "No, I was kind of wondering what you might like to drink."

"All right, that's all right," Skunk Lane Forhension said. "That ain't the entire truth, but I'll have a shot of that clear shit you make at home and most likely keep in a vodka bottle back there somewhere."

"Son, you sure do have a way about you."

The bartender poured Skunk a shot of moonshine out of a Popov bottle.

"Looky there," Skunk said, holding up the shot, "clear as the piss of a swamp country mongoloid."

"How'd you know I got biliary dyskinesia?"

"The way you was holding your hand to your gut as I came through the door. I bet you just ate, too. It likes to act up just after you eat."

"That's a fact."

"That's two facts."

"Huh?"

"Nothing. What you want to ask is where I come from, where I'm going."

"Being as there's nobody else in here, I guess . . . "

The bartender wore a plaid shirt with rough holes where the sleeves had been ripped off at the shoulders. One fat arm crossed over his chest as he belched.

"See that?" Skunk asked. "No relief. One of the signs . . . I'm coming from a little place called Hension, Georgia, and I'm on my way to a job up in a place called Lay Cross, Wisconsin. Lay Cross, that's French."

The bartender leaned on the bar and looked Skunk over, his white T-shirt, his skinny arms, trying to figure out what kind of job it might be.

"What sort of — ?"

"Don't you got a name?"

The bartender straightened, reaching absently for a bar rag.

"Sure," he said, "Ken."

"Ken. What sort of job? Well, it's more in the nature of establishing a presence, if you know what I mean, which you don't. They got a situation up there, Ken, a situation . . . "

"What sort of — "

"Look at the way that dust hangs in the sunlight, Ken. You think dust is especially attracted to sunlight? I don't. Shit's everywhere and we're breathing it in, right now, you and me."

Ken didn't know what to say.

"Feels better, don't it?"

Ken looked down at his gut and nodded.

"Starting to."

"That's the way with biliary dyskinesia. Feels better and better till you eat again. Only thing you got to watch is anxiety, stress. Stress'll set it off between meals. You married, Ken?"

"Yep."

"That'll make it act up."

"What's that?"

"That little kitten you keep at home."

"Maybe you ought to stick to your own story, friend."

"My job?"

"Fine."

Skunk smiled to himself and reached for his shot glass. He threw the whole shot of moonshine down his throat and let out a hiss through his pursed lips.

"They got this situation up there, Ken, like a lot of situations I seen more and more lately where things get stretched and stretched, further and further, and you might want to try and get there and say hold on before it breaks, but there's just no use, it's all gone broke and snapped and nothing to take its place. See, you take this pig and — no, you take a . . . stack of envelopes and you put a rubber band around it and it can't but barely get around them envelopes and then it breaks and you got no way to keep that stack together, and that's a piss-poor example, and you and I both know it, but we both know that's the way it is, too, Ken, don't we? Things bust and don't hold and they get all over the place, and it works the same in law and order and business, which you and me, we know to be the same thing. It gets stretched and stretched, that's the situation they got up there in Lay Cross — got French written all over it, don't it, Ken, Moulin Rouge, the fairy from Paree; you come see me there — anyways it's getting stretched and it'll break and I'm on my way, and when it breaks I'm there and I come sliding up all primal through the cracks, if you see my imagery there, Kenneth — what comes up primal through the cracks . . . that's me."

Ken lifted the shot glass and wiped the bar under it.

"Know what I mean, Ken?"

Ken didn't. He shook his head.

"I'll tell you, then. I had this place down in Algiers. Know where that is?"

"No."

"Cross the river from New Orleans. I had this place above a tavern there no nicer than this shithole of yours — you wince a little there, Ken? See, that's what I mean about stress, anxiety. Can't let the little insults bother you. You want, I'll apologize, but then that would offer credence to the notion you got something to be upset about, which may as well be a telegram to your liver saying it's okay to act up at each and every little emotional upset. So we'll skip the apology, Ken, and get on with the story, since you asked. I lived above this bar facing the alley out back, and every night these two big old cats meet back there, right behind the bar, and tear into each other, rip each other a new asshole every night, every night, same time. This goes on a few weeks, it gets so I'm waiting up there for them, see, and they don't miss a single night. Fight to a draw and turn back the way they come. Finally one night one of them shows up and the other don't. I don't know, maybe he finally crawled off and died from his wounds — both these cats was scarred up good — but maybe he took one look at himself in the mirror and figured it weren't worth it no more; I don't know . . . my guess: he's dead. Nothing else would've kept him from that other cat, from that nightly fight. Well now that other cat shows up and waits around awhile, and he prances back and forth awhile, and he struts, and he's waiting, feeling pretty big, I guess, and after maybe an hour or so he starts up this mewling, I mean serious mewling, Ken, and he paces back there, and he gets to howling a little bit — howling now — and he's getting angry, he's getting angrier and angrier — he wants to fight, he's *got* to fight, and now there ain't no one to fight — I'll tell you one thing, I knew I wasn't going down there in that alley — so he's got to fight and there ain't no one and he starts acting crazy — I'm up there leaning out the window like every night and he pays me but no attention, he's going crazy, he wants that other cat to come back, and he's getting crazy from it, starts leaping up and throwing himself against the back of the tavern claws out and everything and to tell you the truth the first time it was kind of funny cause he jumped at the wall with his claws out and he kind of stuck there for a minute before he disengaged himself and really went berserk on it, I mean screaming — screaming now — crazy, throwing himself at that wall and tearing at it, fighting that wall, and screaming, leaping up, then backing off, running hard at that wall, smashing his furry little head into that wall again and again, ramming his head again and again on that wall until finally one time he backs off kind of stumbling and falls over on his side dead. Plain dead. They threw him out in the morning, Ken. Garbage can. And this is where a guy like me pays attention. I'm up there next night same time waiting to see what happens, and sure enough right at fight time long comes this skunk. He sniffs around kind of waddling like they do, never even stops, and he lets this stink mist out his ass and keeps on walking. Two months later when I left, place still smelled like skunk."

"Nother?"

"Huh? Oh, shine? I don't think I'm getting through to you, Ken. Well there's more than one way . . . One more . . ."

Ken wished he hadn't asked. Skunk noticed his wince as he reached down for the Popov bottle.

"Ready for me to leave, Ken?"

Ken poured the shot.

"I got things to wipe down," Ken said, and started walking toward the other end of the bar.

"No you don't."

"You needn't act contrary, son."

" 'Son,' " Skunk repeated. "No, I needn't, Ken, but you got to be stronger — I mean emotionally. Everytime you upset that little sphincter by your liver — that's right, we all got more than one — that little liver asshole tightens and you get pain. Anyway, that's about how it works."

"I got nothing more to say," Ken said, and turned again.

"That just ain't true, Ken. You got lots to say, but you're scared of me now. Alls I got to do is open my mouth and I can bring you pain, just some asshole off the street, some stranger, maybe a psychopath who just happens to pull into your little town early one sunny summer afternoon — makes you feel a little unsafe, don't it, Ken? Gets to you. And if I was to mention your little kitten alone at home, maybe — "

Struggling to cover the pain, Ken said, "That's enough out of you. You go on your way now. Right now."

"You're hiding it, Ken. It's starting to hurt like a mother-fucker."

Ken dropped the charade, holding his belly with one hand, reaching under the bartop for a baseball bat with the other. He lived in the kind of town where a bartender in his own tavern could club a stranger to a sack of pulp and later be absolved by officials. But Skunk Lane Forhension remained at his stool.

"One swing you can knock me cold, Ken, one swing, but you ain't got one swing in you cause I'm thinking here about your little kitten and how you got to be wondering by now if maybe I got her tied up and gagged in the kitchen and you thinking about me thinking about what she'll be thinking when it's me instead of you and that kind of thinking is too much, too much stress for a biliary case such as yourself . . . "

Ken struggled to rally the anger that would have raised the bat over his head but instead began to yield to the pain that made him want to lay his forehead on the floor. The blood rushing to his head pushed the veins at his temples out like guinea worms and his eyes bulged fishlike with hatred, involuntarily entranced by the calm smirk on the face of the man who really did look a lot like Lee Harvey Oswald, and suddenly he dropped the bat, stumbled backward and doubled up, his arms crossed over his belly, and looked up at Skunk Lane Forhension to say with pain-suppressed fury and a dull wonder, "You're evil."

4

THE TWO FACES OF SANDY CALDERON

You can discover a lot about a civilization by paying attention to where its more determined adherents hole up. I look around my quarters and wonder how soon this will again be considered luxury: this food, this shelter, this . . . electricity. If I were writing a letter to a friend I'd just say: Gerard died, I've taken over his place.

I remember the day Gerard gave me the key. "In case I die up here," he said; "I want someone to find me before too long." To you, Gerard, I say: It would've been a better way to die; I'm sorry, but thanks for the little home and all the little things in it. I didn't have much because I was always leaving and coming back, a very uncertain nomad, too timid a migrant. One time I gave you all my Indian tapes before I left. You gave me two hundred dollars. "So I don't come back, right," I said, and before long I did come back, to find you living here. After a while you died and I had the key.

Much of my old music is unfamiliar here in your office. The sarangi winds like smoke in a bottle up these surreal stairs crammed with boxes of atomic biscuits, but then the stairs disappear into the ceiling; the tabla sends the tune back down the stairs, which only disappear again. You told me this was a stairwell before it was converted into a maintenance closet, but you never told me why, and now at least I'll always have something to think about. Since the stairs no longer invite the landing down to the floor, I use your rachitic stepladder and I call the landing a *loft* — there's room enough for a dwarf to lie once one way and twice the other, just enough room for me, since I couldn't bear to take over your bed.

Sandy Calderon nearly joined you on the other side last night, Gerard. I'm guessing you didn't know that. See, I've been thinking a lot about ghosts lately. Walking around this office building late at night — God knows, the last place anyone would come looking for me, up here, on the fourth floor, remembering those nights the city was drinking itself to sleep and we had to open the bathroom window on a downtown sunk in the color of absinthe if we wanted to hear the sirens mocking the toy accidents, or watch couples fighting their way up Main Street, the byzantine sewer systems of their paranoia always climbing out of the manhole in front of the liquor store near Fifth Street, they had to get the fight over with before they crossed Seventh or they'd risk expiring in separate canyons of hunkering dawn; we'd watch the woman turn north on Sixth, an old ruse that usually worked, leaving the man to flap his entreating arms or hunch his abject shoulders, looking from a block away and four stories up like a bird of reluctant and gangly flight, an albatross in the oil slick of meek choice; and if he followed her they'd soon wind up groping away their irresolution in the doorway of the Triangle Diner, and if he didn't, she'd reappear on the stoop of the Cathedral calling weakly up to where his toes were pawing Seventh Street as if mistrustful of the tepidity of its indifference; we'd limit ourselves to one such happy ending per night, and then you'd take to wambling the terrazzo floors playing your viola loud enough to drown out the insults my fingers extracted from my Durango guitar, which I bought, I admit, because of the name, not really to play it — I still can't, of course — and not so I could wander this rectangular hallway still wondering if the sound you sent down toward the lawyers' office — a melody that bent three times and returned to your viola — was an echo or not, and not so I could long for your approximation of Piazolla's "Regreso al Amor" or Ravel's something for a dead infant. I'm not afraid of ghosts, Gerard, but I can't summon the delusion I fear is necessary to deliver yours. So I don't believe in ghosts, Gerard, and I guess the other side is only that, and you'll send no emissaries here.

About Sandy Calderon, then: I wash up at night when nobody's here, usually around three, just like you used to do. I sleep until noon, wake up, put on my linen pants, permanent-press shirt, sometimes even a tie, and those Florsheim's nobody laughed at when Sonny Corleone kicked the shit out of Carlo, and I splash water on my face, wet my hair, which I keep short and neat, and then it's safe to emerge to take a leak — if anyone sees me I'm just a guy who stepped out of his office to take a leak — which is what I did today. Remember that old guy who worked in the Alzheimer's office? He never looked the same way twice, but it was always him, and he was the only one who saw me today. I took care to say good *afternoon*, and breezed past him like a man coming out of his own office would. I took the stairs down because the elevator still gets stuck once in a while, and I had just reached that polished wainscoting between the second and first floors when I ran straight into the last of the Spleen boys coming up.

First thing he said was, "Did you hear about Sandy Calderon?"

"No," I said, "I just got up."

He looked confused, but let it pass.

"She tried to kill herself last night," he said. "She jumped out of an apartment above the Log Cabin and landed flat on her face, really fucked it up. Fractured her skull right in half, broke her nose, I mean smashed it over to the side, broke her jaw, most of her teeth . . . the doctor said it was as bad as a skull fracture could be without killing her. They'll have to put plates in, she's got all kinds of stitches . . . "

"Jesus," was all I could think to say.

"She was drinking again, had a fight with her boyfriend —
it was his apartment."

"They're sure it was suicide?"

"Attempted. Yeah, they found a note."

"Jesus," I said again, and he started up the steps, stopped,
and said, "She probably won't see anybody for a while."

But I see *her*, Gerard. I can't help picturing her face, the way
it is now. I haven't actually seen her and still I can't get it out of
my mind.

There's my ghost.

I'm fighting the tendency — which I'm beginning to think
of as a more saccharine form of paranoia — to turn my own experience into a universal, yet the notion that who we're really
haunted by is the living suits my mood, especially in public.
And what a turnabout if death can be considered the moment
it's no longer possible to haunt anybody. I will myself to be
haunted by you playing your viola and all I see is the destroyed
face of the once-beautiful Sandy Calderon.

5

HIDING LOLA IN THE VAN

Releasing Lola's thigh, Gerard whispered his plan in her ear, punctuating it with a kiss on her cheek and a smile, hoping to scramble Torgeson's instincts. They both stood and did their best to amble toward the door, which was about nine stools down from Torgeson.

As he opened the door for Lola, Gerard said loudly, "Wait here, I'll go get my truck."

Lola eased out, and when she had stepped clear of the door-window she kicked off her heels, crouched low, and ran like the genuine dickens to the far end of the block, turned right on Mississippi Street, and met up with Gerard who led her into an alley while he looked back over his shoulder for Torgeson who he hoped would be standing outside the Wonder Bar at that point, donning his sunglasses in an elaborate display of false calm, scanning the street for Gerard's truck, which was parked with ad hoc surreptitiousness in a parking ramp downtown, a mile away.

They were about halfway down the alley when Gerard spoke the two words that would haunt him absurdly through the coming night of bad sleep, cheap beer, and paranoia unforestalled.

"What luck," he said when he saw Billy Verité's Surveillance Van shoved into a mini parking lot off the alley. He turned to look one last time for Torgeson, didn't see him, and ushered Lola and her bleeding feet to the van.

"In here," he said, jerking open the back doors.

Billy Verité, kneeling in his sweat-sodden white linen suit, wires coming out of his ears, looked up and with unbidden alacrity made the unconscious decision not to be outraged at the intrusion, nor frightened that he had been caught; instead to be delighted that he had someone to share his breakthrough with.

"You wouldn't believe what I just heard," he blurted.

Then he noticed Gerard's preoccupied face, the face of a man of action; then Lola's off-white underwear between her yawning thighs; finally Lola's bleeding feet as she cradled them.

Billy Verité couldn't help being a mammal. He forgot Lola's feet and stared at the explosion of trapped black hair only partially by underwear contained. An enormous bubble grew inside his skull, swelling from the pressure of a bewildered rapture that though inexpressible if voiced would sound something like, "Gawd."

Something remarkable was bound to happen and it did. As Billy became aware of the way anticipating doom seemed to attenuate time — a literal impossibility — the phrase 'slow onset of gangrene' streamed through his mind behind a tiny airplane, the kind that seem so flimsy yet never crash, and before he could wonder why, Lola barked out, "Somebody do something before I get gangrene."

The coincidence was spoiled by Gerard, who had a tendency towards literalness. He turned from the curtained side-window and explained to Lola, "You won't get gangrene. You have to be infected first and your cuts are still too fresh. The blood's still flowing, cleaning the area. You aren't even at risk of getting infected yet."

The sequence seemed to clear a small area within which the three of them could operate as if they shared a common understanding with existence. Lola pulled her skirt down, allowing

Billy Verité to view the interruption of his snooping from a different angle; and Gerard tended to the mundane matters of explaining how things stood to Billy and figuring a way to get Lola's feet washed.

"They aren't that bad," Gerard said, returning her heel to the carpet that covered every unwindowed inch inside Billy's van, ceiling and all. "Just a little scraped. You won't even feel it tomorrow."

"Well it hurts like hell," she said with a declension of petulance like a dog's return to its natural whimper.

Billy sat on a padded bench looking down at his linen vest, which had the last button undone so you could see some of his blonde subnavel hair snake rakishly out to curl past his shirt, naturally roughed out of his pants looking fine the way they spilled over the linen pants that even as he sat reached to his black Italian Florsheims, shined daily. He looked at all this, looked it all over like a man who owned a horizon, and thought that way 'this is all mine,' and he decided to be direct about matters, Billy Verité, Private Eye.

"So how long's this for and what's the pay?"

"Shut up, Billy," Lola said.

Gerard ignored him.

"We'll go up to Spleen's house, up on the ridge," Gerard told Lola. "You can wash your feet up there and maybe borrow a pair of his wife's socks and shoes."

Billy Verité was demoralized.

"You want me to take you up there now?" he asked Gerard.

"No, we'll wait a little longer."

But something occurred to Lola —

"He'll probably keep my shoes for a trophy," she said. "I kicked them off right outside the bar."

— and it forced Gerard to re-imagine Torgeson's behavior as he left the bar. He would've seen the shoes before donning his sunglasses. He wouldn't be looking for Gerard's truck; he'd be looking for Lola, probably near where they were now. If he saw Billy's van, he'd at least come up to ask Billy if he'd seen a barefoot woman run by.

"Let's go now, Billy, right away."

6

LOLA WAS DEMORALIZED

Lola was demoralized.

Billy said the light had to be on so he could catch up on his paperwork. He had transcripts to type, he said. He had a report to write. Lola had nothing to do, and with the light on she couldn't help looking at Billy's face. Lola had seen photographs of burn victims less ugly. His mouth was the worst part, like a horse with its lips perpetually pulled back. And his face was so narrow it would be eclipsed by its own shadow, if it could cast one. The skin was as tight as if it had a nylon stocking pulled over it.

Lola wished she were wearing nylons.

And this was just the first night. Gerard said it could be awhile. That's all he'd say: awhile. Billy said she could stay as long as she wanted, which no doubt meant as long as he could spend all day looking up her skirt.

Too bad it wasn't Gerard.

"Why can't *you* stay with me?" she had asked him.

"It's Billy's van, Lola," Gerard had said.

It was a good thing circumstances had their own force, Lola figured, otherwise they would be unbearable. One day you're in love with a handsome black man with an athletic build and a line of bedroom patter as entertaining as it is transparent, the next day your memories are all you have — and the naked guy you see in there is a cop. So you're stuck with the ugliest son of a bitch in the city staring at your pussy and the only lucky part is that you have absolutely no choice. Life shifts like there was an earthquake and you're tossed someplace else, that's all.

"A cop," Lola said, shifting her torso angrily and stretching her legs. She was leaning against the rear doors.

Billy looked up from his desk at the other end of the van. The desk was actually a two-by-two plank hinged so he could latch it to the wall when he wanted it out of his way. Usually he pulled his folding chair up to it facing the front, but with Lola back there in that little skirt it made more sense to squeeze in on the other side.

"Huh?" he said.

"Huh?" she mimicked, so someone would know how nasty she felt.

She probably didn't understand what it meant that he was a professional observer, Billy thought. Certainly, for instance, he was looking at her legs every chance he got, they both knew that, the same way they both knew he was dying to get a peek at her very large and lowslung breasts, still slumbering innocuous inside her black T-shirt; but he was doing more than ogling Lola — he was *thinking* about her, and thinking, according to the Billy Verité private eye scheme of things, is the better part of observation.

So Billy knew Lola was unhappy.

But he didn't know how unhappy: twenty-eight years old and a sexy broad and there she was slumped/heaped/dumped at the back of Billy Verité's van, and bored, goddamn bored bored fucking bored. She wanted to throw a foot tantrum, do a rhumba on the carpet with her heels.

"How long do we have to wait here?" she asked.

"Until Detective Stratton gets here, so I can get my money."

Lola shoved her hands up her scalp and drew her hair like a curtain over her face.

Lola blew a part in her hair.

"I'm going to sleep," she said. "Think you can keep your hands off me?"

Billy had the wisdom to let Lola's anger run its course. A lot of guys would find it necessary to protect their manhood by sniping back at her, or they'd try to draw her out, pester her. Not Billy.

"I won't touch you," he said. "You can sleep down there on the sleeping bag — I'll sleep on the bench."

1

WHAT LUCK

Meanwhile, Gerard was quivering his viola up on the fourth floor of the Winchester on Fifth building downtown, growing increasingly frustrated at the intrusion of the phrase 'What luck' into his rendition of "Gypsy Aire," giving up now and then in order to swaddle a forty-ounce bottle of Old Style, hoping an abundance of nipping would throw off his timing enough that the insidious words could not gain access to the tune and hence his head on the principle of the revolving door at high speed or maybe interlocking gears gone awry; but What and Luck were proving themselves a suave and versatile dance pair, so Gerard was forced to reckon with himself as a man capable of uttering a cartoon phrase in a time of crisis. He quit and he drank and he thought and he thought and he found himself staring at the boxes of biscuits. "What luck," he said. There were twenty-five boxes of Civil Defense Ration Biscuits in his office/stairwell/maintenance closet/home that had been in the building, once a nuclear fallout shelter, a sanctuary from which to witness the end of the world, since 1962. Each box contained two tins, each of which claimed to contain precisely 1602 biscuits. The boxes weighed thirty-six pounds. Gerard could think of nothing so difficult as surviving a nuclear attack — and here was the reward: enough biscuits to last . . . about 1602 days if he could limit himself to fifty per day, which would be about four years and five months, or enough time that he could at least hope for a cure, so he figured his chances were pretty good and he started up "La Cumparsita," accommodating the words "Six-teen hun-dred and-two bis-cuits-per-tin that-should-last four-years-five-months . . . before-I-die," playing the opening bars repeatedly until he realized how moronic an exercise he was engaged in, and realized anyway that a notoriously rogue cop whose babe he'd once stolen, and who now had him to blame for fouling an ongoing investigation, was without a doubt gunning for him. And if that eventuality was insignificant beside such a ghoulish escapade as a nuclear war, it had as one of its attributes an unwavering focus on Gerard that rendered it rather less appealing. Fuck the biscuits, Gerard thought. If he survived Torgeson's onslaught he'd buy himself a steak.

And then he thought of Lola.

Lola, Gerard thought.

How you drive a man to drink.

Forty more ounces, what do you get.

You don't get Lola.

Those big thighs, those big thighs of Lola.

Lola surely enjoyed having Gerard's hand on her thigh. And Gerard liked having it there.

But where was Lola now?

Was she in that little refrigerator?

No.

But another forty ounces of Old Style were (was?), and Gerard enjoyed his despair at finally succumbing to the forces he had on hire to get him there. His life was not in a shambles. (Not yet.) (What luck.) But he wanted a woman pretty bad and Lola was just the kind of woman to cause a fairly handsome man to wonder why he never seemed to take her to bed when he had the chance. There was always someone better, but sooner or later you were alone and thinking of Lola.

Lola could be had, that was her special quality.

Gerard checked his watch. It was 11:30 P.M. Lola was probably asleep in the back of Billy Verité's van, hiding from Torgeson.

What luck.

Gerard guzzled beer. Torgeson would be looking for *him*, too. And when he found him he'd say 'you stood in my path once too often.'

Gerard guzzled more beer.

Torgeson would come gunning for him. Torgeson was out there now, prowling the city, a rogue cop with a score to settle. Gerard set the beer bottle on the floor and retreated toward the doorway, surveying his furtive empire. He lacked nothing. He had drinking water in plastic jugs, a mat to sleep on, several years worth of biscuits, a viola, hundreds of books in cases, a melange of electronic devices, exotic tapestries, a mound of coins on a shelf that probably added up to twenty dollars or more, several pairs of shoes, plenty of clean underwear, socks, shirts, pants, a light jacket, a heavy jacket, three sweaters, a couple hundred cassette tapes, nine cans of sardines (from northern seas) in oil with tabasco peppers (from humid lands), enough crackers to outlast the sardines, and maybe a few more things, like a director's chair and a desk and a few lamps, tools, but nothing more notable than that little refrigerator with one more forty-ounce bottle in it that Torgeson didn't know was in there like he didn't know Gerard was up there (here?) — what luck! — backing out of his doorway fully secure in the knowledge that no one stood behind him with a sap, backing clear into the hallway, turning around and letting loose a maniacal howl of hyenal laughter and repeated shouts of fugitive defiance, "I'm all alone!" and more maniacal cackling as he ran around the hallway kicking up his feet, "They'll never find me here!" laughing like an electrified homunculus, his graying hair wild, his eyes watery with unblinking delight, running the halls, a satyrine lust for freedom and action burning on the alcohol in his blood; Gerard, dancing and running with a Zorbic lust to draw ecstasy from petty adversity, retreated to his quarters, removed the last bottle from the refrigerator, drank a good ten ounces at once, letting a tithe irrigate his beard, then inserted a cassette of gypsy music, lifted his viola to play to the tape, saw in his mind the flames of a gypsy campfire, heard the wails of gypsy women and made his viola return their wails, rent their cries with cries of his own, sent muskwaves to the gypsy women from his strings at frequencies inaccessible to the society of civilized women, a mating call to a better life, a life of undulations unsullied by modest calculation, a life of defiant transgression, movement without end or purpose, of hair-raising tenacities unencumbered by the proscriptions of intent, a life of heaving generosity and brazen gestures uninvited, life with an excess of hair and a fricassee of smells risen from the natural spoilage of the earth and the worst that man has made of it, rising free and swirling in the malignancy of recuperation that precedes revenge, a life of comets and other flames and subterranean wails echoing the strains of a viola that calls to the night's estrous dancers to come to him as they did come to him, Gerard, a drunken man, in pairs, or a pair, tapping softly at his chamber door, their eyes dark and smoldering behind a mocking timidity, hair black and wild, strands slapped and stuck by sweat against dark foreheads, breasts draped in golden bells sewn into wisps of felt-bordered cloth, long sloping midriffs down to sheer peach-colored Arabian pantaloons and more bells, bells everywhere, bells on their ankles, wrists, in their hands, and a string of bells slung let's just say below the navel, their navels little dark sockets swinging with the hips, two navels, not in concert, at Gerard's eye level, for when they arrived he sat in his doorway mystified by the conjurence he had faithlessly achieved — for they truly stood there before him, they really did, two beautiful bare-bellied brunettes.

Gerard did not look toward the bottle of beer; he knew these were not genies formed of alcoholic ethers. They were really there. He could touch them.

"We heard the music," one said.

"We were in the bathroom on the third floor," the other said.

"We're belly dancers."

"She's Carla. I'm Bonnie."

What luck.

[32]

"We heard the music," Carla repeated.

No, Gerard did not cast a comic double-take style look at the bottle, but he did remain seated in the doorway dumbfounded.

The women were beginning to realize that even though Gerard held the bow in one hand and the viola in the other, the twain not meeting, they could still hear the music.

"Oh, it's a tape!" Bonnie exclaimed.

"I was playing with it," Gerard said, and thus they knew he could speak.

"Oh, you were playing along with it," Carla said.

"Yes, I was playing along with it."

That much clarified, Gerard had a sudden and brief vision of orange monkeys scuttling up the reinforcement rod that ran along the stairs, disappearing with them into the ceiling. He knew the vision was related in some way to the sort visited upon problem drinkers in varying degrees of majesty by delirium tremens because he wasn't looking that direction. He was looking at the eyeballs embedded in the glorious midriffs in his doorway. His mind was beginning to split according to irreconcilable directives; one being, naturally, to invite these odalisques in, submitting entirely to whatever entrancement was descending veil-like on his midnight; the other, to preserve the inviolability of his furtive lifestyle by preventing the women from discovering that these musical chambers served as well and illegally as his home. And he quietly acknowledged the cruel capacity of consciousness to arrange itself in layers,

THE ORANGE MENACE OF NIGHT

embellishing his regret even as he decided that the lovely gypsies must go.

Gerard stood with the deliberation of the unsober and advanced with an air of intemperance toward the doorway. The gypsy women retreated a step.

"We practice belly dancing in the basement," Carla said.

"We heard your music," Bonnie said.

"We use the third floor bathroom," Carla said.

"It's cleaner," said Bonnie.

"I have to practice now," Gerard said, pushing at them with what was palpable in his bearing; "I'll come watch some day."

"Come watch us," Carla said.

"Every Thursday," said Bonnie.

And they all said goodnight as if a sublime mood had not been ushered off by the exigencies of the dumbest of momentums.

To perpetuate the ruse, Gerard tucked his viola in and went out into the night, vaguely certain that the thing to do was walk until sober or find a tavern where he could get more drunk. A debatably finer instinct sent him shuffling down the alley that ran beside his building, away from the cluster of bars. Halfway down the alley, abreast of the third blue dumpster, he sensed or heard — he couldn't tell — a presence behind him, and he turned.

It was an odd moment. The turn was too abrupt for his inebriate gyroscope and he swung wide, reeled sideways, and came steady with his elbows up so that he looked like a raptor just at the instant of narrowly missing its prey. He lifted his head before correcting his position, since he had yet to come to a point where he could again lend trust to his balance, and what he saw was an orange balloon faffling along the ground toward him.

The alley opened onto a parking lot that struck Gerard in his state as overtly confrontational, an invitation to some sort of disaster that would involve humiliation. He turned right and walked along keeping the rear of his building within arm's reach. By the time he reached Jay Street the orange balloon was gaining on him.

He picked up the pace.

At the next corner, he saw that the fountain behind the bank had been sprinkled with Mr. Bubble again. Immaculately white bubbles, perhaps millions of them, none actually white, spilled over the fountain's round cement wall and headed for the unsuspecting institute of finance. To Gerard, the bubbles were no better than the orange balloon and no worse.

At Fifth Street, Gerard turned right, back in the direction of his office. This time the balloon was slow in following and he had time to gauge the weather conditions. The night was balmy, he decided. Balmy.

He had walked a full block when the balloon finally turned onto Fifth behind him. He was only a half block from the entrance to his building, but the unformulated thought that it would be better if the balloon didn't know where he lived compelled him away from it, down Jay to Fourth Street, where the taverns tended mostly to be.

At the corner of Fourth and Jay, Gerard saw a bald man wearing an orange beanie angling across the street, straight toward him. He turned and saw the orange balloon turn on to

Jay, still following. When he turned back, the man was upon him. Now Gerard could tell that the beanie was the man's head, shaven and painted orange on top. He had large arms that loped hairless about his sides.

"Where's the gay bar around here?" he asked Gerard.

Gerard pointed up Jay — the orange balloon was skimming the sidewalk, heading his way.

"Go up there," he said. "Turn left and it's a block and a half down."

The man with the orange head grunted and moved off, but before Gerard could cross Fourth Street he stopped to declare, "Don't look at me like that — I'm not a fag."

I wasn't looking at him, Gerard thought, and he didn't stay to watch the meeting of the orange balloon and the man with the orange head. Instead he walked all the way down to the river, taking a sort of zigzag route hoping to mystify the balloon.

He walked back and forth along the river, pausing occasionally to scan the night-black grounds of the park for furtive movements. The orange balloon could've been anywhere, but he didn't see it. After a while he gained confidence and took to watching the lights from the park on the opposite shore shatter on the water until they disappeared. The wafting din from the closing taverns consoled him — those people were several blocks away and they were going home now, away from the river.

Perhaps an hour had gone by when Gerard figured it was safe to walk home. The orange balloon hadn't turned up — probably the guy with the orange head had popped it — but now he was sober enough to remember Torgeson was after him and it wasn't a good idea to go wandering about aimlessly.

"What luck," he said aloud, and then he saw coming at him the man with the orange head.

"What luck," he said again.

They met at the intersection of Fourth and Main.

"I couldn't find it," he told Gerard, who kept walking, issuing only a dopplered "What . . ."

The man with the orange head turned to follow Gerard.

"Let's go together," he called from behind.

"I'm not interested," Gerard said, finding it unnecessary to explain that the bar would be closed anyway.

"I haven't forgotten where my car is," the orange head responded, in case Gerard didn't yet know he was a lunatic.

Gerard kept walking, listening to the footsteps quicken behind him.

"I know you want me," the lunatic called predictably, and as if tired of having to enact the same old ritual.

"You're crazy," Gerard told him over the shoulder without stopping.

"I'm not crazy. You're the one that's crazy — You're lucky if I don't kill you . . . "

Gerard kept his pace steady, bracing for the assault by mentally drawing a path that his elbow would follow through the air and into the goon's stomach. He would turn and follow with a short downward right cross.

But the orange man slowed a little and Gerard took evasive action. He turned behind the shoe store that shared an alley with Winchester on Fifth, took the alley back to Fifth, and scurried into his building before the orange head was out of the alley.

In the elevator Gerard recalled a conversation we'd once had about the Mississippi. I told him if he was going to spend his whole life here it made no sense to live anywhere but right on the river. No, he said, the place to be is up on the ridge, back of the bluffs. The river, he told me, is a sewer — that's what rivers are, sewers, collecting all the shit washed from up on the ridges and on down. But I said no, that's not the point, Tom, the river, this Mississippi River, is the only thing that gives this place meaning, real autochthonous meaning, what happened with the glaciers is way in the past, what we have now is the river . . .

So as he got off the elevator, Gerard was wishing I was around so he could tell me what had collected down below the bluffs in the sewer valley. You didn't find any orange-headed lunatics up on the ridge where the wind blows clean and the rain washes all manner of filth down and away. And so, full of himself, he sent a stream of entirely too-clear urine against the urinal in the bathroom outside his office, a happy man with his hand on his hip who knew he was right and suddenly heard with a clarity distilled by the night, "I know you're in there," closer than a whisper and raising tiny hairs up his back.

"Huh?" Gerard replied, jerking and spraying the mirror above the sink to his right, his natural direction.

It took him a moment to collect his thoughts and regain his aim.

"I know you're *in* there," the voice came again, deranged and singsong.

It came from the alley, crawling up the brick wall four stories and slinking in through the open window.

All right, you know I'm in here, Gerard thought with unapologetic banality, but *you* don't have a key. He went to the window and stuck his head out, expecting the man with the orange head to be down there looking up. Instead he was picking amongst the dumpsters, approaching one of them now with hunching stealth and repeating, "I know you're *in* there."

Gerard's relief gave way to juvenile inspiration. He retreated to his lair to retrieve an enamel wash basin big enough to hold two gallons of cold water from the bathroom faucet.

At the window, basin at the ready, Gerard silently urged the orange-headed maniac toward the dumpster directly beneath the window. Come on, you crazy fucker, Gerard encouraged him, just a little farther you fucking homo or homo hunter, whichever the fuck you are . . .

"I know you're *in* there," the victim sang as he crept within range. Gerard let fall two gallons of cold water that found his orange target, which lurched backward and let out a girlish deep-lunged cry.

Gerard didn't watch long enough to determine if the orange washed off. As far as he was concerned the episode was over and he felt damn good to be the one who made that decision.

Later Gerard was in the stairwell at the window between the third and fourth floors, watching the eastern sky to see if the sun had enough left to go through with it all one more time. Torgeson would probably be up soon and looking for him, and maybe he'd finally be asleep in one place it was certain Torgeson would never think to look. What . . . luck. Gerard felt about as lucky as the sun. The matutinal haze was thick enough to veil the bluffs a mile away. Across the parking lot below was the Catholic church, lined by a row of perfectly symmetrical and unpenitent evergreen trees. Gerard could feel the accumulated hours of solitary mental activity leak out from his skull and fall at the invitation of the asphalt lake beneath him. If the sky was lighter, if the haze burned away or was brushed aside like a fine curtain by better air, if the spirit left him was the color of the sky, if he could hear in the tolling of five bells hope, or nestle in the sloping hip of forlorn civilization, anything . . . if anything at all, would Gerard, this thinking mammal, know anything, would he know anything at all?

9

FRIENDSHIP AND THE LAW

A sleek black sedan cruised shiny the color of night, resisting fearful rituals of pacification.

"You eat shit," Torgeson, in the passenger seat, said.

"Come off it, Pard, your luck'll turn," Stratton said.

"There you go with that Pard shit again."

"You'll always be Pard to me."

"That ain't cause for celebration, asshole."

Stratton drove slowly, like someone coming easy back into his fortune.

"I'm going to help you, you know that. But first I'm going to say something, and I want you just to listen, think about it fair and honest. If I'd said to you you eat shit you'd demand an apology on the spot. I'm going to let it pass, no apologies necessary, but I want you to think about it, that maybe you aren't entirely fair with me all the time. I don't say things like that to you, and when I do you get pretty upset . . . "

The sedan was on the 200 block of West Avenue North, but when they passed #226, neither of the coppers were aware that

Nick Ray had once lived at that very spot.

Stratton waited three blocks for a reply.

"What do you think?" he prodded.

"About what?"

"About what I said."

"You eat shit."

Stratton was sailing along on the crest of his finest humor.

"I'm glad I'm able to get through to you."

"Fuck that," Torgeson said. "Two weeks I'm banging that broad, two weeks . . . not that she's that bad, a lot of fine flesh on them bones, and she's got great big tits . . . I mean huge, if you haven't seen . . . and she gives great head, just loves it — but I'm a married man; I'm cheating on my wife — this is business. And that fucker who fucked my wife comes back from out of nowhere and blows the whole fucking thing. I got no *names* from her. I was playing it real cool. I got no names. All I got is I got delivery on *her.* So fuck it, I'll nail her good, maybe plant some to make it worse, good enough, but then that cocksucker ain't satisfied to tip her off, he's got to hustle her out of there and I got nothing . . . He better have got his ass out of town or he's a dead man . . . "

"Well that's what I'm saying. My luck is your luck. That's why you're coming with me. If anybody knows anything it's this fucker Verité. He knows Gerard and I'll damn sure bet he knows Lola. He's a little fucking rat — he lives in the cracks the roaches hide in . . . You just don't worry, Pard, we'll take care of this bullshit."

"All right, look, here's the deal — you don't call me Pard and I don't say you eat shit."

"That's my bud."

"I don't like bud no better."

The winding down of their conversation as the sedan neared the body-shop lot where Billy's van was parked demonstrated the dependence of the Police Officer language/consciousness nexus on the properties of convergence, an acquired skill of sorts neither Torgeson nor Stratton was aware they owned.

Billy's van sat a fat moon gray in the unlit lot in the moonless night. Inside Lola was snoring and Billy was trying to figure out how to prod her awake without Lola mistaking the contact for the unwanted advances of a predator male, foreplay in one of the first four degrees. Her skirt rode up and her undies too, and Billy was not disposed to philosophize over the phenomenon represented by the broad flank of flesh that certainly held more power over him than all the laws in all the lands in all the world. He could look at that thigh and what it became further up a long time, only he couldn't because he couldn't have her snoring when Stratton showed up.

"Lola!" Billy decided. "Wake up!"

Lola slumbered lavishly and Billy wanted her bad.

"Lola! Lola, wake up!"

Lola stopped snoring in mid-intake, as if two tiny oak doors came shut simultaneous and apneatic. She straightened out, rolled onto her back, rocked once, snorted, and curled onto her other side, still asleep.

But not snoring.

"Jesus," Billy sighed lubriciously, and saw headlights strafe the side of his van.

He slid aside the panel that separated the operational from the navigational compartments of the van, locked it behind him, and squirmed out of the driver's seat to greet Stratton, pleased to discover Torgeson's angry slouch in the passenger seat of the unmarked black sedan.

Billy's self-confidence had arrived at a curious zenith. It never occurred to him that Torgeson was along because they suspected he was harboring Lola. Instead he snickered privately about how he was putting one over on his eternal tormentors, these all-powerful high and mighty rogue slimeball coppers who thought he was too stupid to know when he was being pushed around, who treated him like he was no more than a petty little snitch, condescending openly regarding his private eye venture, thinking he didn't know when he was being made fun of. Billy knew you couldn't fight city hall — you *can't* fight city hall — but when these corrupt bastards strayed too far from the building Billy Verité knew it and knew how to take advantage.

Ha! Billy thought. Ha! Fuck with Billy the Kid. See where it gets you.

I'm a two-bit snitch, Billy thought as he approached the sedan, and I'd sell my old lady down the river for a nickel. Maybeee, assholes, but to you I wouldn't sell out Adolph Hitler for a million bucks. Got it?

Billy was on top of the world.

He sported the unrestrainable grin of a two-bit snitch prepared to sell his old lady down the river for a nickel. Only two preoccupied rogue cops of below average perception could have failed to notice by the look on his face that Billy was hiding something.

Stratton had a last private word with Torgeson, then rolled down his window.

"What do you got?"

"I got one thousand dollars worth of information. I got names and dates. You got the money?"

"Yes, I got your fucking money, now don't waste my time. Who is it?"

"Which?"

"Which?"

"Which who?"

"Don't fuck with me, you cheap petty-ass two-bit snitch or I'll stomp a turd out of you and shove you up the tailpipe of your own goddamn van."

"You want to know who the new boss is or who sent him?"

"Both."

"Okay: the guy in charge is Earl Strafe. He's head of Guns Over Zion, you heard of them. And the name of the new leader of B.A.D. is a fellow named Skunk, that's his first name, Lane, that's his middle, Forhension, that's his last name."

Billy handed Stratton a slip of paper with Skunk's name written on it.

"That's in case you wonder how it's spelled. Now can I have my money?"

Stratton's eyes slid sly and reptilian toward Torgeson, then came back aligned with a smirk like two BBs coming to rest in pinholes.

10

BILLY SPIES A NEW FRONTIER

"Sure. Sure Billy, you can have your money."

Stratton pulled a sawbuck out of his shirt pocket.

"Here . . . go on, take it . . . it's all yours."

Billy looked at the bill without moving his hands. This was one thing he hadn't counted on.

"What's wrong, Billy? You did your job, now here's your money. Take it."

Billy could have been an Okie.

"That . . . that just ain't right, Detective Stratton."

"What? Is there something wrong? Is there something wrong with this bill?"

He flipped the bill over and back a few times, withdrew it and passed it to Torgeson.

"That look counterfeit?"

Torgeson flicked on the domelight and passed the bill close before his eyes.

"It's got Billy Verité private eye all over it . . . would still spend, though."

Stratton took it back and thrust it out the window, letting it fall when Billy still made no move to grab it. Remarkably, though such is common, the bill after fluttering wound up *under* the car. Billy didn't watch it fall; he looked with all the cold fury he could forge from his defeat straight into Stratton's eyes, somehow not managing the natural dignity inherent in the silence of doom and wrong. Still, by his behavior it was clear that Billy Verité had come a long way — so clear that even Stratton recognized it.

"I expected a little more whining out of you, Billy. All in all you're taking this very well. So well, in fact, I'm inclined to think maybe you don't want the rest of it."

"We had (— Billy's voice cracked when he said had, or else it would've been perfectly delivered —) a deal."

"Well you haven't lived up to your end."

Billy knew he had.

And knew he could never enforce such a contract.

"You left something out, Billy. I wanted you to find a couple of people for me — remember? Lola? And Gerard? That there ten is good faith money, show you I'm on the level. You want the rest you find Lola and Gerard and report back to me or Detective Torgeson. Then you get the rest, all of it."

Billy had a vision of himself telling someone — maybe Lola, maybe not — how at that point he told Stratton he was a liar, straight out.

"You're a liar," Billy told Stratton.

"Nevertheless, my little — " Stratton said, cutting himself off when he heard Torgeson's door open. He watched with pride as Torgeson walked around the front of the car, approached Billy Verité, grabbed his shirt front, slapped his face, wheeled Billy about and slammed him against the car, held his slumpward body up, said, "Find them," dropped the body, then walked slowly back around to his door, got in, and said, "Let's go."

Billy lay fetal on the gravel thinking that that kind of thing hurts; when a cop throws somebody against a car it really hurts. Billy could see it again and a thousand times before, like an ancient ritual striving to achieve its perfect form; and he could at the same time feel exactly where his spine hit the door frame.

His spine didn't break.

The ten dollar bill that rose in the dust of the sedan's exit came to rest like an exhausted butterfly and Billy saw how he could be chasing it like a child perpetually kicking the ball he's after out of his own reach.

Lola, Billy thought, you stick with me, baby.

EXILE

When Oneball walked into his living room in the old Deke Dobson mansion and saw Skunk Lane Forhension with his feet up on the desk, he charged like a creature bred for savagery, meaning to grab him by the face, yank him over the desk, and pummel him until his bones were mush. Only then would he find out who it was and what he was doing at the very nerve center of the paramilitary motorcycle organization B.A.D.

But Skunk Lane Forhension held him at bay by quickly shoving the desk into Oneball's charging knees.

Like a lot of big red-haired men whose natural strength oscillated under a great deal of fat, Oneball had overburdened knees. The pain made his eyes water, and he was beginning to get mad when he heard a gentle southern voice say, "Well I can see right off why Earl sent for me."

Skunk came around the desk, pulled a chair up behind Oneball, who was still clutching his knees, and tenderly persuaded him to sit. Back behind the desk, Skunk resumed his former position, absently chewing a fingernail while waiting for

Oneball to stop gasping.

Finally Oneball looked up and said, "Who the fuck are you and how do you know Earl?"

"That gun loaded?" Skunk asked.

Oneball looked to his hip and slapped his holster as if a colostomy bag had been planted there.

"You see, Uni-ball," Skunk explained, "this is the age of guns, not fisticuffs. Been this way a long time. Now you come into your home and find an intruder there and instead of calmly pulling your firearm you come at him like a bull with his balls cut off, which in your case makes a certain amount of sense, but I guess you don't realize what organization you represent, and being of a retrogressive tribe of men resorted to the original weapon of primitive man, which had he relied on it entirely would've meant his extinction at the paws and claws of various large felines, which is one of many legitimate reasons why as of this minute you are through as president of this organization, and why you will not simply be demoted to the status of soldier, rather will be clearing out entirely. Is that plain enough for you?"

Oneball stared with a mystification that diminished in proportion to the reassertion of his brutish confidence, restoring itself as he realized he was dealing with a little smart guy he could easily break in half or, as the fellow as much as said, pistol whip.

"Now I see where your thinking is taking you," Skunk resumed, "and I'm going to do you the favor of suggesting why you should go quietly rather than allow your instincts to reassert themselves. Now what you want to say now is 'Huh?' That's because you're a large and stupid man."

Oneball was smiling now. He had decided to kill Skunk with his bare hands.

"All right, then, use the phone here and call up your most trusted lieutenant. You'll need a witness."

Oneball was feeling better now. After years of being nothing more than an intimidating motorcycle gangster, one of Deke Dobson's thugs, he was a leader, he had power, and he couldn't be faulted for not yet knowing how people with power behaved — with patience, for instance. But he was learning, and now he remembered the way Deke acted — with patience — when he was dealing with a condemned man. And when Skunk suggested calling a witness he remembered something else: Deke rarely touched the victim himself; in fact, it was as often as not Oneball who did the dirty work. This Skunk business was shaping up to be a true test of Oneball's leadership qualities and he was beginning to realize it. The thing to do here was call Hobo, his most murderous lieutenant, and have Hobo slice the little fucker to pieces.

Oneball dialed Hobo's number.

"Hobo?" he said.

Skunk looked at his fingernail. He really didn't know what people saw in nail chewing.

"Hobo, we got a man here who — how did Earl put it? — we need to, you know, what was that word . . . no, it means . . . I can't say it over the phone . . . no, it's like a vacation, you know — permanent . . . Huh? . . . yeah — exile . . . Hobo? . . . "

"Let me guess," Skunk said, "he hung up and he'll be right over because this is his kind of job. You're the boss now, you leave the dirty work for others."

Oneball sat down.

"You just keep talking, you ain't got much time left."

"Now that was good. That was a real leader-type thing to say. But now I'm going to tell you something you may find a little too theoretical for your taste, but you'll listen since you're pretty sure you're in control of this situation. The thing about power, Oneball, is that it comes in layers. You know what I mean by layers? Of course you don't. The world is made of layers, kind of like concentric circles and what that means is there's bigger and bigger circles, circles inside circles inside circles. You have power in a circle, but your circle is inside the next circle and you don't know what's going on in that circle and even less the next and the next. Now do you see where knowledge — that means what you know — do you see where knowledge fits in, Oneball?"

"You're running out of time," Oneball said with the absolute confidence of a legitimate man of power.

"You're right. I'll cut to the point. You don't know what's going on and I do. I can see the future. You think you can, but what you don't know is I'm the only man on this earth who can save your life and even though I know you won't listen I'm going to tell you anyway. What you're suffering from is called an intracranial aneurysm. Now in layman's terms, which is especially necessary in your case, what you have is a tiny bomb at the base of your brain. When it blows, you die, just like that. There's no symptoms. You know what fulminating apoplexy is, Oneball?"

"You got one hell of a mouth on you, boy."

"All right, then, let me get to the point. Rupture, or in our terms, explosion, may follow trauma, exercise, coitus, fear, or any other condition that elevates blood pressure. My guess is exercise is what's going to do it in this case — should be fear. The only thing that could save your life would be to get on the operating table as soon as possible, but if you believed that you'd be scared as a hen in a foxhouse and you'd probably rupture in a fulminating apoplexy before you got there. Any way you look at it you are a goner and you don't know it and I do and that means, what I was saying about circles, you're in a little circle and I'm in a big one and the minute you realize that will be the minute you die."

"This is great!" Billy Verité exclaimed.

Lola didn't say anything. She was on her elbows and knees, supporting her face with her hands right up next to the earphones, so distracted by the melodrama she was not horrified by the proximity of her face to Billy's.

"They're not saying anything now," Billy said, "I wonder what they're doing."

"Waiting for Hobo."

"Yeah, Hobo. I know that guy — he's one mean motherfucker."

"I know him, too. I gave him a blow job once at a party. In the bathroom."

Billy wished it had been him. He pulled away from the earphones to lean back on his hands and look up Lola's skirt.

"He pulled my hair when he came and I damn near bit him. He liked it rough."

Lola kept her ass up in the air precisely because she knew what it was doing to Billy.

"You must be Hobo. How's your back?"

Hobo felt a foot-long slant of lightning cross his lower back. He looked over at Oneball, wondering why he'd tell this asshole about his bad back.

"Exile the motherfucker, Hobe."

"Shut up," Skunk said as he stood up. He walked directly up to Hobo, a dark-skinned man with straight black hair pulled into a ponytail and the facial menace of a Hollywood Apache.

"Now what you want to do," Skunk said as he dropped to the floor onto his back, drew up his knees and held them so that his body formed an egg, "is get down like this? And rock back and forth — not just for a minute or two, but for about a half hour every morning. Cause what you got is compression, the disc's compressed and you need to stretch it out, and this is the way to do it."

Skunk rocked forward and sprang to his feet.

Oneball watched the whole thing, wondering why Hobo was just standing there looking like he was actually listening to this prick.

"It's a funny thing, Hobo, you got all this pain and there being such a simple solution whilst Oneball here has no pain at all and — you know what an aneurysm is?"

Hobo, still assessing the situation, said, "Sure. My old man died of an aneurysm in his brain. Healthiest man alive, never sick a day in his life, then one day just like a time bomb went off in his head, he slumped into his breakfast cereal dead. Just like that."

"Had a fight with your ma?"

"That's right."

"Blood pressure. Eventually it'll go anyway, but a rise in blood pressure'll bring it on quicker. I been trying to tell Oneball — "

"Would you kill the motherfucker like I said. What the fuck are you waiting for — what the fuck are you *talking* to him for?"

Oneball's face was turning red.

One of the danger signs.

His blood pressure was being elevated by a combination of anger and fear.

"Just stand there a minute, Mr. Hobo. You got plenty of time to kill me. Watch this." He indicated Oneball with a terse swing of his head.

"Hobo, you kill him right now or I'll fucking kill you both."

"Watch," Skunk said.

Hobo didn't move.

"Here goes," Skunk said as Oneball lurched lumberously to his feet, fumbling at his holster, his face rushing to assume the red of brick. He drew the gun and advanced on Skunk Lane Forhension, who merely slid his hands into his pant's pockets.

Oneball shifted the gun in his hand so that he could hold it by the barrel and bring the butt crashing down onto Skunk's head, but as soon as the gun reached its apogee, he grunted into his penumbral hesitation, a moment shorter than a second during which he had time to realize that pain unprecedented did not necessarily eclipse thought, nor the warm feeling of absolute collapse into truth, and his eyes of course wide and staring at Skunk as he would his maker he fell with surprising quiet sideways dead on the carpet.

Skunk nudged Oneball's cheek with the toe of his boot, then looked up at Hobo.

"Here lies one stupid and unfortunate motherforsaken fool."

"Jesus," Billy said, "I don't even know what happened."

"His brain exploded, you idiot," Lola told him.

"How did his brain explode?"

"Weren't you listening? He had an aneurysm."

"But what *is* that?"

"It's like a heart attack only in the head — a head attack, caused by high blood pressure. When you get mad you pump more blood into your head and the veins expand and expand and finally it's too much and they blow up like if you pump too much water into a balloon. It explodes and you die."

"Jesus," Billy said.

12

FOUND OBJECTS / SANDY CALDERON

I found a silver and black pen on the sidewalk today. I hope it didn't mean too much to anybody because I kept it. It has a lot of scars and says U. S. Government on it. It's been in my hand all day. I'm using it now. I don't examine this pen and extend myself logically down the dark dead-end alleys of a labyrinth — I don't make too much of it, not intentionally. The concentration I lavish on it is effortless, so that I can without dishonor or a sense of degradation assert that to me it means something, even without considering the tight concentric circles of reflected light that radiate from its silver tip onto the page.

More and more now that I'm back the world is breaking itself up for me that way, into objects and their shadows and angles of optimal pose and beauty of juncture and tissues of reflected light, time of day, size and transferability, intent or means of resisting such as was ever evident. I find at a particular corner seen from a particular bench in a particular park that the shadow of a streetlamp, unable to resist the glare of another streetlamp, lifts itself along the wall of a building in the noble pose of a *War of the Worlds* alien craft. Only there, on that corner, and though the pull these (what I must lump together to call) Externae have for me makes me, naturally, I think, fear the proximity of psychosis, they are not hallucinations, and, mathematically, I think, to the extent they are indifferent to me offer themselves as well to others.

In a way, of course, I'm speaking of ghosts, whose existence cast an absence beside me in the shape of someone with whom I walk to a certain hollow near where two rivers meet, and to whom I say, "See, see how the river bends there; see how the marsh grass sweeps into the grove — see how that great tree twisted as it fell, the death of a mighty cottonwood, across the river . . . "

And I am asking, too: how many apocalypses more, how many more will it take before it's all really over. I know we're nearing the end and the End consists of an infinity of tiny ends, but just as in Zeno's paradox the formula that precludes an end takes its posit of an end from the knowledge of the End. So we know where we're headed and maybe that's why I can hardly see people anymore, the shadow of a streetlamp cast by a streetlamp becomes the composite corpse of men as from Pompeii on their way to work, the pen mysteriously stamped U.S. Government, cheap comfort, but profoundly so.

I would like to look at the eyes of a lady I pass on the street, knowing that, say, her stockings are a trick, that they barely cover what her long dress doesn't, look at her eyes and see them utterly blank, or see all the way to the back of her skull, or have them turn their green rays on me without malice, without love, without any sense at all of a shared participation, however equal, in horror — but I see her, again and again, and I know all about those knee-length stockings they wear, and I look into their eyes and whether they look at me or look away or slip their eyes into their hiding place in a vast warehouse constellated by an infinity of plastic eyes, every time I am forced to be honest, to recognize that they *are* eyes, all of them, and they are all real.

If it struck me as strange I would examine myself, I would extend myself down the dark dead-end alleys of a labyrinth — and I would find Sandy Calderon there, and under the shadow of a streetlamp her eyes would throw the rays of light reflected off the back of her skull, made green by the horror we share, throw green rays of light into my eyes.

Sandy won't see me; not yet, or not ever, I don't know. I've been to the scene. I've heard more about it, more details. Everybody was drunk: her boyfriend, the two men who lived with him, Sandy, all of them so drunk nobody knows what happened. If it weren't for the suicide note everyone would be entirely in the dark, where I sometimes think they'd be better off, where they were when it happened.

I'm still haunted by her face, but the face is restoring itself little by little. For instance, the old nose is back, no longer smashed over to the side. And the jaws are back in line. Now there's only the green eyes, the crack running from the top of her head down to her neck, and the missing teeth. At this rate by the time I see her she'll look awful, the once-beautiful Sandy Calderon. I think more about her now than I do about Gerard, I suppose a sign of less faint hope, occupying myself more with thoughts of the living than with the dead; yet I was down at the corner of Fifth and King earlier tonight, near the park, to look at the shadow of a streetlamp burned into a wall, and I thought I saw Billy Verité's old van parked down Fifth Street, painted over now, and I employed all my yogic powers to avoid looking at it, to prevent myself from noting any comings or goings that might've been in some way related to it, kept my focus zealously trained on the shadow of the streetlamp.

13

BILLY AND LOLA IN THE VAN

"Now *there's* a babe," Billy said as the woman walking across the street passed in front of the van. The light had turned green, but Billy waved her on.

"Who is that?" Lola asked. What she wanted to say was 'Who is that hussy?'

For the past week Billy's lusty glances had been trained on her alone and she didn't much appreciate some bimbo who was free to walk the streets as she pleased wriggling her designer blue-jeaned ass for Billy's eyes, even if she did find the notion that both she and Billy were part of the same biological equation repulsive.

"Sandy Calderon."

"Oh, I know about her. She fucked her way through all the men in A.A. and then started drinking again. So that's what she looks like."

Not that Lola cared, really. Even as she gave in to her pettish impulses she was more disturbed by the itching caused by her fake beard, and the annoyance of having her long thick hair, finally washed, tucked up into the black homburg Billy had bought for her.

She didn't like looking Amish, either.

And she didn't like wanting Billy Verité to want her.

And she didn't like waking up the night before, finding her blanket thrown off and not knowing if it happened while the light was on, thus not knowing whether a connection existed between her undie-clad body and the furtive crepitations taking place under Billy's blanket.

Lola didn't like going for so long without sex, especially since she was never awake when Billy was asleep — she didn't like that Billy could masturbate and she couldn't.

Lola didn't like the van just sitting there when the light was green so Billy could look at Sandy Calderon's ass walking down the street.

"Would you fucking go!" Lola snapped.

And Billy went, thinking who needs Sandy Calderon when you got Lola Montell in her undies every night sort of all to yourself. And even though you could say let's face it a hot chick like Lola would never go for an ordinary working stiff like Billy Verité, that's only what's normally the case, not applicable to extreme circumstances when Lola's defenses are under duress until like cement they crack and the dark orchids of Billy's hope burst from the interior rot toward the sun of Billy's inner glory.

As if cement had interior rot.

14

BATHROOMS PUBLIC AND PRIVATE

Billy knew where the cleanest public bathrooms in the city were, which ones had reliable locks on the door, which were seldom used, and which Lola could come and go from unseen even by the rodent eyes of sullen amoral clerks. He knew that on Wednesdays the Honeymoon Suite at the Holiday Inn was given a thorough going over, and that it was always vacant that night and that Melissa Stripton vacuumed the hallways and would for five dollars leave the door to the suite unlocked, no questions asked. And even if Lola insisted on being alone in the whirlpool, she was grateful enough to finally get her hair properly washed that she said for the first time in a week, "Thank you."

Now she was in a pissy mood again and Billy had to wonder if maybe it wouldn't take another year stuck in the van together before she finally fell for him. Not that he was overly sensitive. He knew people, and being able to read Lola enabled him to remain detached. The important thing was not to doubt himself. Lola was upset because the night before she spent three hours in a honeymoon suite, and this morning she woke up in a van, which offered her a compressed glimpse of the calamity her life persisted to inhabit. She's thinking about her downfall, is what Billy figured.

And he hatched another plan to appease Lola. First the beard and the hat so she could sit up front instead of spending the entire day cooped up in back, and, now that dusk was almost nigh, he was going to take her to the best bathroom in La Crosse. You got to think about these things when you're on the lam or half on the lam, whatever the two of them were together, and Billy was proud to know as much about bathrooms in the city as he did, and he was certain that by now bathrooms were coming to mean a great deal to Lola.

Billy had talked once with a former fellow cabbie about bathrooms and the quotidian (the other hack's word). A lanky man, this cabbie, we'll call him Anonymous, saw Billy in his van one day and, in a rare sprightly mood, hopped into the passenger seat.

"(Anonymous)," Billy said. "I ain't seen you in a while."

"That's because I've been avoiding you. But good Christ I'm feeling good and you're just the guy who'd understand. Remember Dave the Dispatcher?"

"Dave?"

"Dave — the one Bev said smelled bad."

"Dave, the college guy. I never worked there when he did."

"Yes. Well let me tell you he's smelling pretty good these days and I'll tell you exactly why: because he and his girl Vicki have the best goddamn bathroom in town. I just came from there and I tell you this because I know you're a guy what knows his way through the Byzantium we know as the quotidian, through like I say the maze of the mundane, which is nought but a collection of blind alleys some of which a man comes to know as necessary resting points, most obviously the toilet, the dinner table, the bed, places which we tend not to give their due, especially at the time of construction — these, my friend, these should be our palaces, these our Taj Mahals, our cathedrals, our Fenway Parks. So I tell you, Billy Verité, I just came from there, and in the best of all possible bathrooms I took the first decent crap I've had the opportunity to self-satisfactorily call complete, final, and wholesome, the first decent crap in days, maybe a week . . . "

Mystified as he was, Billy managed to write down the address — 932 Cass #1 — on a scrap of paper he filed in his wallet and never brought himself to throw away; and now, nearly a year later, he pulled his van up to 930 Cass and told Lola to go ahead and remove the beard and, if she wanted, the hat.

"You let me do the talking, sister — "

Sister? Lola thought.

" — I'm going to get you into the finest bathroom in La Crosse."

Number 932 was the side entrance to the house, where a stairway led to apartments on the second floor. Billy pressed the buzzer and within seconds footsteps came bollacking down the stairs.

The man who pushed open the door had a beard and the kind of face people recognized as one they'd known a long time but couldn't place. He said, with a preemptive strike of wryness, "Yes?"

"Hello, my name is Joe Foreman and I'm a reporter for the La Crosse *Tribune*. This is Lola Larson. We're doing a feature story about bathroom facilities and we've been referred to yours by someone who wishes to remain anonymous. What we'd like — "

"Hey spongehead," came on the carom down the stairs a voice that could bend window panes. "Who is it?"

Dave turned his familiar head and shouted back, "It's Billy Verité. He says he's Joe Foreman and he wants to use our bathroom."

Dave turned back to Billy and said, "You're not going to steal anything, are you?"

"No," Billy said, refusing to allow his mind to give play to the word "setback."

Lola rolled her eyes.

"And you must be Lola Montell," Dave said to her in courtly fashion.

"You're a fuckhead, Billy," Lola said.

"That's all right, I'm a spongehead. Come in and use the bathroom. We won't blow your cover."

"Who's Billy Verité?" the voice upstairs asked.

"He's coming up," Dave told the stairs at precisely the same moment Lola muttered, "The biggest fuckhead in the world."

Billy hung his head and followed Dave and Lola up the stairs. Vicki was furled on the couch, looking like she was without appendages.

"Come in and use the bathroom," she said, "whoever you are."

"It was his idea," Lola said.

Billy was at such a loss he had plenty of room to marvel inadvertently at the way momentum had landed them in a strange living room, their most important secret spilling like blood from a steak hidden under a poor man's hat as he walked out of the store wondering how he was going to get caught.

Dave closed the door behind them, Billy and Lola skipping awkwardly aside like timid paupers. Nobody knew what to do next. A silence had insinuated its way into the scene and it was trapped there now; everyone was left to recognize their own particular way of belonging better someplace else. Billy and Lola both looked toward the windows, beyond which an obscure sort of reckoning was falling with the night.

Vicki and Dave were the first to come out of it. After knitting their brows separately, they did it together, looking at each other, then at their guests, then back at each other.

"What do you think?" Vicki asked. "Think they're on the lam?"

"They must be. They're using fake names and it's obvious they're upset we saw through their little hoax. He said he was a reporter doing a feature — he used the word feature, which was good — on bathrooms."

"Well it's about time the paper wrote something decent. I think a feature on bathrooms would be a fine start — you people might want to mention that's where I keep your insipid rag . . . for obvious purposes . . . "

"No, Vicki, it's a hoax, a scam — they're not reporters — "

"I can *see* that, spongehead, but why do they want to use our bathroom?"

"It's a great bathroom, Vicki."

"Yes, I know, spongiform, but why *our* bathroom. You'd think fugitives would use bathrooms at the Texaco or the library. Who'd've thought they'd go door to door?"

"We don't really know they're going door to door. All we really know is they came here. I think word got out about our bathroom, that's why they came here."

"I'm not convinced. I'm far from convinced. I feel like I've forgotten what it's like to be convinced. You think fugitives would put so much energy into getting into one special bathroom? I don't think so."

Billy and Lola could make out the words, but once the conversation got going without them it seemed not to be their province, or as if their role as the observed and discussed was a sort of house rule.

"What it probably is," Dave offered, "is a means of maintaining a sense of dignity in the face of adversity. They — "

"Yeah, yeah, I know what you mean, but you're romanticizing them. They aren't Bonnie and Clyde. I'm sure the answer is something much more mundane, like they just got tired of shitting in public bathrooms . . . "

"And they just happened to end up here . . . "

"Why not? They *are* here."

"That can be used in support of my theory, too. They *are* here, not someplace else. And he did say he'd heard we had a great bathroom. That'd be a bit much of a coincidence. Besides, what if we had a lousy bathroom? He'd be taking quite a chance. I don't think he's *that* stupid."

"How stupid is that, compared to this, coming to the door of someone who knows him saying he's someone else the reporter — "

"He didn't know I'd remember him — "

" — doing a story on *bathrooms*. A story on bathrooms? What could be stupider than that?"

"Obviously that took him by surprise. Anyway, what difference does it make how stupid he is? If he's on the lam he shouldn't be weaseling his way into bathrooms this way."

"What about her — what's her role in this?"

"I don't know, though it's clear this wasn't her idea."

"Well what, is she a bimbo or what is she doing with this jerk?"

"That may be the key to the whole thing right there. If we can establish — "

"Look," Lola said, "I really gotta piss."

15

STRATTON DIAGNOSED

"That was a very nice meal," Lola said with unaccustomed civility. "They were really nice people."

She was propped against her bedding, rubbing her belly and belching with relish.

Billy, sitting opposite, removed his earphones.

"Anything yet?"

"No, just some noises, the tape starts and stops right away. Probably that Skunk guy's alone in there . . . The thing I don't get is that bathroom didn't seem like anything to me. I mean, it's a little bigger than average, but the toilet is off center — there's nothing great about it, don't you think?"

"It had a bathtub, that's all I care about."

"Anyway, we're lucky — I don't think they'll squeal."

"It was still stupid," Lola said, so Billy wouldn't get the wrong idea about her postprandial languor.

"I said I was sorry a dozen times," Billy said, to which Lola delivered a belch to close the discussion.

Billy put the earphones back on and Lola stroked her midriff, neither of them giving the least thought to the way the adaptability of primates is enhanced by resistance to the nihilistic lure of metaphysics. Billy listened for B.A.D. secrets and wondered when Gerard would arrive with a plan that would bring ruin to his seedy little paradise; and Lola sat belching and happy at least to have Billy to belch to rather than someone like Gerard, who she'd have to let belch first, if she could hold out.

Outside the van the last heat of the day rose wanly from the sidewalks toward the indifferent medium of night. The oblate moon rolled heavy and irregular in the southern sky and the scars of meteors vanished forever like the paths of vaporized fireflies.

The schism between the short-term intentions of the people of the city and the hope derived from their inventions was growing wider, a yawning more palpable than what they already knew of what next they would clutch. Were bravery required to propel a human into that night, there would've been hundreds, perhaps thousands, willing to throng the streets or worse, to clamor for the directive that would send them back the way they thought they were going. In Stratton's case it took greed and a feudal spirit to wend a rogue's path to Skunk Lane Forhension's door.

"Stratton's there!" Billy shouted.

"Is Torgeson with him?"

"I don't know; I don't think so."

As she scooted forward on hands and knees, Lola asked, "Isn't there some way we can listen without the earphones?"

"Sure," Billy said, "Just unplug them and it comes out the speaker."

"You little bastard."

"Turn around, Detective . . . don't worry, I won't drygulch you . . . just turn around and do like this . . . "

Skunk hunched his shoulders forward, stretching his shirt across his back.

Stratton did as he was told, biding his time. This skinny guy looked like Lee Harvey Oswald, and he appeared to be unarmed, without a bodyguard, and as harmless as Billy Verité, for instance . . . But Earl Strafe had sent him and that had to mean something.

"Just what I thought. Go ahead and sit down now. You got a sebaceous cyst up on your back, probably about ten years old and just a little bigger now than when you first noticed it."

"Look, I didn't come here — "

"Shut up, now. I know why you came here, but you don't know why I let you. Let me start by telling you what one reason isn't, and that's so I can hear you talk. I don't want to hear one word out of you, not one. One, and I mean one, one single one and only one single one and our meeting is over. Now to establish the power differential and your capacity for obedience and willingness to submit to authority if you perceive it to be financially in your long-term interest, I will ask you: do you understand?"

Stratton opened his mouth, abbreviated his utterance, and nodded.

"All right, all right, that's fine. I'm a man of my word and I didn't say nothing about grunts or moans or any form of non-word vocals — so that was good. But back to that cyst that you never have checked for fear it might be cancerous, a tumor or the like, and perhaps more deeply for fear it might be diagnosed a sebaceous cyst, thus unlocking the focus of your hypochondria, unleashing it like a rabid coon dog to roam mad about the rest of your body where it will likely come to rest back at the same spot, from which pain radiates at unpredictable intervals and in varying degrees because you have also got yourself a case of bursitis, and I mean chronic and scapular, a result of throwing baseballs or getting yourself knocked down, cumulative or incidental trauma I can't say, and sure enough don't see the point in saying, except if it were incidental it may have been spawned by the same incident that spawned your chief medical problem which is called involutional psychosis if you don't know and occurs in men sometime after they get up around forty and see they are losing vigor both physical and mental so that, try to follow me now, they see they can no longer so effectively strong arm fate, which is to say they see finally it is most definitely true what they have heard about death, to wit it will happen to them. I like to see it as they, and I mean you, Detective, waited too long to come to terms with death so now it's too late and they panic. You will not believe me because I am talking about a subtle phenomenon that prowls on the paws of a wildcat at night in your mind. You will say I know'd I's going to die all along, and that's true, but deep down you never believed it, and now you see events gone out of your control and it's getting harder to get what's rightly yours, take this here visit as a case in point — I see you squirming like a blind baby strapped in a high chair wondering when I'm going to get to the point — and I'm some stranger who's got you by the gonads, well this here's the sort of thing that'll cause your involutional psychosis, which will manifest itself as agitation, hypochondria — is that a tumor, Detective?; nihilistic ideas — are things here in Lay Cross the way they used to be, or're they going down the shitterhole for good?; delusions and hallucinations — where, Detective, are the shadows of the outlaws of yesteryear? where is your passport for this particular little nightmare? where's your authority? is this really happening? do I really look like Lee Harvey Oswald?; and of course you have your obsession with death — are you really not thinking about your death every minute of every day? you deluding yourself there, Detective? Remember, don't say nothing. I'm going to give you a minute to think — "

"Is Torgeson there, too?" Gerard asked.

"No, just Stratton," Billy said.

"Where the hell have you been?" Lola demanded to know.

"Laying the groundwork," Gerard said. "I've got a plan."

"What plan?"

"We have to get him before he gets us."

"How long do I have to live like this, with this . . . creep?"

"Until we straighten this out or you decide you'd rather leave town."

"Where would I go?"

Billy watched Gerard and Lola, suspecting that Gerard's natural command arose from physical attributes, giving him a natural advantage over Billy, who could easily offer Lola the same advice, yet could only earn her submission through a series of trials circumstance had yet to devise for him. It wasn't fair.

The word phrenology snapped into Billy's mind — he'd read some books in his time — turned in a silver flash, and disappeared.

"Can I talk to you alone? Can Billy go somewhere?"

"Wait — let's listen . . . "

"You want one thousand dollars a month, which my predecessor Deke Dobson gladly paid you and which my uni-testacled predecessor denied you and now you have contacted me in order to bring back the good old days, a desire symptomatic of involutional psychosis — you cannot — "

"All right — that's enough," a thoroughly fed-up Stratton decided, standing as authoritatively as he could after allowing Skunk to go on for so long. "I still represent the law in this town, especially as far as you're concerned, and you either pay me or I'm gonna be all over you like stink on shit, and that's a fact. I may operate alone when I'm in your employ, but you piss me off and you got an entire department on your ass."

Skunk chuckled genuinely and leaned back in his chair.

"Detective Stratton. I'm irked. I might have let this outburst go, never mind what I said about one stinking word, I'd have let it go if you hadn't lapsed into that pale imitation of the colorful southern vernacular which you might've noticed I employ with the good-natured ease of a cottonmouth slithering through the legs of a picnic girl. Like stink on shit; Christ Almighty. There's that, and that police threat, which is as idle as my pappy's snores the day after he spent his paycheck. Detective Stratton, you and I both know that there's no police department in our universe. They're over there in the old one, that old universe in atrophy we each in our own way aspire to escape. But I guess you don't really know that. Let me put it to you in a way you might understand. I got a hard-on in a bathtub full of flies — they all want on and that's all right with me cause it feels pretty darn good. But once that volcano blows them flies is gone and I don't want them back. Detective Stratton, you are a fly on my pecker and I'm about to blow."

With the speed of a card sharpie sliding an ace off the bottom of the deck, Skunk pulled a switchblade from a drawer in front of him. All Stratton saw was that where Skunk's arm ended up was a little to the side of where it started; the knife only flashed in the light of the desk lamp as an afterthought.

"What I'm going to do now," Skunk said, "is let you walk to the door. When your hand touches the knob you will feel a sharp pain in your right calf, which is where this knife will be stuck in up to this here hilt."

Stratton had his revolver tucked into his pants at his spine, but he cringed when he thought of the last two times a criminal had gotten the better of him, and cringed another cringe only he knew was separate from the first when he realized he'd already hesitated long enough that it was fair to say he stood stupefied.

"Not that I don't enjoy your predicament, Detective, but I'll make it easier for you by saying if you go for the gun you get the knife in the heart and you die. It's a lot worse than the knife in the calf, though that's gonna hurt like hell, probably more than just about anything you ever felt . . . "

"Stratton's gonna pull the gun, I'll bet ya," Billy said.

"No, he's too chickenshit," said Lola.

"I don't think he could get the knife in up to the hilt," Gerard said, "the calf has a pretty dense muscle, especially — "

" — a skinny little fucker like you. You put that knife away or I *will* pull my gun — and I'll use it."

Skunk snickered gleefully —

"Weak," Billy said.

"He's a pussy," Lola agreed.

"He's trying to buy time," Billy analyzed, "waiting for Skunk to look away, or — "

" — interesting, I'm not even going to give you a time limit. You have all night to make up your mind. Will he kill me? Will he stick the knife in my calf? Am I afraid to die, like he says. Am I a coward? Am I going to be taunted into making the fatal mistake of reaching for my gun? Take your time, Detective . . . "

The thing to do was remove himself from the situation with dignity, but Stratton was scared and found it difficult to think. The word foremost in his mind was "please." What he did not know was that he was learning a great deal about time from his predicament — as he watched himself watching his own stupefaction, brought about by watching himself, he was a man trudging and chopping through dense green folds of experience, the machete once so heavy in his hand now an extension of it, the trail he forged leading to a lost clearing with an emerald spring surrounded by lazy beasts drenched in a surfeit of time — a clearing by virtue of its utter desolation of consciousness heir to the title center of the universe. And all he could think was: please. And all he could do was curse petulantly, "I'll be back, you fuck," and turn slowly and walk with the mechanical saunter of a man who mustn't let on he fears what lurks behind, and reach for the doorknob casually because, really, it could not be true that just as he touches it, as it turned out it was true, a knife would close the mathematically uncloseable distance from points A to B and embed itself in his calf.

No one says ouch when that happens.

Stratton screamed away his apperceptual doldrums, hopping about reaching again and again for the knife, each time straightening abruptly as if trying to catapult the pain from his body, finally lashing out at a standing lamp that until then had served as silent sentinel, hiding the microphone that Skunk spotted as soon as it was exposed and approached with some consternation.

Stratton sat against the door — he hadn't managed to get it open — clutching his calf, from which he had just pulled the knife. His face was damp from sweat and tears (though he wasn't actually bawling), and pale from the sight of blood spreading like muffled laughter on his hands.

Skunk picked up the microphone and held it to his lips.

"Testing," he said, and followed the thin black cord to where it disappeared into the floor.

He looked at Stratton, who remained entirely self-absorbed.

"Say, Detective . . . Don't faint on me . . . who did you hire to bug this place? That's how you found out about me, right? What gonadsucker using primitive methods of surveillance — albeit successfully up to now — is listening to us here?"

Lola giggled.

Stratton didn't respond. His stomach felt emptier than his explanation for being where he was. He was at the juncture of nausea and death, or so he thought.

"Detective?"

Stratton looked supplicantly up.

He saw no angels.

Skunk held the microphone forward with one hand and pointed with the other.

"Billy," Stratton managed to gasp like a thirsty man, "Verité."

"Thank you," Skunk said, focusing his attention on the microphone.

"Billy? Billy Verité. Can you hear me? My name, as you know, is Skunk Lane Forhension, and I am sending Detective Stratton to get you. I'd like to speak with you, Billy Verité, kind of man to man. I'd invite you to stop by, save us all a lot of trouble, but my guess is you'll run, maybe you're already running . . . "

Billy Verité's Surveillance Van sped across the Clinton Street Bridge to French Island. In back Gerard and Lola listened to Skunk's final threat.

" — in proportion to the length of time it takes to find you, say each day buys you an hour of pain you would previously have thought unendurable. Billy, my friend, you will learn something about the capacity our species has to adapt . . . regardless . . . so run,

16

SEMINAL MOMENTS IN FLIGHT

Billy Verité, run . . . "

"Let me stay with you," Lola pleaded, "I can't stand another night with that ugly little fucker, and now they're after him . . . I'll be safer with you . . . "

Gerard put his arm around Lola.

"You'll be all right. You'll be comfortable in my boat tonight and I'll be back in the morning to take you to the island — "

"Island? What goddamn island? You're planning to leave me stranded on some goddamn island with — "

"You'll be safe there. Nobody goes there. And it's big enough you can't be spotted from shore if you're careful. Nobody would ever think to look for you there. I'll gather supplies tomorrow and I'll keep bringing food, maybe once a week, until this whole thing's settled."

"How will it ever be settled? I can't go to jail, I can't. I should leave town — let's leave town, tonight, all three of us. We're close to the interstate, we can just get on it, take turns driving, go out west for the rest of our lives . . . "

Gerard held his index finger to his pursed lips, which he liked to do when he was thinking. Lola was amazed at how big the first segment of his finger was. She never noticed that before.

"Let's go out to the Sail Club first. When we get there we'll vote on it, see what Billy wants to do . . . "

11

LOLA WAS A HARD-LUCK WOMAN

Lola was a hard-luck woman. She had what it took to inspire a man to break his back providing for her, that is if he didn't lapse into a dolor before the soricine quotidian of her company and one day, the day she selected the first truck driver she could love all the way to the coast, wade into the black oil pool of oblivion — like in Herzog's *Stroszek,* the only movie that can make me cry, when Stroszek comes unmoored and finds himself alone with a dancing chicken that he understands so well he blows his brains out . . . poor Stroszek, so determined an adherent, so unlucky not to have found an office like Gerard's, like mine. In the right place, at the right time, Lola could've made men understand dancing chickens. But something invariably went wrong during the selection process, and now she wanted nothing more than to flee to the coast, yet found herself at the mercy of Gerard and Billy Verité, who fancied themselves men of action — Gerard perhaps the more noble in that his delusion did not grow from the desire to establish himself as a hero capable of extracting floundering damsels from dire circumstance — and voted in favor of staying in order to right a wrong, even if it meant facing evil and danger head on. If Lola wanted, they'd ship her out on the next bus, but they were staying, and together they'd see Stratton and Torgeson behind bars.

Billy's role would be to hide out on the island, Red Oak Ridge, with Lola, while Gerard would remain in town using his considerable resources, operating from his secret chamber, to nail the renegade cops.

18

FINALLY, A FIGHT

The first thing Gerard had to do was ditch the van. He left Billy and Lola hiding in his sailboat, a twenty-foot sloop docked at the French Island Sail Club, which occupied the extreme northern tip of the city and from where the as yet to be inhabited Red Oak Ridge Island was but a stand of trees rising from the water two miles to the west. He figured the cops would have an All Points on the van by the next day. All he had to do was make it to the Albright Bros. storage facility at the south end of the island, where he could fit it in his shed if he piled to the side all that shit he'd accumulated over a period of some thirty years of preparing to open his own machine shop.

He was wrong about the All Points, which was already out. A French Island patrol copper spotted him moving south on Flegler along the west side of the island. Gerard feared the worst when he saw the cop pull onto Flegler behind him, even though he was unaware that Torgeson himself had already been notified and was on his way down the causeway, just two miles from the island. But when the cop turned off on Spillway Gerard relaxed, remaining calm even when he passed another patrol car squatting in the lot of Scragmire's Ballroom, where Flegler makes the bend toward Bainbridge. That cop stayed put. It would've been the height of paranoia to think he was being team-tailed, especially since the next patrol car was moving north on Bainbridge and Gerard passed it heading south.

Albright Bros. Self-Storage was an irregular row of garages, on a southward slant, built in the darkening zone beyond the last streetlamps on Bainbridge, where the last scrofulous houses gave way to dredge yards and chemical tanks and other industrial secrecies that made money for people no one ever saw. Gerard pulled onto the gravel in front of the sheds, cut his engine, cut his lights, and had just opened his door when Torgeson pulled him from the van, yanking him with such force and so abruptly that he couldn't hold on as Gerard went stumbling sideways, his feet managing to remain under him until he had his balance back and was facing Torgeson in the crouch position.

Torgeson assumed the fight was on.

"Come on, baby," he said, unselfconsciously.

Gerard straightened and approached slowly, thinking, more or less, What the hell, I'm caught, I haven't really committed a crime (have I?). His mind had gone slack into a pattern of simple logic, discounting the more reliable indications of such unquantifiables as instinct, common sense, even memory. It was the polar opposite of panic.

"What do you want?" he asked with civility, there in the dark lot, approaching a rogue undercover cop with his arms to the side, shoulders hunching their innocence, and palms facing forward, yet retaining just enough instinct to tighten his stomach muscles in time to receive the blow that Torgeson thought would leave Gerard doubled up on the ground so he could kick him in the eye, but instead merely pushed Gerard back a foot or so.

"You could kill someone that way," Gerard said. "There are all those organs that keep us alive in there and when you punch there if the muscles don't tighten up" — Gerard demonstrated with his hands the forced and sudden diaspora of organs that could kill a man — "the organs all could get pushed like this. You could kill him. It could stop his heart — "

Torgeson didn't want to talk. He stepped into Gerard to deliver another blow, this one a direct right aimed headward that Gerard deflected with his forearm.

Torgeson's next move was to throw a wild left that swung well over Gerard's ducking head, followed by an Okinawan side kick attempted from too-close quarters, so that Gerard, keeping his wits about himself, was able to capture the leg, pulling it upward and back, leaving Torgeson's arms flailing fecklessly free of the ground and unable to prevent his skull from smacking the gravel.

Gerard was getting angry. He released Torgeson's leg and stepped back.

"I haven't committed a crime," he said in a de facto rush as Torgeson converted the scramble to his feet into a head-first charge toward's Gerard's gut, already tender and unwilling to take another blow, forcing Gerard to resort to a brutal uppercut that smashed into Torgeson's forehead and flipped him backward onto the softening spot on his skull.

The alembic of violence transmuted Gerard's reluctance, his peaceable nature, into a nearly insane zeal — but only for a second or two. He rounded Torgeson's inanimate legs and drew back his foot to deliver a kick that would splinter Torgeson's ribs, maybe even kill him.

But he couldn't do it.

The potion wore off.

"Aw fuck," he said.

Torgeson was unconscious.

Gerard leaned over him, found a neck pulse, hopped back into Billy's van, and drove south without lights, turning onto an overgrown unpaved road that merged into the forest. He dodged trees as long as he could, then ditched the van, found his way to the railroad tracks, and followed them over the swing bridge off the island and back into the city of his undoing.

19

WILLIE CICCI PAYS A VISIT

Solitude can do funny things to a man. I lock myself up in the office and watch the rhythms of the day march by, watch myself watch for a way out of time, or back in. I'm propped against the wall, on Gerard's bed. The fourth-floor bathroom for men is on the other side of the wall. I know that the old way out of time was the precise recognition of time, the elaborately choreographed mime of the heroic; one false move and men were condemned to the world of men. At 1:30 in the afternoon the lawyer speaks to me from the other side of the wall. At 1:45 he has his final say. At 2:15 the real estate mogul enters the bathroom, groans his lonesome disgust through the wall and chooses the other stall. At 2:18 he, too, only flushes once, and then I'm alone again until 4:30 when the lawyer returns, flushes both toilets repeatedly, and lingers until five. He talks to himself in there, but I don't know what he says. After five I hear nothing. I sit there until suddenly I notice a bright light out my nailed-shut frosted-glass and chicken-wire window — a light from the east as the sun sets, I have to admit, in the west. I rush out the door, down the hall to the stairwell that's not a maintenance closet yet, lift open the window — and it's only the sun plastering its crepuscular vomit against the vast expanse of the Cathedral. By the time I get back to my cave it's dark outside.

I'm deep in the belly of the city of Gerard's undoing and it's getting darker, I think it's October and it's getting darker; I crouch through the day at the foot of Gerard's bed — this green sleeping bag on top of foam pads, this Gerard cocoon, laying here cheated of his corpse — and I can't find a reason to get up and turn on a light, and I get to thinking about Sandy Calderon and her cracked face which I still have not seen and I forget how sad I feel and crouch at the foot of Gerard's bed, the light muffling through the door-window from the hallway assuring me an enduring dusk, and I refuse to turn that way even though I feel the heavy presence of a dark intruder; without looking I can trace his outline — another impressive fact about ghosts — I keep my head turned away, yet he emerges into his outline clarified and dapper in midnight blue pinstripe suit, jellied hair and moustache, triangular head and terse, surprisingly gentle manner. "That was no suicide," Willie Cicci says, for it's him and no other, stepping forward, having his say, turning, throwing his cigarette to the floor, mashing it with his foot, and stepping back like someone who had, impelled by the reluctant force of obvious truth, broken without regret a vow of silence.

And then he left me abandoned like a fetus that just wouldn't die, a little urban fetus, slamming my eyes shut and refusing to consider the fronds of the umbilicus frayed in dark winds.

The ancestors are gone, lost avatars all, buried outside the cities . . . They tell me nothing. I have to wait until Willie Cicci shows up to dismiss my reveries with the stamp of his foot on the cigarette butt of my despair. I know who sent him. It's his kind of joke. I ask for ghosts and I'm going to get the full bollixment that results from a glut of the incorporeal. Willie Cicci is gone: I look at the entryway and his outline has faded onto bare trees, a mound of dirt and rocks (no grass will grow on that grave), and a headstone of pocked cement, unengraved. The earth is shaking, sending tiny rocks tumbling from the mound . . . seminal tremblings sending notice to the assassins that what they failed to understand about death is how long it really takes, that if millennia of human striving have done nothing else, in bringing on our untimely apocalypse an attenuation of death has been accomplished and a new species has risen as will Barlow, that loudest of loudmouthed mouthpieces of justice, that bearded and long-jowled Quixote, who earned his rest beneath the dirt by baresinglehandedly failing to bring down Deke Dobson, menagist and former president of B.A.D. who hired Richie Buck to stem the tide of consequences that bred like rabbits expressly to thwart his designs, hired hit man Richie Buck to do in Barlow, as he did, that Barlow might rest briefly in dirt that trembles when I look at the entryway where bare trees ache in rarefied gloom around a bare tombstone perched to mark a grave inside which Barlow, now on his hands and knees, has rolled at the news of Sandy Calderon's failed suicide, but "That was no suicide," Willie Cicci said, and there's Barlow rising: rise, O Barlow, rise like the great forfeiture of curved-spine apehood, rise like the fickle progress of the true ramapithecan limping along the evolutionary chart from bad intractable decision to slump-shouldered erectile thinker of inutile thoughts, rise, O Barlow, rise like and come to me like the slow uncrouching of inevitable madness.

"Jesus H. Fucking Christ on a hardroll, you are a moron," Barlow said, and I knew there was no corking the bottle . . .

"Suicide attempt? Well filch me a new pair of drawers, I never would have thought of that myself, get utterly bombed and leap from the second story apartment o'er a tavern, making sure to land on my face since that's the only way you'll die from such a height, cept maybe top o the head, which is a lot harder than you'd think if you ever tossed a knife at a wall and had it slap up uselessly against . . .

"So you see what I'm trying to get at, my fripperous stooge? Or don't you? You don't. Wicked Houris of the Hourglass, my death was premature. Her neck, boy, have you thought of her neck?"

I hadn't thought of her neck.

"Can a gal fall one full story to her near death, landing flat on her fulsome face so's that her skull is in twos cracked, and not do the slightest damage to her neck? Think about it, simp, her face smashed up like that and no neck damage? The cops called it suicide, right?"

What did he expect me to say?

"Right. The cops. What the fuck do they know. Call a doctor. Talk to her doctor. Since you're in sort of a groove of obtusity, just to show you I'm not a hard-hearted guy, I'm going to tell you what to ask the doctor: Doctor, in your opinion, gauging by the damage done this woman, could it be she simply dove onto her face from a second-story apartment above a bar? But first, lame-brain, drag your sorry ass down there to the scene of the crime, look at where they found her, unconscious, her face on the step, where all the blood was. She jumped off the ledge and — what? The wind blew her back toward the building? Or did she jump onto the chain holding the tavern sign and kind of swing back that way, landing gently enough on her face that it kind of nuzzled into the cement and split in two? I suppose it's not impossible — but then again: the only damage done was to her face? Her skull? Not even a stubbed toe? You believe that? Semites of Circumspection, grant me patience. The woman was beaten, don't you see? The prelate's poltroons are not doing their job, for Christ's Caroming sake. Witnesses? None. All drunk, all blacked out. Her boyfriend, my choice for culprit? Terry McDonough — passed out. Roommates? Eddie Deacon — passed out. Tommy Marco — passed out. Read the goddamned police reports. Officer Ratrace, whatever the fuck his name is, says in the morning when he went to talk to McDonough McDonough seemed to fake like he found the suicide note just then. 'Seemed like he knew it was there already,' Ratrace writes. Understand you the significance of this fact?"

I did, but I wouldn't offer him the benefit of my complicity. If the worst a ghost could muster against me was the sort of abuse I'd come to expect of it while it was alive, then it was a disappointment indeed.

"Of course you do, of course. The coppers got a cut-and-dry case. A few things don't add up: the note is vague, perhaps not a suicide note at all, the injuries don't fit the story if they care to look into it, which they don't. They got three coincidentally blacked-out witnesses, one of whom, Mr. Marco, the only one of the three who is not a cardcarrying soldier of the local two-wheeled army known as B.A.D., and consequently the vulnerable spot you will attempt to exploit, Marco is on record stating 'Last thing I saw before I blacked out was Sandy standing out there on the ledge.' What, señor, do you make of that?" The truth is I made a lot of that. As Barlow meant to imply, if I were to pursue the case I would need to find its weak spot. No litany of inconsistencies would pry open the clamped maw of justice. The cops don't give a rat's ass about necks that should be broken. The good old days when they'd roust a sleeping biker and haul him downtown, stand him up in the elevator and take him to the top floor where the jail is and roll his fetal body out with the confession spilling like a string of drool from his lips are gone. If I wanted the cops to reopen the Calderon case I'd have to present them with something tangible to go on. Something they couldn't ignore. I could send a team of doctors to the police department, but I already knew they would quickly file out demoralized by the ascendancy of thuggery over science, which they certainly would have suspected all along, and which would, in truth, have prevented them from going in the first place. But Tommy Marco was a different story, he was a man, and if he was a man he had a conscience — and he would have a breaking point. Arcing over it all was the lie he already had on record. It would be unusual for a man in the process of blacking out to record in his mind so precise a memory, so precise a moment, and all the more unusual for a man, no matter how drunk, to see a woman as beautiful as Sandy Calderon on a window ledge and not come to her aid. There isn't a lot of beauty around such as Sandy Calderon's used to be, and one of the deeper instincts of man is not to squander it.

Marco was lying. He knew it, I knew it, and so did Barlow's ghost.

"Flaming Genitalia of the Female Saints, I believe I finally got you thinking."

"Fuck you," I said.

20

BAD BREATH

"Open that screen, I can smell your breath."

"You can't smell my breath, and Gerard said to stay put till he gets back."

"I'm not going anywhere, and your breath stinks and I can smell it."

Billy chose to ignore that thrust, but it hurt despite himself, it being the first thing in the morning and all.

Lola funneled her violence down into her foot, kicking off the fold of the sleeping bag that smothered it.

"Your breath stinks and I want more air in here."

"Then do it yourself, but don't leave the cabin — like Gerard said."

"I'll leave the cabin if I want — you're not my boss."

"Gerard said not to."

"Well Gerard didn't know how bad your breath would stink. Besides, who's going to see me out here?"

Billy'd had more than he could stand, and now he was awake enough to adopt the manner he figured the behavior of this irrational twist called for.

"Look, sister. Maybe you don't get it. This is a sail club, and it's summer. People come out here to sail. Any of them could be here at any time. As far as my breath goes, I wouldn't kick about it — I've been smelling yours for over a week now."

"Fuck you, you sniveling little weasel," Lola replied.

If the sun was up it was still dispersed in a heat haze of early summer morn, in a sky yet fuzzy, cool, and blue.

The sun was up and the air was warm and undulant.

Billy felt weak and hurt. He couldn't stop his eyes from tearing. He had an erection and he wished it would go down.

Billy felt like a circus freak.

He clamped his legs tight and rolled to face away from Lola.

Lola knew Billy was crying by the way he sniffled.

Their berths curved with the hull so that though they were generally about two feet apart, their feet had come together and mingled in the night. Maybe that accounted for Lola's foul mood — she was disgusted.

"I guess maybe it's not your breath," she said. "It's probably dead fish."

Billy sniffled until he could no longer put off blowing his nose into a towel he found in one of the compartments under his berth, the dry end consoling his turned cheek until he fell back to sleep like a child whose parents had come home finally but still didn't like him very much.

21

ILLUSIONS & OTHER PHILOSOPHICAL OPPORTUNITIES

If Gerard were more philosophical he might have urged his mind to distinguish or arrange a correspondence involving the pervasive odor of dead fish at the north end of French Island and the way the heat united all the blues of waters and sky with the greens of trees and distance, a phenomenon charged with a suspicion of weight that could've been accused of refusing to allow the fishrot to rise. Instead he smelled the dead fish and simply allowed that such was not unusual on a hot summer morning where the land pointed listlessly to a shallow lake from out of a congress of stale sloughs. That, and he himself had been one with the stagnance of the river valley as he paddled a rented canoe across Lake Onalaska to the Sail Club, cleverly having chosen a roundabout method of return to his boat. After debilitating Torgeson and dumping Billy's van he had with brio assembled his wits, calling a cab from the Causeway Joie de Gas and returning to his truck, removing the license plates, exchanging them with the plates from a similar truck he often found parked near his in the ramp downtown, driven his truck to his brother's garage, removed the bogus plates, dumped them in a neighbor's garbage can, put on plates from a truck his brother never drove, returned downtown, and drank himself to sleep, smiling all the while and allowing himself to feel just a little mean.

But one thing that can be said for Gerard is that he wasn't the type who's overly eager to relay to others his latest exploits. He drank himself to sleep as always, and while he was at it he did recall his victory over Torgeson and he did smile, but the next morning he was all business, he wasn't anxious to tell the story to Billy and Lola, he was not suffused with pride, well-earned or not; he was not thinking about the past at all, no, he was thinking about Billy and Lola and what supplies they'd need to take to the island. He moored his canoe on the other side of the dock from his sailboat and called out to Billy Verité to help him with supplies, receiving as a reply only Lola's "Oh God!" of disgust, for Billy's morning of disgust had resumed — and culminated, Lola hoped — with a waking fart that was like a little man's cry for help abbreviated by, say, a boulder, a little man, that is, with a tiny bullhorn, a little man smaller than a homunculus, much smaller, so that the noise, though loud, was not loud enough for Gerard to hear, though to Lola it was louder than her own oh god, which, again, was all Gerard heard.

Gerard was simply glad they had heeded his warning to stay in the boat, and cared nothing for illusions. He was the kind of guy who, though not without wonder, would respond to an expression of wonder at some wonder of illusion or other by saying, "Of course," and then explaining it away.

But when Lola came out to help with the supplies and saw across the slough lit by the sun on the darker green of far shore tree reflection a white heron, a snowy egret, and cried out, "Look! Look at the white bird — is it an albino?", Gerard responded with the eager alacrity of a kid who knows too much. "It's an egret," he said, " — they're all white;" which, he thought quite involuntarily, makes one wonder what an albino egret would look like, or mean, or indeed if such a thing were possible.

"It's so pretty — why's it just standing there?"

"It's hunting," or fishing, I guess, you might say, he thought, wondering at his equivocation.

"It just stands there?"

"What?" Billy said, emerging from the cabin.

Lola answered, which was a good sign.

"Over there, an egret."

"Oh yeah," he said, not without wonder. "I seen lots of those."

The egret stood fifty yards from shore in a few inches of water interminably still, a living zenic icon, unswelled by the majesty of ancience and unperturbed by uncountable years of failing to solve the food cycle dilemma. Impervious to frustration, the simple white bird stared at the absence of life in blank waters, prepared to remain in place as long as it might take for a fish to swim within range of the deadly split dagger that was its beak.

"They can stand like that for hours," Gerard said, "without moving. They're extremely patient."

Just then the egret strolled forward a few paces.

"That's unusual," Gerard said.

And the bird was now so still it was impossible to be convinced it had previously been elsewhere, especially as around from behind the trees beyond swung with vigor an osprey that harbored different ideas regarding the hunting of fish. It was a more excitable bird by far that suspended itself in the air sixty feet over the water, a hundred yards or so from the egret (which didn't look, or pretended not to); suspended itself, that is, as long as it could, for the osprey is no hummingbird, and tended to drop about ten feet before fluttering back up near optimal altitude, yet never taking its eyes from the water, repeated this exercise for ten or twelve drops before finally spotting a perch of dubious size, whereupon this interloping osprey dropped abruptly, splashed hard on its belly while its talons sliced through the water into the no doubt horrified fish, flew up again from the water with the apparent ease of a helicopter, and flew back out of sight around the trees, rigid scimitar of a fish in its claws.

"Wow," Billy Verité said, "I never seen that before."

The egret shifted like a man uncomfortable in his overcoat at a bus stop.

"That was an osprey," Gerard said, "Or fish hawk."

"I never seen one before," Billy said.

"So much for all your patience," Lola said, as if to the egret.

The egret strolled a few more paces and bobbed its head a few times.

"He must've noticed the osprey," Gerard said.

"She," Lola corrected. "It's a she. And any broad who thinks patience'll get her what she wants is a bimbo."

At the word bimbo both Gerard and Billy shifted their eyes askance and back.

"See?" Lola persisted, as the egret continued to stroll and bob. "Now she's lost all patience cause that other chick showed her how it's done, by going out and getting it . . . now she's all confused. A girl's got to be like that other bird."

Gerard and Billy tried not to think about how Lola applied her philosophy to her own life.

"Let's get the supplies on board," Gerard said.

He had brought along two sleeping bags, a tent, a kerosene lantern, a propane stove, a box of candles, several jugs of water, seven cans of sardines, a box of crackers, two forks, four rolls of toilet paper, a flashlight and extra batteries, a box of stick matches, a Swiss Army knife, a Filipino machete, binoculars, a bag of apples, two fishing poles and a full tackle box, a can of ground coffee, a buck knife, a spade, two loaves of bread, a jar of peanut butter, a carton of cigarettes, a length of rope, a frying pan, and a sponge.

As they were loading it all into the sailboat, Gerard explaining what everything was and why it was there, Lola found herself waiting for him to produce more food, growing increasingly fearful when he didn't. By her calculation they had just enough food to last a day or two.

"What about food?"

"I'll be back with more supplies in a week."

"But what'll we eat till then?"

"I think I've given you just enough — "

"Plus we'll catch fish," Billy said.

"I hate fish."

In danger of becoming redemoralized, Billy set about following Gerard's curt orders, while Lola plopped down on the sternside bench in the cockpit, the sudden sight of men at work enough to prevent her from whining 'I'm hungry *now.*' She saw no way the situation could become less bleak.

"Untie that line and throw it ashore," Gerard said, and when Billy had done it they were adrift. Gerard used a tiny electric motor to back the sloop away from the dock and direct it toward the open waters of Lake Onalaska.

Billy and Lola and Gerard had the overwhelming yet subtle fortune to be present intimately on waters newly created yet fulsomely resisting all hints that the change in geography had been arranged by men. Lake Onalaska, five miles at its longest and generally three miles wide, had been bottomlands, marsh, and farms, expanding to Red Oak Ridge, which sloped down on its western side to a further littoral of bottoms and eventually the banks of the great Mississippi at its near narrowmost. In 1938 or thereabouts an organization passing itself off as the Army Corps of Engineers dammed the river in order to bring it under commercial control. They needed a deeper channel and they achieved it, but the river was forced to find expression outside its former bounds, and what was once land became of a sudden watery. Red Oak Ridge was now an island an eighth to a quarter of a mile wide and one mile long, and the bottoms became a shallow, stumpridden lake, in places unnavigable even by simple sloop. Gerard would have to approach the island with care, using precise maps, for besides the submerged tree stumps there was an old stone bridge a foot or two under the surface. It's been said an old sawmill was on the ridge or nearby, and somewhere on the island could be found the foundations of ruined farm buildings, including the foundation of the silo where during World War II a draft dodger named Amos Mosely of the longtime single black family in La Crosse (cobblers) was hunted down and shot the same way all deer stranded there had been — and by the same people. Versatile farmers formed a line at the north end of the island, swept south, at no point ever a sight-gap between links of the farmer chain, all the way to the southern lip, where a sheer drop of thirty feet met rock-ribbled shallows nonetheless inviting to the frightened Mosely who leaped and turned in midair twice upon being blasted by the two bounty hunters who got clean shots and afterward said this to each other: "Rather kill a deer." "Sure ain't much to outwit a scared nigger."

The circumstances of the Mosely hunt lurk today as verifiable fact, while the rumors of the sighting of a white man up a tree by a couple of the farmers run murkily concomitant back into the same neglect, forging a regional alliance of myth and shame.

"Nobody ever goes there?" Lola asked. "Nobody since that time?"

"Sometimes," Gerard said. "I've been there looking for arrowheads a couple times. Not for several years. Probably no one's been there at all for years at a time. No one'll ever think of looking for you there. You've just got to stay away from the shore on this side so no DNR guys spot you."

Red Oak Ridge Island ran parallel to the north end of French Island, two miles away. Clear of the shallows off the promontory, Gerard cut the motor of the mini-engine and undertook his manipulations of the mainsail and jib, ruddering toward the center of the island. The breeze was a slow, heavy draft from the southwest.

Billy sat on the bench opposite Lola, watching for French Island to recede, unconsciously assigning ten minutes of travel to the short distance they had to cover. Ten minutes later French Island hadn't moved, nor had their destination. He examined the riffling wake and then a floating speck of flora to assure himself their boat was indeed moving. Inside he swelled adventurous with upwelling pirate yarns from his youth. His consciousness lapsed happily into the neither here nor there and the heat wilted the seams of landscape, rendering all forms peripheral where no longer are green trees distinct from blue waters. He stood tall and removed his shirt to feel the sun and breeze on his chest, sat down erect, his prow-face cutting fearless the banal air, when a wind gust shifted to broadside and Gerard swung the boom, which slammed across Billy's temple area, Gerard muttering unconsolatory only, "That'll happen," as Lola laughed vengefully. Billy chose the stoic course, dismissing bone on metal as rough trade no more to be acknowledged by a man of adventure on high seas than a stable fly biting a foot, though the stable fly, biting his foot, could no more be ignored than the run of a cutlass throat-through, and Billy slapped it anon, cursing, "Fucker."

"Stable fly," Gerard said. "Shouldn't be following us this far from land."

"Ouch!" Lola cried, slapping at her ankle, "These flies bite."

"I hate those little fuckers," Gerard said, laughing like a man whose hoary suspicions regarding human folly were being borne out before his eyes.

The ruckus abated and Billy again scanned the horizon for evidence of their movement. Red Oak Ridge Island loomed no larger, but behind him, he found, French Island was shrinking. The horizon kept its distance, but as they pursued their course the boat was receding into itself, and all three experienced a shift into a vaguely more elemental consciousness. For Billy it was an amazing new sense of vastness and of a thrilling danger no less thrilling for its superciliousness. He could see twenty or thirty miles upriver the undulations of bluffs that rounded out the north, no seam belying the fact of a longer river. Somewhere up there the river slipped through the heat-misted bluffs and somehow the illusion of closed space made the world appear larger. For Gerard it was an acute mechanical knowledge of their specific circumstances as the descendants of the engineers of the technology that would take them across a placid lake that could easily be their death if one of any number of conceivable disasters should befall them. For Lola it was the confusion brought on by having enlisted yet sensing forces of kidnap sailing her to a place from where she could never return, what now lay behind at some mysterious nexus passed unrecognizable, what lay ahead unknowably wild and dimly suspected, clipped of wonder by her knowing the estrangement between her self and its volition.

Well into the lake and no perceptible wind, the boat's wake no more than the recession of fixed points of lonesome debris, a hollow eruption of genuine horse latitude sensation lolled Billy and Gerard the sailors to wondrous feary quietude. A cormorant limned low a furious streak from shore to shore, black and (barely bulbously, ducklike) doomful.

"What's that?" Billy whispered.

"Cormorant."

Lola dared not speak, nor knew why.

They watched the cormorant disappear past the north end of the island. They felt no wind and the shores were soft and sensuous strangelands in the distances.

"This is really the river, isn't it?" Billy asked.

"Yes," Gerard said, "But that doesn't mean it's always moving."

An hour had passed since they'd embarked, long enough to relieve them of what certitude they harbored regarding the relations of speed, distance, and time. And they felt in their stomachs the significance of their loss, and the way all losses attained the same logic, that if they were not yet there they may never get there. They looked to the island and knew all history was generated by its fact and could barely suppress groans of abject despair.

Even Gerard, for whom these mysteries were as rocklike as he.

No wind.

Thoughts as dissipant as the conglomerate wilds.

Fish were an inconceivable fright and birds emissaries of dark notional continents cast unto dream.

None knew by what untrustworthy fortune the island shore so suddenly grew a nearer impenetrable, a humped vaster stand of trees, leaves of grapevines rising from the waters, crescents of sand laid at the defeat of sheer land surrounded. Island no more: they were in a bay inside land that betrayed no limits. Creatures hooted and trilled jungly, unwary it seemed of the coming transgression.

Orders came.

"Drop anchor!"

"Load the dinghy!"

Lola's mind eased at the proximity of land and the sight of its continuance under the shallower lake. She saw, too, how this could be paradise, magazine images of exclusive beach soirees coming to mind under neon glyphs: Cancun, Acapulco, Rio, Hawaii, Tokyo . . .

Make me a drink, Lola would say.

Billy felt an explorer's patience, and he had to, for it was a long walk into the unknown, every step a confrontation with the new, a hero's encounter with forces heretofore unconquerable, though yielding, Billy knew, at the frontiers of the nature of man.

And Gerard, cognizant of many similar such follies played out on shores thought of as pristine, employed his faculty for detailed concentration to keep from shaking his head. Once arrived to the brambly shore, he unloaded the goods then dinghied back to the sloop for his refugees. Gerard had not oared far when Lola glimpsed the first proof that this was not her Eden — clumps of green weeds like inverted featherdusters infested the sands nearer to shore, rising trembly in the water, bending at the surface to avoid the world of air.

"I can't swim in this shit," she said.

"We ain't here on vacation, babe," Billy said, to which Lola avowed privately 'you will soon pay for that, you skinny little fucker.'

Climbing out of the dinghy behind Billy, Lola suddenly understood that Gerard would remain in and soon be gone.

"You're not coming with us?"

"I have things to straighten out on shore."

"Oh god," she realized, with too much of defeat in her for panic.

The goods were huddled on a dry lip of sand before a tiny massif. Billy sat on a sleeping bag, his hands hung hapless between inward slanting knees.

"Can't you help us set up?"

"I have to go. Billy'll know what to do."

Lola looked back at Billy, a slumped puppet bleached albino by the sun.

"All right," she said.

The fishing poles leaned against the tent sack. She could sit next to Billy on the other sleeping bag, or on the other side of their mound of goods on the little plastic cooler. She chose the cooler, hanging her hands hapless between her inward slanting knees.

"Bye," everybody said, Gerard adding, "See you one week from today," rowing twice before calling: "Keep track of the days."

Billy and Lola watched the sculler diminish in proper proportion to the sloop, skiff alongside and board, load the dinghy, haul anchor, turn the sloop about, and beckon wind for home, little more than a little man in a boat. Neither moved nor spoke, watching long the way the sloop didn't shrink, each in a private way asking after all this time, and again after all this time, If I can still see him how long is a day?

Gerard did not look back, for he still saw what he feared he'd forever see, Billy and Lola, shipwreck stunned amidst the goods, a forlorn study of what we made, what still it boiled down to, and what could never be more, and what could never ever be enough.

22

EDDIE THE FBI GUY

Gerard returned to the city harboring unfinished a plan to gather enough evidence against Stratton and Torgeson to get them both thrown in some federal pokey for the duration of their lives. He figured this Skunk guy would have to go down with them, but having in mind the relatively incompetent persona of Deke Dobson, he figured Skunk could easily be rendered harmless, maybe even induced to turn state's evidence. Gerard, a concrete type, was not good with vague thoughts.

His first step was to enlist the aid of the local FBI office, which he found in the basement of the Post Office Building at the end of a corridor in a room still labeled MAINTENANCE. Chief Agent Eddie Legree stood just inside the open door beside a stack of fruit crates bulging with what papers weren't leaking through the slats, regarding with angelic absorption the report of a field agent long since fled.

Legree was revisiting the past.

"Excuse me," Gerard said, and Legree looked at him pleasantly. A visitor was not yet too great a surprise.

Both men were forty-eight years old.

"I'm Agent Legree, can I help you?"

"FBI?"

"FBI," Legree said. He paused to let a memory drift by, reached up to place the report in the top crate, and stepped forward extending his hand.

"Eddie — call me Eddie."

Eddie's head was hairless but for graceful side tufts connected by a thin fall of turf behind. His dome was rounded eggless and he wore wire-rimmed glasses.

"Tom," Gerard said, "Tom Gerard."

"Come in, Tom. Never mind the disorder, we're just moving in the new office here."

It occurred to Gerard to look about the stacks and back through the narrow aisle down which he was led for the people Legree referred to. He saw no one.

Eddie's desk was behind the disorder, a bare metallic quadruped without head or drawer. A narrow cot was pushed against the back wall and Eddie gestured to it.

"Sit down," Eddie said, and Gerard sat.

Eddie produced a notepad from the vest he wore, a corduroy job that brought Gerard back to the days when such things could be had at discount clothing stores downtown.

Gerard wasn't ready to talk business, not until he was convinced this was a real FBI guy. He figured he'd either have to ask straight out for an ID or get Eddie to say something only the local Chief Agent would know. He thought a moment and couldn't imagine what that might be.

"Look Eddie" — he somehow did not find such familiarity hard to manage with this guy — "I'm sorry to do this, but I'm here with some — well, this is hardly what I expected. Could I see some identification?"

Eddie smiled and out came an actual puff of kindness that Gerard couldn't help but receive as a sort of osmotically transmitted message: Here is a good man.

"I'm sorry, Tom, I should've figured. This doesn't amount to much, does it? I mean considering what you might, of course, expect."

He pulled out his wallet and extracted a card that he handed to Gerard.

"This do?"

Gerard looked from the card to Eddie and back.

"You had more hair then."

"They won't issue new ones."

Eddie sat in his desk chair and swung to face Gerard directly.

"I'll be frank with you, Tom. This is an officially sanctioned, one-hundred percent FBI office, but it's not funded by them anymore. It's funded by me, off my pension. When they moved to eliminate the La Crosse office I worked this out with D.C. I can keep it open on my own, but they'll not send money, or even a caseload. But I can report to them and I do represent their authority, such as it is."

"Such as it is?"

"What?"

"Such as it is."

"Such as what is?"

"You said their authority, such as it is."

"The FBI's?"

"I believe so."

"No, I mustn't . . . I must've meant my representation of it, or some such. I think. I don't know why I'm telling you all this."

Engaged in the conversation as he was, Gerard was not as agape as a nagging feeling told him he should be.

"I haven't told you why I'm here, but I came to see the local FBI and you're it, right? Just you."

"I'm all alone, Tom."

"But you have authority."

"I do."

"So if I have a federal case against some people here you can call upon the Agency to assist in — "

"I believe I can call in the big boys, yes."

"Conspiracy to commit murder."

This Eddie received as a non sequitur. He blinked and waited politely for Gerard to continue.

Gerard thought Eddie was thinking.

A great deal of time passed.

Gerard cracked first.

"Is that a federal case?"

"Is what?"

"Conspiracy to commit murder."

Eddie recapitulated the sequence in a nearly silent mumble. Gerard thought he saw his lips form the word conspiracy.

"Oh!" Eddie said. "I see. Yes, sure. We love conspiracy."

"Involving two police officers."

"That's excellent."

"Two police officers mixed up in drugs."

"Do you have evidence?"

"Probably not. A few words on tape. I came to see if you can support me, help me gather evidence, apprehend them once we got enough . . . "

"We. Or I. I mean I can't let you head the operation, that would be irresponsible of me. This is dangerous business."

"Tell me about it. One of them attacked me."

"Any witnesses?"

"No. It was just him and me, in the dark."

"Are you a criminal, Tom?"

"No, Eddie, I'm not."

Gerard wanted to tell Eddie he lived in a maintenance closet, too.

"Eddie? You live here, don't you?"

"Tom, I believe in what I do."

"Then you'll help me?"

"Help you?"

"With the conspiracy case, the two police officers."

"Oh, I thought you were — oh, will I help you with the case. No, I'll op it, and you'll help me, if you like. I can't pay you. And there could be some dangers."

"Like I said, one of them attacked me."

"One of the cops."

Gerard nodded.

"Right, right, I got it."

23

A CAPER, OR OP

Gerard checked the flashlight.

It worked.

But the feeling in his stomach didn't go away.

He tried the flashlight again and it worked again.

Still he had a bad feeling.

So he checked again and it worked and while he shivered on the roof of the Winchester on Fifth building, waiting for the lights to come on in the corner office on the top floor of the Fifth on Jay building, Eddie was scurrying out of there. They had not discussed how they would meet up if something went wrong, only that the distress signal would be three curt beams from Gerard's flashlight.

Outside, Eddie looked up at the office he had just left. It was still dark, which was odd since the only reason he could figure Gerard would give him the danger sign was if he'd spotted Skunk and/or his leather-jacketed commandos on the way into the building. Now the problem was where to meet Gerard, something they had — unforgivably, considering Eddie's experience — neglected to discuss.

On the roof, Gerard wondered what was taking Eddie so long. He didn't think even an experienced agent like Eddie could wire an office in the dark.

Eddie decided that sooner or later Gerard would have to show up on the fourth floor, where his maintenance closet was, so he paced the rectangular hallway until he managed to dispel in his mind the succession of disasters he spent his time dreaming up. What it came down to was this: Skunk must have shown up, turned on the light after some delay; and Gerard was keeping an eye on his movements, no doubt wondering where the hell Eddie was.

Gerard hadn't shown Eddie the way to the roof, but it doesn't take long for a guy like Eddie to figure such things out. On the fifth floor he found a utility room with stairs rising to a hinged trap door secured by a padlock and chain. The lock was still locked, but Gerard had unscrewed the chain. Clever, Eddie thought: his own first instinct would've been to pick the lock.

The door did not open onto the roof as Eddie expected. Instead he found himself inside a mysterious sixth floor, a warehouse for building fixtures of bygone days, which wasn't visible from the street below. As his eyes adjusted to the closeted gloom he realized he had stumbled onto nothing more significant than hundreds of doors, windows, and light covers. Disoriented, he searched the ceiling for seams that would betray the secret way onto the roof, finally arriving at a door affixed mockingly to the back wall, which he unceremoniously tumbled through to find himself skating on the roof gravel, in the process jolting Gerard out of his vigilance.

Gerard was at the far corner of the roof behind the parapet.

"What are you doing up here?" he asked Eddie.

"You signaled," Eddie said, too good-natured in his earnestness to wonder at the question.

Gerard understood right away.

"No, I was just checking the flashlight. I figured you were in there wiring it in the dark."

"What? You signaled because you thought I was wiring his office in the dark? So you didn't want me to do it in the dark."

"No, no. I . . . no, I didn't signal, I was just checking the flashlight."

"Why?"

"I didn't want anything to go wrong, so I checked to see if it was working in case I had to use it."

"Three times?"

"Did I do it three times?"

"That was the signal."

"I wasn't signaling. I was checking the flashlight."

"What was the signal?"

"Three consecutive flashes."

"That's what you did."

"Okay, I signaled, but I didn't mean to."

"Right, so we've effectively bungled the op, but no harm done. The best thing to do is call it off for now. The easiest way to destroy an operation is to push ahead once it's gone awry. We'll try again tomorrow night . . . You're a good man, Tom."

24

BUNGLED OP, NIGHT TWO

Gerard rarely liked a man as much as he already liked Eddie.
There he was, like a little kid, his face pressed to the glass, his
hands rendering his head parenthetical. He was moving his
mouth, trying to tell Gerard something, and Gerard had no idea
what it was. Eddie had entered the office, turned on the light,
and gone directly to the window. Gerard exaggerated a shoulder
shrug and Eddie moved his mouth more deliberately, as if to attenuate for Gerard the incomprehensible. Greater beings might
have mistaken their charades for a futile sort of mating rite or an
early step on the evolutionary road toward the time when all of
men's lives would be one prolonged gesture. A lip reader would
have read Eddie's lips asking: How's the flashlight working?

Gerard shrugged one last time and Eddie waved him off to
assure him it wasn't important, then turned to see Skunk Lane
Forhension and his henchman Hobo enter the office. Gerard
watched the whole scene play out behind the glass like a fish bal-
let: Eddie slumping his shoulders, assuming an innocent posture
apparently intended to persuade Skunk and Hobo he belonged

where he was, perhaps as janitor or late-night electrician; smiles being exchanged, Skunk's for Eddie's; Hobo standing warily to the side, arms crossed like a cigar-store Indian; Skunk smiling, nodding, gesturing Eddie by with his head, glancing once toward Hobo, who seized Eddie from behind; Eddie turning and landing a toe in Hobo's groin at precisely the same moment Hobo cuffed the side of Eddie's neck; Eddie stunned for several seconds, backpedaling noodle-legged, and Hobo in a reflexive crouch, Skunk looking impassively on; Hobo recovering in time to step inside Eddie's next kick, performing some hand-to-hand combat maneuver that looked to Gerard inordinately complex and seemed to involve more elbows than Hobo had yet was executed so quickly that as Eddie was on his knees grasping his throat, Hobo was already crouched again in resumption of groin pain; Skunk patting Hobo on the back; Hobo rising, Skunk indicating Eddie, still clutching his own throat, still on his knees; Hobo walking up behind Eddie and chopping him unconscious with a more standard karate blow; and Skunk and Hobo removing Eddie from the office, Skunk turning off the light as they went.

25

ROGUE MELANCHOLY FOR A DETECTIVE

"You ever think about death, Lew?"

Torgeson looked down at his chicken sandwich, from which he'd lifted the lid to find five or six rhombuses of wilted lettuce sunken like creatures of long ago into congealed mayo. Stratton's question seemed both apt and foolish.

"Everytime I think about Gerard," he said. "I'll catch the son of a bitch — and I'll kill him slow. I'd like you to be there."

Stratton fluttered warmly about the sternum.

"I've been thinking about death."

"Gerard's?"

"Mine. I've been thinking a lot about my death."

"I been thinking about Gerard's."

"I know, but you ever worry about yours?"

"It ain't happened yet, how can I worry about it?"

Stratton looked down at his sandwich. He was seldom hungry these days. He folded the wrapping paper over to cover the top bun and handed it to Torgeson.

"Want this?"

"You sure?"

Stratton nodded.

"I don't know . . . "

He squinted his eyes at some obscure apparatus suspirating irregular and dreary back in his mind.

"I don't know . . . "

Torgeson chewed an enormous mouthful of sandwich, staring at Stratton as if he had his lips on backward. After swallowing, he said, "Look, my friend, you have got to get off this. A crook got the best of you, gave you a little scar. Happened before — what am I talking about, it just happened to me. We get over it. We kill somebody — Gerard — and we get over it. You and me got the best job in the world, you forget at times like this, but look: we make a good salary, get to set our own hours, wear our own clothes . . . there's no real limit to how much money we can steal if we set our minds to it. So get off this. We're going to solve these immediate problems and we're going to have fun doing it. You hear me?"

Stratton turned from the morose expanse of cloudless sky and smiled weakly.

"There," Torgeson said. "You see?"

"It's not that, Lew — it's not the wound or any of that. It's not that at all."

Stratton squinted again.

"You know the other night I had a shot at a nice looking waitress, you know? You know the type once they find out you're a cop, you can see it in their eyes. All I had to do was ask when she's off. That's all."

"Where? Which restaurant?"

"Was that diner down on French Island."

"Right."

"You know that chick? Weeknights? Brunette?"

"Seen her."

"But you know what I mean."

"Sure, go on then."

"Right, so alls I had to do was ask, and I just, I don't know, I just didn't feel like it, you know? I thought about my wife, and I don't mean I felt a resurgency of love or anything, but I just kind of thought, maybe didn't think even, I just kind of thought, maybe it'd just be easier if I just go home and fuck Claire . . . "

"That's all right. We all do that sometimes. I fuck my wife. Why not? I mean, else why's she there. Jesus, the other night, when was it, we ate at that taco place, that night I went straight home and fucked my wife. We all do it."

"So I get home and she's grateful or whatever. I mean sometimes she's got to put me through the motions, and I give it a minute or two and it's fuck you I'm out the door. But this night she's ready for it and we get going — and you know I told you how she likes me to slam her pretty hard, and hell, it turns me on when she screams — we can go on for a half hour like that, long as my arms hold up; but the other night after maybe five, ten minutes my arms are tired, I'm out of breath, and I start thinking what's this all about? I'm going to get off and be done with it and then wonder why I even wanted to in the first place, right? So I hustled it up and went and had a drink — "

"Hey, we all get bored, partner."

"I went out and had a drink, and remember that wild filly named Fran from the D.A.'s office, that did that dance?"

"That was some bitch. I'd like to get me some of that again."

"Again?"

"Yeah."

"You never told me."

"Go on about her, then."

"You never told me, Lew."

"Just fucking go on."

"All right, I saw her that night, down at the — I can't believe you never told me; was it that night?"

"Yes, and I'm sorry I forget to tell you so go the fuck on."

"Well it's just that — "

"Go . . . on . . . "

"Okay okay — I saw her there and she remembers me and says she sees me in the building all the time, all this as she's pulling me onto the dance floor, where she starts grinding against me, and I just didn't have the stomach for it, Lew. She's got this gauze dress on and I can feel her panties, tiny silk ones I bet, and I felt her up a little, but Christ, Lew, my heart wasn't in it — I didn't even get a real hard on."

Torgeson rubbed his crotch, smearing a drop of mayo that had landed there.

"I'm getting a hard on just listening to you. You get her number?"

"No, fuck it, just get it from the D.A.'s, or call her over there. Just don't mention me."

"Why's that?" Torgeson asked, licking his hand.

"She wasn't too impressed with me. I just kind of stopped dancing and said I'm gonna go finish my drink, and as I'm walking away she says where the fuck you think you're going and the song stops and even louder she says if *you're* not gonna fuck me I'll find somebody who will, someone who can still get his dick up — "

"She said that?"

"Yes, and — "

"She really did? Loud? Right there in front of everybody?"

"Yes, but I didn't care, because anyway I couldn't stop thinking so I fuck her and it's over and what's the point? You know?"

"The point is she's a hot and wild bitch and that's the point. What's the point."

"You don't understand."

"I'm happy to agree to that."

"Okay, forget it. Let's say it's nothing. It means nothing. One bad night, that's all. But it never happened before, you know? I never got tired like that. I never refused a waitress like that one — you know me and waitresses. And Fran — Jesus!"

"Stress. You're under pressure. Once we get through this thing you'll be your old self."

Stratton looked down at his lap, suddenly perplexed. "Where's my sandwich?"

"I ate it. You gave it to me."

"That's right. That's what I've been thinking: once this is over, then what? Same old shit? We're not getting any younger. I mean, what's the goal here, Lew? What do we do when we get too old to fuck?"

"You don't get too old to fuck. Old people fuck."

"But I mean these other chicks. Like Fran. Chicks like that aren't going to fuck us forever. So what do we do, fuck our wives? Watch TV? Watch TV, eat, fuck our wives? Is that what lies ahead? Is that our goal?"

"I imagine . . . I know what you're saying . . . shit . . . I don't know, I imagine after a while that's what we'll want to do, fuck our wives. You know, like when we're in our fifties or sixties. We'll get desk jobs and fuck our wives and the four of us will go out to dinner and play cards, and you and me'll go fishing sometimes, go whoring around up north . . . I know it sounds wrong now, but when we get older we'll change, and that's what we'll want to do. We'll make more money; we'll steal more, too, and we'll take a trip down to the Bahamas and fuck our wives — "

"And they'll have their fat asses in their bikinis and all these young chicks'll be there and we'll want them, but we'll be too old for them, and we'll go back to the hotel and have sad fucks with our wives, and you and me'll go fishing and come back and they'll have been shopping all day and want to show us all these geegaws — it'll — "

"Geegaws? What the fuck's a geegaw? Look, I'm telling you to forget this shit. It's going to be all right. You'll feel a lot better once you get your hands around Billy Verité's throat. And we'll find him, too. We'll take care of him and Gerard — and fuck Lola, I don't care about her — she's out of town, I'm positive. And once we get those fuckers, then we'll meet up with this Skunk asshole. Nobody does that to my partner and gets away with it."

Stratton drifted off again to gaze toward his crepuscular horizons; Torgeson leaned back, stretched his legs as far as he could, and tried to picture Fran's face as it was the one time in ecstasy beneath him.

Torgeson grew bored first.

"So what's the deal here, then?"

"Skunk threw this one our way. Says this guy seen Billy Verité a few weeks ago with some chick. That's all I know."

"What's the price?"

"He said there may be some gang trouble ahead and he wouldn't mind if we — "

"He wouldn't mind?"

"That's how he said it: he wouldn't mind."

"Wouldn't mind. I can't wait to meet this cocksucker."

"He wants us to kind of spread it through the department it's just a gang thing, no civilians get hurt, no big deal. He assures me it'll all take place in private."

"Does he think Skinner's some kind of goddamn pushover?"

"I don't know, but you know he's backed by Strafe and that's big."

"What the fuck's Strafe care about some asshole like Skunk fucking motorcycle asshole?"

"Strafe *sent* him here."

"Right, you said that. Well fuck Strafe, too, then."

"Strafe is nationwide, man."

"Yeah, I hear he's got someone in the department."

"He's got people everywhere."

"That's what I hear."

"D.C. too."

"Fucking Jews, partner."

"I don't know, I think it's more than that. I think Strafe isn't even a Jew. I think the organization's a front."

"This our guy?"

"That's Fred."

A lumbering middle-aged blonde man was climbing into a taxi in front of the Guest Villa Motel. Stratton was parked in the motel lot, facing the street.

"I know this guy. Had to pull him off that fat mean fucker one time — Bill. Fred liked to have killed him. Over at Al's Sports Inn. Bet that's where he's going."

"We'll be there first."

Stratton shot past the cab, across Fourth Street, through the Texaco lot onto Market, turned south on Sixth, and pulled over eight blocks down, in front of Al's.

"Here he comes," Stratton said, looking in the rearview mirror.

"Bill's probably already in there."

"They're great friends."

The cab didn't bother to pull over, stopping even with Stratton's sedan. Fred paid the driver and got out.

"Hey Fred," Stratton said, "come here."

Fred had a pleasant face, red and pitted and handsome to the extent his milky eyes falsely reflected an innonence of brutality. He wore a crisp white shirt and gray polyester slacks.

"Detective Stratton, is that you? Why don't you step out of the car and let me knock you on your ass."

Fred leaned on the door, thrusting his face in close to Stratton, who leaned away.

"Hey, you got your nigger partner with you. What say, Lew? Like to go a few rounds? You and me? Put on the gloves? No badges, no witnesses?"

Torgeson eyed Fred coldly, with great dispassion.

"One day, Fred," he said, "we will meet."

"Look forward to it, officer," Fred said garrulously. "Well," he went on, straightening, "If there's nothing else . . ."

"There is, Fred," Stratton said.

"Yeah? What's that?"

"You know somebody named Skunk?"

"Skunk? Why sure, damnedest little feller I ever met. Doctor or something. Met him over at the Wonder Bar."

"He told us you maybe saw Billy Verité not long ago."

"That right?"

Fred looked puzzled.

"You know Billy Verité?"

Fred looked to the stars, his powers of recall stored up there somewhere.

"That's right, ugliest cuss on the face of this earth. And you know who I saw him with? Lola. Know her, good-looking broad. Nice pussy. You ought to get you some of that, hey Lew?"

Torgeson felt walls of blood flood his skull.

"Where'd you see them, Fred?" Stratton asked.

"How the fuck should I know? Coming out of a house somewhere."

"Where?"

Fred tossed a simian arm.

"Back there somewhere. Market Street. Cass. State. One of those."

"What'd the house look like?"

"Like a house. You know, had doors and windows."

"What color was it?"

"Same as all the others at night. Look, Jimmy, I don't mind all these silly little questions, you being a cop and all, but I'm getting a little thirsty. So why don't you come on in I'll buy you a drink."

Fred moved to get around the car.

"Fred?"

Fred stopped.

"Whatwhatwhat."

"When was this?"

"Damned if I know. Nighttime."

And he walked around the front of the car and up to the door of the tavern, where he stopped on hearing his name one last time. He turned, letting some of his natural meanness show.

It was Torgeson.

"Yes, Lew."

"Next time I see you I'm gonna hurt you bad."

Fred laughed and went into the bar.

26

WHY EDDIE WASN'T LISTENING

"I have rarely, Eddie, rarely seen as fine a physical specimen as you. I can look at a man, this talent I have, and I can say just exactly what's wrong with him. From the moment I saw you I said to myself this fella's in perfect shape, soon as I saw you in the office. Well that's the FBI for you, clean living, that fine sweet knowing you're on the side of right, a life of action . . . fulfillment. A good life. I'd say you're a good man, Eddie."

Skunk stood up from his desk and lifted the aluminum cone so the light shone directly on Eddie's open downcast eyes.

Eddie didn't blink. Nor did he look up.

"I suppose I ought to be sad in a way, Eddie. It ought to be sad, the last of anything. Ah, but it's a long way from J. Edgar Hoover, isn't it? A long way. You got a picture of him at home? That's right, you got no home. Well, don't answer. Thanks to you giving me the key, I'll just go have a look myself. Like to get a look at those files, too. I bet you wrote the neatest reports. Neat little reports sent off to Washington where you knew eventually nobody ever read them — who cares about this driftless no place? Who cares about Deke Dobson, who did some of his dirty work right down here — did you write about that, Eddie? You knew, didn't you, that it was futile, but you never gave up, you held the fort, even after you knew no cavalry would come, you held on to the very end. But Eddie? Don't look up. Eddie? Long gone are the days when a steely will abideth over wrongdoing."

Skunk dropped the light, which snake-danced a riot of arced lights about the dark basement room before coming to rest. He walked up to Eddie and tilted his head back by lifting his chin. His body had eclipsed the light, but Skunk could still tell that Eddie's eyes did not look up.

"Ropes too tight, Eddie?" Skunk asked, letting go of Eddie's chin and laughing.

"Ain't this classic? Hardwood chair, single light in a dark, cold room. Cigarette? No. You just want to sleep. Don't let me keep you up. Just a few more questions. Now that you know what it's like over there, was it worth it? Are you redeemed in your faith in the goodness of man? Do any number of rights make a right? Here's one: Where did everybody go? How many, Eddie, are huddled about? Is there a line for those of you with regrets? . . . A knocking at the door — that would be Hobo . . . "

Skunk took Eddie by the chin again.

"What's that, Yorick? A knocking at the door?"

Hobo entered and immediately scrunched his nose.

"What's that smell?"

Hobo approached them, sniffing like a bloodhound.

Skunk let the head drop again, wondering at the weight of what so often seems so little.

"I think he crapped his pants," Hobo said.

"They'll do that when they die."

21

WILD BUNCHES

A vast ocean of air dislodged itself from the Arctic Dome and slid willfully to meet head-on a scythe of tropical bluster uprearing from the southwest over the Driftless Zone. Together they produced a steady and cold summer rain that focused with bleak and wide intensity on the valley south of the city where Skunk Lane Forhension had engineered the last great battle of driftless motorcycle gangs. A narrow gravel road, sinewy and forlorn, slunk from the river road four miles to Skunk's B.A.D. paramilitary training grounds. Skunk had let it be known to Outlaw scouts that on July 14 would occur the last full drill before all-out attack on the Outlaws, and as he stood hatless in the matutinal raingloom listening for the engines he expected would roar down from the north slope, he sniffed of the phenomenal world for evidence of a future soon to conform to his vision, there found none, and saw in that void his command of events.

Hobo, clad in a jungly green poncho, joined him.

"You think from the north?"

"They'll try the north first. We'll inflict casualties on the first wave. Skinner will survey from the ridge. This cold rain will do his arthritis no good."

"Skinner has arthritis?"

"I believe he does."

"What'll they do when they discover the ramparts?"

"Skinner will note their horseshoe shape, and he will decide to retreat and come direct along the road, as he knows we are defying him to do."

"Won't he know that's what we're prepared for?"

"Yes. And that's the way he is. A bold and fearless warrior. He will say fuck you, and attempt to overpower us with his superior numbers."

"Nearly three to one."

"Not after the first attack. We'll reduce their number by thirty."

"Two to one, then."

"Skinner will lead the charge and I will shoot him directly between the eyes. That is the way of war."

"Will the others keep fighting?"

"Not for long. We let in maybe a third. Those will be slaughtered. The battle at the fence will cost us a few men. Gradually it will dawn on the remaining Outlaws that their leader has fallen and they face annihilation. They will retreat up the road and you will trap them at Bad Ax Creek and finish them off. All of them. That is what is meant by war of attrition."

Hobo looked at his leader, this bedraggled Lee Harvey Oswald who gazed up at the ridgeline with eyes that saw beyond the mundane affairs of men, eyes that even as Hobo watched were penetrating rain and mist and gloom to observe the autochthonous machinations of the universe in which men such as Hobo were but the derelict and simple spawn, ever unenlightened and laboring glumly, secretly laying in wait for such a man as this, a truly great man.

It was all Hobo, a proud man himself, could do not to ask: What do you see, boss?

Instead he asked, "Aren't you cold?" for Skunk wore naught below his hatless head but jeans.

Skunk looked his bare ribbly chest over, then saw his feet planted queasily in rising muck. He looked up at Hobo, deep into his eyes and beyond, all the way to the most obscure origins of his motivation.

And Hobo knew it.

"I have a fire in my belly, Hobe."

Hobo suspected as much.

"Everybody in position?"

"All set."

"Cause they're here."

Hobo squinted against the rain, listening with his eyes. Even his ache for action and slaughter could not prevent him from swelling with the atavism of the solitary man amid the infinite applause of rain. But he heard no engines.

"Ah," Skunk said, pointing up at the spiked helmets appearing atop figures clambering hunlike to the ridge on motorcycles, "the kaiser's men."

And down the slope they came, stout leathery visigoths on wheels, sliding godlike and heedless in mucked undergrowth, flattening the smaller trees. Slung on their backs, automatic rifles; tattooed to their massive arms, inverted skulls; covering their faces, beards brambly wild.

One or two got their helmets knocked off by low branches. None were daunted.

Down they roared, they rode, they slid, and as they came within one hundred yards of B.A.D.'s encampment, as they reached for their weapons, Skunk's camouflaged sentinels sprung fences of chicken wire and wood which slapped upright into the mad on-rushing wheels, heaving heavy huns head over wheels and Skunk's berets rose from the undergrowth under helmets of bush to riddle the beasts with small metal pellets that tore through their flesh and bones and organs and killed them, one and all.

The second wave was nearly halfway down the slope when they saw clearly enough what happened to the first, when they saw their surprise attack had been met with ambush, and all but the most foolhardy tilted their bikes into long and nightmarish slides that were in nearly every case too late, three or four managing to clamber bike and all back up the hill while the rest were shot in the head or back. One of the most foolhardy was Skeddy Boone, a frail madman who greeted the bad news with a quick draw and a murderous yowl, skittering and yawing down the slope with both hands gripping his machine gun, firing a spray of bullets that finished off two of his own and three of the enemy, while his front wheel went increasingly berserk until the bike jerked sideways, bucking him off before landing on him, madman and mount skidding on the careen into the fence, where he was mercifully plugged in the skull by a silent commando.

"Skeddy, you fucking maniac," Darryl Skinner chuckled with great pride, for he was a man who knew men and the world of men and knew right then that for such a man as Skeddy Boone there was no better way to die. He scanned the valley from his mount atop the ridge. The trees were thick as rain, but he had to figure the ambush fences covered all three slopes. Most of the fighting was over, though two or three of his soldiers were agonizing in private dramas, clawing at the muck, grunting and panting, waiting for one of the bullets to hit, which soon enough enough did. Skinner could just make out a man wearing nothing but jeans standing in the open on the floor of the valley, watching the action. The man next to him looked like Hobo. That must be that Skunk guy, Skinner figured. "Well, fuck you, Skunk," he said aloud. "You want us to come in on the road, we'll come in on the road. Fuck you."

It took two hours for Skinner to gather his remaining troops, descend the opposite slope, file back to the river road, and find the road into the valley of his certain doom, and once he came roaring into B.A.D.'s camp it took just a few seconds for him to die. Skunk picked him out of the crowd of enraged beastengines, a black wedge-shaped cloud of fury with Skinner at point, and from his position crouched behind a barrel drilled him between the eyes. Skinner sat dead in the air a moment, his cycle boring ahead, before landing in the midst of his fellows, who pressed on, mulching Skinner into a stew of anonymity.

The size and density and sheer rage of energy of the Outlaw attack easily overcame the attempts of Skunk's minions to bar the road — the gates exploded aside and the keepers were murdered on the spot. And when Skinner fell the troops were not dispirited — they were further enraged, and fought with cossackian fury. It took many bullets to kill them. The cloud gained the encampment, losing only Skinner and a few on the flanks of the wedge, and once inside dispersed like a shrapnel bomb, rushing fearless every B.A.D. cover, storming benches, sheds, troughs, the spray of automatic weapons undaunting, if at times deadly; and they managed quickly to overwhelm the B.A.D. forces, rooting out all who were not off with Hobo preparing the final ambush, and Skunk Lane Forhension, who had climbed into the barrel as soon as it became apparent the battle was not going as he had planned.

One by one the Outlaws, bodies soaked, clothes ripped, most bleeding profusely from multiple wounds, straggled into the center of the compound, still toting deadly guns. One or two still had their helmets. None had their bikes.

They had no leader.

Skunk watched them eclipsing back and forth through the slats of the barrel. These were fine men, the best of an old order, vikings, goths, nomadic raiders off the steppes, mongols, men of great brawn, instinctual savagery, tolerators of little nonsense, beasts who honed with uncanny precision in on the elemental, the profane, men for whom that which could be squandered could be more easily crushed, men for whom the varied forms of their sustenance neither required nor brooked explanation, men whose words were few and in the face of great odds becoming fewer, men for whom bravery was the violent and incidental residue of a vague myth inhabited by men of great brawn and savagery, come down the steppes untamed untameable, men who feared nought, took what they damn well wanted, their thievery, their plunder, their rape paid for by an absolute disregard for life, even their own.

Skunk regarded these heroes through the slats without wistfulness, for to have been so would've been to deny the brutes the finer piquancy of their moment of passing. O the grandeur of valor squelched by time, the tectonic force of change, the effusion of meaning, blunt and moribund; sad the

mingling of lost and bloodied heroes, victors, the damned; horrific and sublime the simplicity of demise — the self-corralled
and exhausted barbarians offered up before the phalanx of
Hobo's troop come down the ridge quiet through the trees and
the lazy eyes of the last true Outlaws defying mirth and misery
as they acknowledged the row of inevitable barrel holes pointing at them in the rain and not without kindness.

28

THE DETECTIVE WHO LIKED PAGANINI

Likewise I regard Gerard — through slats of memory and conceit — as much as I know he would never have wanted to be admired as the last of anything; he would have preferred not to have been outstripped by time; and he would revile my tendency to see him as a great incarnation of the industrial/urban myth of estrangulated humanity hounded by monsters of its own creation, the post-apocalypse a perpetuation of mere shells of species that peaked too early, the ghosts haunted by anti-remnants like Gerard, who stayed around merely because they had no choice and haunted with a vengeance, if not a vengeful heart, since if Gerard knew anything he knew what was long wrong yet knew as well that he could only hate what he hated as much as he did for the equal measure of love it deprived him of. Damn it, Gerard, I'm sorry, but I've found another one of your tapes — Paganini, a caprice — to remind me of all those frigid Nordic nights we huddled godless but for the violins that rent the sorrowful veil of bleak night; yes, Gerard, our god was an absence, and not the sun, for even behind the blackness there was no sun — it was on the other side of the world — no, only more blacknesses, one after the other, and you gave me music that found them, one after the other, and for that, for those moments, for the opening slices of Paganini bow on Paganini strings, for Paganini's incomparable way of opening the piece by announcing you're already in the Dionysian midst of it for good, or more likely evil, for that I long for those black cold nights when even your death has its savor, when I can do nothing, be nothing, and remain in the cave for days on end and nights, or days — I lose track, and wake up without the conceit to call it day or call it night and it's Paganini I want, Paganini I play — I found it, Gerard — and the music lends me its life, its fearlessness, its frenzy, and I go out — out — into the day, for it is indeed day, and the sun — the sun, Gerard, the sun — is out and it's only October and it's warm, and I find I've forgotten whatever it is to be a man alive in a world of men, but no more, not out there in the sun, the warm October sun slapped onto the world of men, and I have that Paganini life in me, and that's the demonic jaunt to my step you may have noticed, for I am off to see about a cracked skull, the cracked skull of Sandy Calderon.

The costume was easy. Italian Florsheims, cheap dress pants, permanent-press shirt, bad haircut. The shoes were too much, yet just the kind of mistake you'd expect from an FBI guy, an undercover cop, a private eye. I brought it all together with a pair of sunglasses — not mirrored, of course.

Sandy Calderon lived in a one-story, one-bedroom house on the north side. She didn't recognize me. I didn't recognize her, either. She held a towel over her face, from the nose down.

"Sandy?"

"Come in," she said, allowing me to pass. "Does this mean they're going to reopen my case?"

I took my sunglasses off.

"It's me."

"My god, I took you for a cop." She let the towel drop, caught it in time to lift it over an expression of horror, as if she'd seen what I had. The worst seemed to be her mouth.

"I'm sorry. When I get my new teeth it won't be so bad."

We were in a small, bleak living room crowded with worn furniture.

"It's not as bad as you think. I can still tell it's you."

"Well I haven't changed from the neck down."

"I'm grateful for that, sister."

Sandy caught herself standing with one hip thrust out, as if her face wasn't ruined, and sat down embarrassed.

"So you've taken steps to try to get your case reopened?"

"I didn't try to kill myself — I've never even thought of it."

"What about the note?"

"It's vague. I was drunk and hysterical. All it said was he'd never see me again."

"I hope that's true."

"He called me. I've got it on tape."

"He called you? Since? What'd he want?"

"He heard I was trying to get the case reopened and he didn't want me to."

"Did he threaten you?"

"No. I think he figured I might be recording it."

"How'd he know you were trying to get the case reopened?"

"Are you kidding me? That gang is thick as thieves with the law. The D.A. got on the cops and next thing I know I get a phone call. Fucking bastards."

She reached to the coffee table in front of her for cigarettes.

"You want me to turn away so you can smoke?"

"Would you mind?"

I turned to face a bleak hallway that I presumed led to a bleak kitchen. This was where Sandy Calderon moved about avoiding her reflection.

"You got all the police reports?"

"Why?"

"I'm going to get your case reopened for you, and we're going to nail the son of a bitch that did this to you."

The police reports read like they always did, as if they were written by bad and stupid children striving laboriously with great impatience to earn their way out of detention. The line that stuck with me was: "Suspect exhibited no abnormalcies pertaining to this officer's regard," which in context meant that Officer Ratrace believed everything Tommy Marco said. It was this same Ratrace who had been suspicious of McDonough's discovery of Sandy's alleged suicide note. But what Barlow's ghost failed to mention was the addendum Ratrace provided at the bottom of his report, to wit: "This officer feels the incumbency to note that Mr. McDonough's behavior referent suicide note was due to the nature of his distraught condition." And that must have been enough for the investigators because they didn't. At least there were no reports that indicated the case was pursued after the three potential witnesses were interviewed the morning after the crime.

All I could prove so far was that the prefect's myrmidons never should've been licensed to carry a pen. If I wanted to get the case reopened I'd have to start by getting Sandy's doctor to put in writing that her injuries could not have resulted from a fall. Then I'd have to convince the D.A. that they could win the case, which would involve turning one of the witnesses.

The doctor was a pushover. I saw him in his office, Dr. Leonard Aziz, a man with a fine bullet-shaped head and extraordinarily hirsute arms.

"I'll write your letter," he said, "for all the good it'll do. If it would do any good they never would try to tell me in the first place she jumped from the second story. They tell me this, I look at her five minutes and say this woman did not jump from anywhere, she got her face smashed in. Then I forget about it, fix her face. Now you come here and tell me they still think she jumped from the second story. Why should they believe me now? Sure, I'll write your letter."

Dr. Aziz was as good as his word. He had me sit in the waiting room while he dictated the letter, then called me back into his office while his secretary typed it.

"How is the girl?"

"I saw her this morning. She doesn't like to show her face."

"She'll be better when she gets her teeth. With that body, I think her face will be fine. Now I'll tell you what I think happened. This man, he grabbed her by the hair and smashed her face into the cement. That's it. No trauma to the rest of her body. She did not jump. The man, he smashed her face into the cement, like this — ”

Dr. Aziz enacted the mime several times with relish. He looked like an orchestra conductor.

“Yes, this is exactly what he did.”

It was nearly dark when I left Aziz. All that was false about an autumn day was sliding rapidly beyond an inscrutable horizon. I was already cold a block from the hospital. I thought of Gerard and his absence and considered returning immediately to the office. Tommy Marco tended bar at the Harem Club, a badly misnamed tavern on the corner of Third and Cameron. It would've been the simplest thing to bypass it by cutting up to Fifth; Gerard, I trusted, would never know the difference, and Barlow's ghost would be welcome company, another visit from the as yet undamned. And out there in the cold as I was, I did not feel for Sandy Calderon. She was warm and she'd had her face smashed. She was in her bathroom at the mirror sucking her lip over her gums. She was lucky. It was not for her I remained on Third Street, nor for myself. Perhaps it was because I suspected, instinctively, that the only authentic intensity of feeling exists in a void of motivation.

I was at the Harem Club. I did not in the least believe in what I was doing. I put my sunglasses on as I entered the bar.

The bartender was my height, six foot two or three, and much broader. Worse yet, his hands were abnormally large, as if he were still growing. His face had been hardened by a surfeit of silence, and despite a clear proclivity for menace I detected at least a slight capacity for reflection.

He asked me what I wanted.

“Bourbon,” I said, without quavering, “on the rocks.”

Our only company was a woman halfway down the bar sporting a supercilious consciousness of her own physical adequacy, and a gam that could at least be lovely in tavernous twilight. Leaning forward, her tits pressed against the bar, she bore the proud forestallment of attrition of a broad wallowing in the sloppiness on the other side of need.

Soon she would need a light.

Liquor slopped over the rim of my glass when Marco set it before me on the bar.

"Get me one of those napkins," I said, affecting a facile authority that I figured would establish me as Marco's enemy as well as superior. I was careful not to slouch.

Marco tossed several Harem Club napkins beside my drink. "Have a few," he said, a trifle surly.

"You're supposed to say 'That'll be two-fifty for the drink, mister.'"

"It's on me."

"Good, now we're getting somewhere."

Obviously my disguise was working. Marco would be waiting for me to get to the point of my visit. It occurred to me the best move might be to finish my drink and leave without another word. But I had to wait for the bimbo to slide down the bar for her light. I tried to facilitate things by turning to her and nodding, but she was already pouring her ass off the stool. She was about twenty-five years old and had a nice walk. I took my sunglasses off for a better look, then put them on again. She reached me with the cigarette held beside her head like it was something she'd just found in her ear.

"Nice shoes," she said, as I reached in my shirt pocket for matches.

"They have fake wood on bottom and rubber tread," I told her. "I'd show you, but in some cultures showing the bottom of the foot is considered offensive."

"I'm not easily offended."

"I'm glad you said that."

Her black dress was designed to waft against her figure like a sheer curtain. She wasn't wearing stockings.

"I'm Carly," she said.

"Run along back to your seat, Carly, your bartender would like to talk to me."

She stood with the cigarette poised before her lips, which were curved in a smile that was clearly a last stance.

"You haven't lit my cigarette."

"I'm going to send them along with you," I said, handing her the matches.

"Join me later?"

I was pleased with myself so far.

"I doubt it," I said.

Tommy Marco was busy approximating the sedulous caprices of a man behind a bar. His back, naturally, was turned.

The least I could do to justify his suspicions was to wait.

I sipped my drink and remembered what it was like to be so annoyed with a woman I craved it. I looked down at the near-sultry Carly, and, to be fair, acknowledged that she was not the kind of woman who could drive a man to drink.

She smiled.

I returned to my drink.

Marco diddled with a clean tumbler.

My confidence was growing.

He's going to turn now, I thought, tumbler still in hand, and say something about a badge.

I cut him off as he turned.

"What's that, a Tom Collins glass?"

He looked down at it, already prepared to forgive its betrayal.

"Right," he said, "you want — "

"I think it's dry by now."

He stood directly before me, still wiping the glass.

"All right, what do you want? You with the D.A.?"

"That's more like it."

"I've already been interviewed. You want me to come down and give a statement? I thought the case was closed."

"It's closed, Tommy. It's closed because you lied."

Marco gave me what I presumed was his hardest look.

"I could break you in half."

He was right. I took my sunglasses off and looked at him flatly.

"No, Tommy," I lied persuasively, "no, you couldn't break me in half."

"Look, what the fuck do you want? You got a badge?"

"A badge? That's kind of cliché, don't you think? That's as bad as asking for a warrant. Why would I need a badge if all I want is to enter your place of employment and call you to your face a chickenshit liar?"

"I'm not changing my story."

"That's better."

"I already said everything I'm going to say."

I finished my drink.

"Buy me one more, Tommy, only don't spill this one. Maybe if you don't fill it all the way . . . "

"You can buy your own fucking drink."

I looked down at Carly, who wasn't missing a word.

"Tell him why he should buy me another drink, Carly."

"Cause he's a cop, Tommy."

"What kind of cop, dear?" I asked. "Local or federal?"

"He's a fed, Tommy, buy him another drink."

Tommy poured me a drink.

He didn't spill.

"Why," he asked me, "would the feds be interested in this case?"

"What would this country be like, Tommy, if it was all right for people to simply go around smashing the faces of beautiful women? We'd run out of beautiful women, wouldn't we, Tommy?"

"She smashed her own face. She tried to kill herself."

"That's what I read. Tommy Marco saw her on the window ledge before he passed out. That's a lousy story, Tommy. You think we're all stupid? You remember what you saw right before you passed out, which is kind of rare, and on top of that you saw a distressed woman about to leap from the window and you did nothing to stop it. That's not very chivalrous."

"I was drunk."

"That's kind of a problem. You were too drunk to understand the implications of what you saw, yet you remember it clearly. I thought maybe you'd say you didn't want to interfere."

"That's right, I didn't. It wasn't my business."

"If McDonough was fighting with his woman."

"Right."

"But then I figured you wouldn't say that because that would leave open the possibility that McDonough pushed her out the window — after you passed out, of course — wouldn't it?"

"He didn't push her, she jumped. She left a note."

"I've seen the note. It's not a suicide note. Why haven't you told me McDonough was already passed out when you saw Sandy Calderon about to jump? Isn't that what you told the cops?"

"I don't remember."

"Don't remember which, what McDonough was doing when you passed out or what you told the cops?"

"What he was doing. I think he was passed out."

"But, see, you just told me you didn't want to interfere with them fighting, so they must have been fighting, so he wasn't passed out."

"I don't remember."

"You remember Sandy pretty clearly, so you can't plead drunkenness on that one. So what I'm wondering is why you don't remember. And why you told the cops McDonough was already passed out. Why did you?"

"Because that's what I remembered."

"Where was he? Where did he pass out?"

"In his bedroom."

"You were in there?"

"No."

"Right, you were on the couch. How'd you know he was passed out?"

"He passed out earlier."

"Then *you* must have been the one fighting with Sandy Calderon. Did you smash her face?"

"I'm not a suspect."

"No, Tommy, you're not a suspect, but you know what? You never told the cops McDonough was passed out. You told them you didn't know and they didn't push it. You want to know why I was able to trick you there?"

Marco stared at me.

"Because you were lying, of course. Your story wasn't real. So you have to remember not what did happen, which is fairly easy to remember, but what you said the next morning happened, which is more difficult. Especially since you had a hangover, and it hadn't been all that long since McDonough told you what to say."

"Terry didn't tell me to say anything."

"Well, maybe he asked nicely. Imagine a big fella like you scared of anybody. I understand. And you're right to fear the wrath of B.A.D. So the trade-off might be a good one. If you're really scared they'll kill you. Because we won't kill you. We'll pile up charges and seek the maximum, or maximi. Obstruction; felony obstruction; accessory before, during, and after; maybe even conspiracy — to commit murder, using the springboard of accessory before and during. We can compile thirty years for you at least. Of which we can find a way to guarantee you'll do at least ten. You'll get ten years for being afraid of a guy who smashed in a woman's face. While you're in the pokey I'll see if I can't procure some pictures of Miss Calderon's naked body, so you'll have something to think about."

I figured it was safe to let Marco see that I was enjoying myself.

"You don't have a case," he said.

"If the case depended on you, Tommy, I'd have had this talk with you in private. I got a friend who's specialty is extracting statements from nogoodniks, petty hoodlums such as yourself. But we got a couple things. Doctors — juries love doctors. Doctors will testify that the scenario originally presented is an impossibility. You don't do that kind of damage to the face and not damage the neck, scrape up the arms a little, skin the knees. That's one. The other is the guy you're protecting is a stupid man who shoots his mouth off in taverns. We've got it, Marco, it's only a matter of time and not much. I came here to size you up, see how bad we want to nail you."

Marco tried glaring at me, but was thinking too hard. I guessed he was wondering how bad we wanted to nail him.

I turned and put my sunglasses on. I thought I saw resignation relax Carly's face.

"Carly," I said, "you ready to go?"

She was.

"You got any Paganini at your place?"

"We could pick some up on the way."

29

LIVING WILD ON THE ISLAND — DAY ONE

A stable fly bites Lola on her left calf as she loses sight of Gerard, who has sailed around the north point of French Island.

Billy Verité leaps to his feet as if she had swatted him. "I'm going to explore the island," he says. A small cloud of mosquitoes follows him up the escarpment.

To Billy, the island is vast and untamed.

To Lola, the island is tiny and every creature alive on it knows she is there.

Blue jays call from tree to tree.

Billy tramps through thickets of barbed foliage, a snarled undergrowth laced with spider webs. At its highest point Red Oak Ridge Island is thirty feet out of water. Where Billy is crossing it is one-eighth of a mile wide. Once up the scarp, he finds the land rises gradually. He finds no path through the woods but that of least resistance, which leads him to a pocket blocked by a felled tree, walled by a hanging garden of thorny vines. He retreats and goes around, stepping high through the undergrowth, tearing through countless spider webs. He doesn't notice, in his enthusiasm, how many mosquitoes he is swatting on his arms and neck.

Billy is excited. There is no telling what mysteries thrive on this island, what mutations fostered by sudden and unnatural isolation, cats once domestic gone wild again, savage inbred cats, cannibals. They might be pretty big. He has heard rumors, back there in civilization, of pithecoids in jungly places who are *descendants* of man. It makes sense. He figures rattlesnakes, once abundant in the Driftless Zone, will be on this island.

Upon his first glimpse of blue water through the trees, Billy knows a rare ecstasy. He can only articulate laboriously and aloud: "This is spectacular, this is . . . spectacular." He is right in suspecting that he has been made privy to the same emotion experienced by the first white man to set eyes on the source of the Nile. Billy has not read of such adventures for many years, but he can still say, "Ujiji."

"Ujiji," Billy says.

He stands still.

Water through the trees.

A monsoon of mosquitoes arrives. Billy deals with them harshly, methodically. He knows that paradise has its pitfalls. He and Lola will have to battle the elements.

Billy hears the bloodcurdling shriek of an Amazon and a great crashing sound through the underbrush that reminds him of the time when he was a boy in the north woods and startled a large buck. He could tell by the crashing sound it made how heavy it was. He barely got a glimpse of it, but you can only tell when you're right there how big some of these creatures in the wild get to be. This is a big Amazon. He feels a surging fear mingle with his heroic explorer's determination. He grabs a big stick and locates the source of the dopplering sound.

It's Lola.

She's running southwest across Billy's field of vision. Billy can see that her white shirt and black skirt are already badly torn. She's screaming and flailing as she runs. She has mosquito hysteria, a cousin to claustrophobia. One mosquito landed on her and she swatted it. A few more landed and she swatted them. More came. She stood and swatted, but still more came.

She waded into the blue water and they followed her, this time accompanied by several stable flies. She made a mental calculation: No matter how much I swat, the number of mosquitoes increases. In the meantime, their numbers increased. She swatted while calculating: If I can't stand it now and it's only getting worse, I'll never be able to stand it.

Lola panicked and ran.

Now she's running along the spine of the island.

Billy gives chase.

Lola angles toward the western shore. The sight of water through the trees means nothing to her, yet she aims for it. Billy moves to cut her off. He leaps high over a fallen log, lands in a depression camouflaged by a thicket of grapevines, falls and rolls with his momentum, scrambles to his feet and continues running, managing at the same time to think of himself as oblivious of the scratches he's accumulating, the dramatic tears his shirt suffers.

Lola runs wildly, shrieking, flailing. She doesn't fall until she runs off a shelf five feet higher than a spit of sand that sucks at her feet, detaining her long enough for Billy to catch up.

Lola recognizes Billy through the parted curtains of her hysteria. "I can't stand it," she screams. "The fucking mosquitoes'll eat us alive. I gotta get out of here. I'd rather be in fucking jail. Get your filthy hands off me."

Billy slaps Lola the way he knows strong men slap hysterical women.

"You have to get ahold of yourself," he says because he knows they do.

Lola stares at Billy. The little fucker slapped her.

Lola punches Billy in the cheekbone, knocking him down. She leaps onto him. Billy curls fetally to defend himself. Lola pummels at his torso. Billy tries to rise and Lola lands a punch on his jaw — his head slams back to the sand. Billy fakes like he's going to rise again, Lola throws a wild punch, Billy jerks up, grabs Lola by the hair and pulls her down. They grapple, rolling like a single mythical beast into the blue water.

They are the loudest animals on the island, even though they aren't saying anything.

They have spent themselves. They look at each other, on their knees in the water. Lola's breasts hang free of her shredded shirt. Billy looks at them, glad that the worst is over.

Lola slaps Billy hard one last time.

Something pops in Billy's ear.

Billy leads Lola back to their goods in silence. The mosquitoes are as ferocious and plentiful as before, but somehow they have lost the power to cohere into an abstract force greater than their numbers.

Billy tells Lola to wear long pants and a long-sleeved shirt.

"Cover everything you can," he says. "The rest we'll cover with mud. They won't bite your eyeballs."

When Lola is covered with mud, Billy tells her to sit while he searches for a campsite.

"We best get set up before sundown," he says, setting off with the machete.

Billy chooses a relatively clear and flat area on the northern ridge of the island. Dense woods slope down from the clearing. He has the high ground and plenty of cover. He clears the brush assiduously, slicing every plant over an area about fifteen feet by fifteen feet. He gathers wood and starts a small fire. He finds a log and sets it near the fire.

Billy retrieves Lola and sets her on the log.

"Mosquitoes don't like smoke," he tells her.

Billy lugs all of their belongings to the campsite by himself while Lola stares at the fire.

For dinner Billy and Lola eat peanut butter sandwiches.

Billy tries to make conversation, but Lola stares silently in blackface into the flames.

Few mosquitoes persist in attacking. They search Lola for an opening, then move on to Billy, who kills them.

By nightfall Billy has set up camp.

Lola crawls into the tent and traggles into her sleeping bag.

Billy remains by the fire. He makes coffee, smokes cigarettes, listens to the wild night beyond the shifts and snaps of the flame, the wood, the ash. He hears a loud slap on the water. It must be close, he thinks, hoping it's a beaver, for he has heard they do that to frighten away bigger animals.

Billy wonders what the bigger animal might be.

He puts out the fire and goes to bed.

"What's that?" Lola asks later, shaking Billy awake.

"Huh?" Billy says.

Lola keeps shaking him.

"That noise."

It sounds like monkeys, strange wild noises in the night.

"Sounds like monkeys," Billy says.

The night is close and hot, the air in the tent is stifling and Billy and Lola smell each other's sweat. Neither has ever heard such sounds before.

"It's not monkeys," Lola says, "there aren't any monkeys here." She wants to hate Billy, but she's frightened.

"I don't know, maybe wild cats."

Lola listens. The noise is guttural, but more like a series of hoots than the whining she expects from cats.

"No, it's not cats."

"Probably fox pups."

"Yeah, I bet that's it — fox pups."

"Sounds like little men, though, doesn't it?"

"There aren't any little men here."

"No, I know, but I mean that's what it sounds like, wild jungle men, like Pygmies or Hottentots."

"Hottentots *are* Pygmies . . . Aren't they?"

Billy dares a glimpse of Lola, sees her wide white eyes and is briefly overcome by the sensuality of remembered adolescent dreams of negresses. Her shoulders are white and heavy.

"I don't know. I don't think so. Pygmies live in Africa. They're the last descendants of early man, I mean just when they first stood upright but were still small. Hottentots live in New Guinea — they're cannibals. Pygmies don't eat meat at all."

"That's why they're so small. I mean it, I've heard that's why we're so tall, cause we eat so much meat. And that's why the Chinese are getting taller all of a sudden, cause when Nixon went to China they started importing meat from us."

"That's why the Hottentots are small, cause they eat human meat and it's not as nutritious because it's like recycling — each time flesh is eaten it loses more of its nutrients."

"That's what I've heard. They say these primitive people are dying out because of attacks on their forest, companies harvesting their trees, but what it really is is they're using up their resources because they refuse to move."

Billy isn't sure he agrees, but he can feel Lola's knee pressing his thigh from inside her sleeping bag. It excites him. She may not know she's doing it. It's a very small tent.

"They can't move," he decides, "because their gods are there. But then they see the white man on the tractor and most of them have white gods who ride big machines and they're waiting for them. So a lot of them are getting civilized now."

"They like classical music."

"Some of them like jazz."

"Isn't that where jazz came from?"

"I think so."

Billy involuntarily presses his thigh into Lola's knee. She rolls onto her back.

"Listen," she says, "it's kind of like music, with the crickets in the background."

"I can hear a train."

DAY TWO

The first morning on the island is difficult for Billy and Lola. They wake up at dawn and feel as if every bone in their bodies is as sore as it's ever been. They can't find a painless position. Everything hurts and it takes a long time to get back to sleep. The ground, they think, was not this hard last night.

The next time they wake up it is late morning and the heat nearly suffocates them. They hear the screeching of herons, which sound like ducks touched by hysteria.

It's a new day and each hopes the other will take charge of it. But for the pain it would be easy to imagine staying in bed all day, sharing wordlessly the slow malignancy of torpor.

It's Billy who takes charge, instituting a policy of divided labor. After breakfast, Lola will go fishing and Billy will explore the island.

After breakfast — peanut butter sandwiches, coffee, cigarettes — Billy sets off to explore and Lola starts looking for worms.

Billy finds what he's looking for, the ruins of an old farmhouse. Here the earth has made mock of man's attempt to settle.

The limestone of the foundation fell afoul of the inscrutable designs of the land. The timber ramparts are breached, rotted, and askew. Stacks of leprous wood lay about. It could still be a fort, Billy figures.

He hopes to find mammals, or snakes. Instead he is set upon by insects, and when he makes his way to shore he finds sandpipers running up and down. Later, as he stands on a ridge at the southern end of the island, he sees a bald eagle in flight over the river. He sees a barge toward the Mississippi's western shore, cars at the base of the Minnesota bluffs on the river highway. Between the island and the main channel stumps rise like husks of totemic sentinels. Narrow islands border the main channel on the east along the lake, some, barren green humps, created by dredge spoils. The barge disappears up the main channel behind the trees. A train comes out just above the water line.

Another barge is pushing through the locks to the southwest. Billy is fascinated by an idea, something about the way civilization functions around him while he surveys these machinations from afar, invisible on his wild island. The nearest human is a mile away, his Amazon, fishing for their supper. He knows he's being watched by creatures of remarkable stealth that harbor great powers in their unrevealed monstrosities, probably the way hunchbacks carry their secrets.

Soon they will accept him.

Lola quits digging after finding three worms — short, skinny ones. Billy told her to find a sunny spot and start fishing — mosquitoes don't like the sun.

Stable flies love the sun. They like flesh warmed by the sun.

Lola wonders if she would appear as an apparition if anyone happened to spot her from shore. She hopes so, because there's no way she can both fish and stay entirely out of sight. She's standing in her underwear a hundred yards from the island and the water has just now risen to cover her knees. Her theory was that the stable flies wouldn't find her if she were out far enough. She was right, though a few followed her. If anyone saw her, then fuck it, just fuck it.

The stable fly perceives the world differently from men. The man, as stable fly, approaching Lola from behind, would choose to bite her thigh, towards the inside, where it has made its final upslope; or one of her nates, where it is uneclipsed by her undies, at the precise locus of the mystery of fulsomeness and suspension. But the stable fly is out to rip through the thinnest skin that conceals the most blood. They like hands and feet. The last stable fly bored into the vein behind Lola's knee with disproportionate fury. Lola smashed it.

Lola once had a boyfriend who made her fish. She knows how to do it. Every worm comes up lucky, yielding a total of three fish, two bluegills and something she can't identify; it's about a foot long and has two spiny ridges on the back like a sturgeon. It's brown like river muck, even on the belly, and has had a bite taken out of its tail fin, which is heterocercal.

Back at camp, Billy and Lola discuss whether or not to eat the third fish. Two bluegills aren't enough for dinner. If they eat the spiny oddfish they'll have enough, and their supplies will last longer.

"It's not a bottom feeder," Billy says.

"So — I'm not going to eat that thing."

"You eat the two bluegills and I'll eat it."

"You'll probably die. That thing probably eats mud."

"It's not a bottom feeder."

"How would you know?"

"Its mouth isn't on bottom like a catfish."

"It could still eat off the bottom."

"What do you care if I'm the one that's going to eat it."

"I don't. I don't care if it kills you."

Thus they eat all three fish.

After the main course, Lola gets the idea of roasting apples in the fire.

They both decide the fish would've tasted better with salt.

31

DAY THREE

Billy has decided they might as well remain camped where they already are rather than search for an ideal location, but they need to erect some kind of shelter to cover their goods in case it rains.

He asks Lola to refer to their camp as Base Camp. Lola rolls her eyes.

Billy tells Lola of a tiny sheltered bay on the east coast about a quarter mile down from Base Camp. He suggests they bathe there and call it Bath Bay. Lola asks Billy to escort her there. He leads the way with the machete, hacking out a rudimentary path. This time it takes them an hour to walk from Base Camp, but soon it will be a matter of a few minutes.

Billy hacks his way back.

His project for the day is to build the shelter. He begins by gathering branches. When he thinks he has enough he starts to think about tying them together. Gerard left them some rope, but Billy will use that to secure his roof to three trees.

He tries grapevine first, but it's too weak. All the vines he tries turn out to be too weak. He thinks maybe he doesn't need to tie it at all. He tries to imagine how that might work.

He remembers the rotting wood at the ruined farmhouse. Rotted wood leaks. But maybe he can find a rattlesnake there.

He decides some tasks need to be thought through before they're executed, so he starts thinking about the next step, covering the thatch. He'll wipe mud all over the thatch first, stick grape leaves in the mud in a sort of fish scale pattern, cover that with river grass, which abounds in the large bay on the west side of the island, and, as a safety measure, finish it off with strips of bark. While exploring different bark options he stumbles on a solution to the twine problem: the inner bark of certain saplings yields strips of sufficient strength to tie his thatches.

Billy makes short work of weaving and tying his roof. It is intricate and ungainly, and very thick. He piles the sticks on wherever he sees a space. His lack of construction experience liberates him. He uses a great deal of barktwine, always double-securing designated points of juncture. The finished product is six feet by ten feet, though slightly rhomboid.

Finding good mud is difficult. Most of the island's soil is fine sand, deposited back in glacial days when the river was much wider, perhaps so wide that's why the glaciers were frightened off. Billy isn't sure.

He wonders where Lola found the worms the day before, but he can't ask her — he hasn't seen her since he left her at Bath Bay. She never came back for the fishing gear.

Billy decides they must invent a secret call.

Billy has a watch hidden among the supplies, but he would like to feel that time means nothing to them out in the wild. It's civilization that makes him want to know what time it is, how long Lola's been gone. They can invent a new way of telling time. Lola's been gone since the sun was where the eagle likes to sit on yon island; she returned when the sun split the great black locust tree by the farm ruins. Billy never liked Indians because they beat people up with ax handles, but now he figures he could if he met one who was by himself.

Billy gets an irresistible urge to whittle, but Lola runs up just as he sits down with a knife and a stick.

"I walked around the whole island!" Lola exclaims, as happy and excited as Billy has ever seen her. "I saw a bald eagle and something else — I think it was an owl."

Billy is surprised at himself. He wants to scold her for abandoning her fishing duties. He wants to say, 'While you were off fucking around, I was making a shelter.' But he holds back. Instead he says, "Let's have a snack and then go fishing together. You can show me where you found the worms."

They catch a three-pound largemouth bass that was slumming near shore.

Mosquitoes attack en masse just after dinner.

32

DAY FOUR

Billy wakes up with an erection. The warmth of Lola's heavy flesh rides on her breath. He lays awake, in motionless turmoil, for what seems like hours.

When Lola rises, Billy pretends to be asleep. He gives her ten minutes, then makes his way toward Bath Bay after her. He watches Lola bathe from atop a ten-foot hump, his body partly hidden by a locust tree. Lola is about thirty feet away. His pants are at his ankles and he's masturbating. Lola washes her hair by bending toward the water with her legs straight, her ass aimed at Billy. "God," Billy says quietly.

Billy wonders if primitive island people masturbated. He wonders if the men could just take the women whenever they wanted them. He figures on some islands the women took the men, especially the ones with Amazons. On both kinds of islands both the men and the women probably liked fucking. It wouldn't be any fun if they always had to force the women to do it. Billy wonders if Lola will ever want him.

When Lola returns, Billy has already made coffee and is

busy packing mud onto his shelter. Lola eats apples and drinks coffee and smokes cigarettes. After a while she sighs loudly.

The day is hot, like every other day so far. Lola watches Billy's single-minded industry awhile and becomes annoyed. She sighs again and is acutely aware of her body. She doesn't know what to do with it.

"What day is this?" Lola asks Billy.

Billy doesn't look up from his work.

"Day four," he says.

"What time do you think it is?"

"Morning."

"Yeah, but what time?"

"I don't know." Billy looks at the sun. "Probably ten, or eleven."

Lola sighs, smokes another cigarette, sighs again.

"What am I supposed to do, go fishing all goddamn day?"

"No, you can go later."

"What do I do now?"

"You could go for a walk in the woods."

"I'd have to wear long pants. It's too hot."

"You could go swimming."

"I just took a bath."

"You could help me with this."

"I don't want to."

"Then what are you going to do?"

"That's what I'm asking you. There's nothing to do."

"There's plenty to do."

"Like what?"

"I need some of those seaweeds that grow in Seaweed Bay over on the West Coast."

"What?"

"I'm going to put that on my shelter."

"Seaweed? From Seaweed fucking Bay?"

"Yeah, it'll work."

"You want me to go pick seaweed?"

"I'm just saying it's something you could do."

"Well I'm not going to."

"That's all right, I'll do it."

"Then what am I going to do?"

"You could practice knife throwing."

"What?"

"Knife throwing. In case we see any rabbits or squirrels. Then we could have meat."

"You're a fucking idiot."

After a while Lola sighs again.

Billy goes to the Place of Worms to get more mud and when he returns Lola is throwing the Swiss Army knife at a tree.

33

DAY FIVE

Billy and Lola wake up about the same time, each silently entertaining the phrase 'If you were the last man on earth.'

Billy bathes first. While he's masturbating with soap in the waters of Bath Bay, Lola is masturbating in the tent. They reach orgasm about the same time.

Billy finishes his shelter by early afternoon. It takes him about three hours to secure it to the trees. By then most of the bark has fallen off, as well as a lot of the seaweed. The two trees that comprise the rear of the shelter are four feet apart. There the roof is five feet off the ground. In the front, where it is secured to a third tree, the roof is seven feet off the ground.

Billy spends the rest of the daylight hours tying logs horizontally between the two rear trees and saying 'barktwine' over and over in his mind.

At dusk Lola returns to Base Camp from Fisherman's Point with a thirty-inch northern pike.

"I caught this little perch," she says, "and it was too small to eat and I was out of worms, so I hooked it under the spine back by the tail and after a long time letting it swim around I caught this. It must've taken about an hour to reel it in."

"That's a northern pike."

"I know what it is."

"It's a small one. They can get up to seven feet long."

"Well it's big enough for dinner tonight."

"No, it's a good fish. I just mean they get really big, but you can't eat them then because of all the garbage they eat."

"You're thinking of muskies."

"That's the same thing. When a northern gets over five feet it's a muskie. Up north they eat dogs sometimes. There's even been times when they've eaten children."

"I've heard of some that were cut open and things like tires were found inside. And clothes."

"That's why you can't eat the big ones. You can get tetanus cause they eat rusty cans and shit."

"Well this one just ate a perch so I guess it's okay to eat him."

Billy gets the idea to start a fish log. On back of an old parking ticket he finds in his wallet he writes:

> D2 . . . . . Bluegills — 2, Prehistoric fish — 1
> D3 . . . . . Largemouth Bass — 1 (5 lbs)
> D4 . . . . . Perch, N. Pike — (20 lbs)

After dinner and a long silence, Billy says, "If we had a big net we could catch birds. That's how they do it in Argentina."

On her way into the tent Lola says, "I want to be alone for a while. Don't come in for a couple hours."

Billy sits by the fire in the dark. From where he sits his shelter appears shabby and insubstantial, hardly worthy of his several days of enthusiasm and industry. He's devoid of a sense of accomplishment and he knows it. It looks like it's going to fall any minute, and even though you could say the Leaning Tower of Pisa is that way too, at least the Leaning Tower of Pisa has been that way for two thousand years.

Billy decides two more walls might do the trick.

At least their goods will remain dry when it rains.

The mosquitoes aren't bad tonight.

Lola hasn't complained about them for two days. Maybe it's true, Billy thinks, that they don't like the sun.

The song of the crickets seems organized. It ebbs and flows. Hundreds of them, maybe thousands, all in time with each other. Sometimes hundreds or thousands more come in at a different time, like a cross wave. It never sounds disorganized.

Billy wonders how closely crickets are related to termites, if at all.

When the fox pups, if they're not Hottentots, start up, Billy realizes that lately he's been too busy to think about ideas. Now he thinks how loud the crickets are, and even the fox pups, and when he hears a train he thinks how he can hear the train, but nobody out there in the world can hear these crickets and these fox pups; so it's like there are two worlds and he's the one who's in a secret one and he's the one who must be free because the people out there don't know about this world.

Without even wanting to Billy feels he's being watched. Two eyes — behind him and a little to the left, where the light from the fire gives way to the dark and the trees. If you keep thinking about it you can hear a slight rustling, something moving, shifting a little bit.

It's scary.

Lola screams, bolts from the tent, dashes moonluminescent to the fire, jumps up and down, her great unquarantined tits aflop and slapping, screaming something's in there, she thinks it's a rat, it crawled on her, at first it felt like a spider but it's too big, like a rat . . .

Absurdly, the first thing Billy thinks of is rattlers.

"Keep your eye on the tent, in case it comes out. I'll get the flashlight."

Here's where you're really tested, Billy thinks. He also thinks: I'm glad it wasn't me. And he gets goosebumps.

He returns to the fire with a flashlight and a stick.

"Did it come out?"

"No," Lola says. She's hugging herself and shivering, making quavering breathy sounds through her teeth like someone who can't shake off the incorporeal.

Billy concocts a plan.

"You hold the flashlight on the opening. I'll drag the tent closer to the fire."

The tent collapses as Billy drags it, but nothing comes out.

He wonders if Lola might have had a nightmare.

"Were you sleeping?"

"No, goddamnit, something's in there."

"Okay, get ready," Billy says, and he reaches in and pulls one of the sleeping bags out and leaps away as he drops it.

Nothing happens.

He unzips the sleeping bag and flips it open. Nothing's there. He turns it over. Nothing.

Same with the second sleeping bag.

What now?

"Give me the flashlight."

Stick in one hand, flashlight in the other, Billy starts walking on the tent, flattening it towards the opening. More than once he imagines stepping on something deadly and more powerful than he.

Lola watches from the other side of the fire.

Billy walks very, very slowly, like an apprentice fakir his first time traversing broken glass.

About the time Billy has flattened three quarters of the tent a dark and magnificently hairy spider the size of Billy's fist — not including its legs — runs directly into the fire, leaps out the other side, and runs with remarkable speed right past Lola and into the woods.

All Billy can do is stand there staring. All Lola can do is let out a curt scream.

"Better make sure there isn't another one," Billy says. He feels like gravity stopped working.

Lola can't believe what she just heard. She sinks to her haunches and weeps, albeit with an alert eye scanning the ground around her.

When Billy has the tent inside-out and has rechecked the sleeping bags, he sets the tent up again, this time nearer the fire. With great tenderness he lifts Lola by her elbow.

"Watch," he says. "Old Indian trick."

He draws a line in the dirt all the way around the tent. He pours kerosene from the lamp they haven't used yet anyway in the dirt, all the way along the line, all the way around the tent.

"No spiders or snakes will cross this line," he says.

Lola believes him.

Billy gets nervous and puts out the fire.

Lola has both sleeping bags open, one spread out on the other. She wants Billy to hold her.

"Just tonight," she says.

When she feels his inevitable penis against her, she wishes it were smaller, but presses back into him to let him know it's all right.

When Lola is asleep, Billy risks touching her pubic mound.

He can't help thinking about the spider.

34

DAY SIX

A sandpiper races up the beach ahead of Billy. As he comes around the bend to Seaweed Bay he scares up a heron that leaves with a display of flapping and screeching petulance. The sandpiper maintains a distance of twenty to thirty Billy Verité paces as they follow the shoreline of Seaweed Bay. Where the bight breaks off into the long south lip of the island, the sandpiper looks back once at Billy and runs full speed out of sight. When Billy reaches that spot he finds a single print of a large bare foot, laid fresh into the sand. It's coming his way, but he has seen no one.

He takes off his left shoe, for it is the print of a human left foot, and places his own left foot into the depression. There is a half inch to spare on all sides. He makes a print beside the one he's discovered. They look equally fresh.

"We are not alone here on this island," he says softly, with great portent.

Billy finds a thick, straight stick and whittles it into a spear.

He walks back to Base Camp through the woods, spear held at the ready. Several times he thinks he detects movement in the forest far ahead. His vigilance pays off when he sees a squirrel trying to blend into a tree, the first verified mammal sighting. As Billy is rearing, the squirrel bolts. The spear does not miss by much. Billy is pretty sure it was the biggest squirrel he's ever seen, bigger, he begins to think, than some raccoons.

Should he tell Lola about the footprint? He doesn't want to frighten her. Or does he? For her own safety maybe.

It doesn't matter: Lola doesn't believe him.

"Jesus, Billy, you're just like a little kid playing deserted island. First it's Hottentots and now it's Robinson Crusoe."

"I'll show you the footprint."

"I'm not going to walk all the way to the other end of the island just so you can have your little joke on me."

Billy sulks. He wants to carve a spear for Lola, but what for if she doesn't even believe him?

What Lola doesn't tell Billy is that sometimes when she bathes she gets the feeling she's being watched.

D5 . . . . . *Bluegill* — 1
. . . . . *Perch* — 6 (!) *remember to ask for* salt

35

DAY SEVEN

A day of great excitement attenuated by the way disappointment asserts itself gradually, defining the substance of the day's equilibrium, as well as its properties.

Does Gerard come today or tomorrow?

By about 10 A.M. Billy and Lola are set up at Drop Point Bay, facing French Island with their fishing poles and shameless display of acquiescence.

It's hard to believe a week has gone by, they try to think.

A week hasn't gone by.

"Hand me the binoculars."

"Is that his truck?"

"Is that something?"

"There's a sailboat."

"Probably he'd shop for supplies today, so he could still be coming."

"I think he usually sleeps late."

"He gets up at noon, gets ready by one, shops for two hours and takes an hour to get to Bryce Prairie, add one hour

just to be safe — ”
    “So he doesn't even get started till 5 or 6 . . . ”
    “I'll bet when he drinks a lot sometimes he sleeps til 2 or 3 ...”

D6 . . . . . Bullhead — 5+
. . . . . Catfish — 2+
. . . . . Perch (baby) — 5#
. . . . . Bluegill — 9 baby+ — 3 adult*
. . . . . Bass — 2*
. . . . . Northern — 3(!)+
(* dinner) (+ = let go) (# = bait)

DAY EIGHT

Gerard arrives early, before the sun reaches the island's spine.

D7 . . . . . *Bluegill* — 1

Billy and Lola run through the shallows of Drop Point Bay to greet him.

Billy speaks first.

"Don't you think it would be a good idea if we have a secret call?"

"He's naming everything," Lola complains.

Gerard has brought citronella candles because he thinks the mosquitoes might get bad. The complicity Billy and Lola share doesn't last.

Gerard has brought water, salt, oranges, beef jerky, bread, sardines, crackers, and Chinese carry-out for three.

At Base Camp they sit around the firepit eating the carry-out while Gerard fills Billy and Lola in on events in the city.

Eddie the FBI guy has been kidnapped and Gerard plans to get him back by kidnapping Stratton.

Lola asks if they have to stay on the island.

Gerard says yes.

Billy tells Gerard about the footprint and wants him to help search the island.

Lola tells Billy to go search by himself, she wants to spend some time talking to Gerard in private.

Billy won't go.

Lola says she won't stay on the island unless Billy leaves her alone with Gerard for at least an hour.

Gerard tells Billy to go ahead and go. After an hour or so, he'll help Billy search the island.

Billy knows what Lola wants. He walks until he's out of their sight, then sneaks back.

Gerard and Lola are already in the tent.

Lola's moans are loud and follow rapidly upon each other. The only actual word Billy can make out is "More."

The sun is west of the island when Gerard and Lola emerge from the tent.

Billy can't stop crying.

Gerard finds him sitting against a tree, sobbing.

Billy won't get up to search the island.

Lola walks Gerard to Drop Point Bay.

On the way back she sees Billy still sitting against the tree.

When Lola retires for the night Billy is still sitting against the tree.

37

NO ONE-EYED MEN

A man, any man, all men, everyman, must inevitably exit the revolving door of his middle years to find himself in the great lobby of his decline; and yet, this man, as all men, wishes nothing more than to be unique; for it is only now, in his decline, that he looks back and realizes that until now he *had* been unique. It was never in question; he lived as such, under that assumption, and so was . . . until now, in his decline.

Thus more or less mused Stratton as he strolled along the sidewalk on Twenty-Eighth Street in the postcrepuscular sultriness of a summer's eve, as he strolled along as, come to think of it, never before, like an old man habitually abetting his digestion. And what wicked loveliness is ushered in between the stars. The air is warm and the trees are soft and no one but he is stirring. This may as well be heaven, Stratton thought, the way it all tends toward blue, and the way the lights in every house signify the lingering and closeted concerns of mortals still enduring the trifles they nibble on like salted crackers, but especially the way no one else is about. Yes, this is Detective Stratton's long, lovely, twilight walk, and he's a-going to the cemetery.

Stratton stopped at the corner of Twenty-Eighth and Elm to light a cigarette. A cat jaywalked past him, paused under the streetlight to look back, then slunk between houses. The cat, too, might've been blue, Stratton said to himself. And the cigarette tasted bad. He was conscious of an emptiness that had been making room in him lately for something he despaired of ever naming. He felt both restless and inutile. All had lost savor with him.

But, he realized as he continued his walk, flicking the cigarette into the street, along with this depression arrived a blessing of sorts: old concerns were falling away. Billy Verité ran loose out there and he didn't care. He'd lost his moonlight income and he didn't care. He'd screwed no one but his wife for weeks and he didn't care. The pain in his calf was like a constant hum that couldn't be located, and he knew he was afraid of Skunk Lane Forhension, but not tonight, not on his walk. He didn't care. He would of course have to play it all out — he'd have to find Billy Verité and Lola, and help Torgeson take care of Gerard, and maybe he'd get some dirty money out of it and maybe he wouldn't — but it would no longer be him doing these things, it would be his rogue shadow; he would be right here on his twilight stroll, easing without care toward the graveyard . . . and for a moment as if something large and slippery had flipped inside-out, his emptiness became a wistful sort of pleasantry.

But that didn't last long. Stratton was a man for the world and could not know self-containment. Stratton had an insight at the southeast corner of the Twenty-Eighth and Maple intersection, just at the Maple Street curb — an insight truly granted a very very few men: he knew that his emptiness was called freedom, knew both fully/emptily for the first time and knowing this was the only portion of his revelation he would never forget. This he called wisdom and he knew that with this wisdom came blindness; and he knew that with this freedom, knew that with this wisdom, knew that with his small portion of his vaster lost revelation, knew that with this which could only be called loss and agony, knew that with this came a desperate need for God; and he knew that he could not have God. Stratton knew briefly the precise dimensions of his tragedy.

38

WHICH MAKES KIDNAPING SEEM A MINOR THING

The untrained mind cannot hold such molten extravaganza for long. Soon he was just a little sad, but otherwise his old self. He turned back toward home just short of the graveyard, walking with his head down, his hands in his pockets — shuffling more or less — yet not so demoralized or self-absorbed that he did not notice the TV repair van that wasn't there before, the old detective having his wits still about him, though not to the degree that Gerard found it difficult to sneak up, overwhelm him with chloroform, and spirit him into the van that said Tom's TV Repair in rather hastily painted letters.

39

WHY EDDIE CAN'T BE TRADED AS A HOSTAGE

Hobo, who refused to wear a suit, opened the door from inside Skunk's new office.

"Carly," Hobo said, "Mr. Forhension will see the gentleman now."

And he shut the door.

Carly stood behind her desk holding a clipboard. She had a willowy sort of figure unfettered by undergarments. Her dress was white and very short. She walked well in her heels.

"Mr. Torgeson. Mr. Forhension will see you now."

"Yeah, I heard something to that effect."

Carly led him through the door Hobo had just shut and retreated to her reception area.

Skunk's office was painted white where possible. A horizontal strip of varnished wood lined the walls about four feet up as a way of suggesting that the affairs of men could be contained, organized, and parceled out in that very room. Above the line the walls were glass, all the way to the ceiling. The furniture was all leather in a variety of brooding, recessive colors that all looked the same. Like anyone who first entered the office would, Torgeson looked at the Mississippi River out the window. He looked at the Cass Street Bridge, seven blocks away over lower roofs and parking ramps, and he felt envy.

"Detective Torgeson," Skunk said, rising from the chair behind his massive oak desk and sluicing around to shake Torgeson's hand.

Skunk patted Torgeson on the arm and gestured at a burgundy armchair set aslant across from his desk.

Torgeson sat.

As Skunk made his way back to his desk he looked across Jay Street at the roof of the Winchester on Fifth building and felt vaguely that he knew something about it.

Hobo stood beside Skunk's desk, his bare arms crossed, staring at Torgeson.

The tan carpet beneath each of them was so fine and subtle none knew it was there.

Torgeson did not know what was intended by the appearances he was being offered, but he could appreciate the kind of people who were so evidently conscious of style. He felt in his element. An air of intelligent silence underscored by menace was central to Torgeson's notion of style as it pertained to himself.

And he really liked Skunk's suit.

"That a silk suit?"

"Yes."

"Nice."

"Thank you; if you'd like I could give you my tailor's number."

"Unless I come into some money soon, I do not believe I could afford one like it."

"We are subtle men, are we not?"

"I like the suit, but with you in it on a given day I'd as soon wipe my ass with it. But we got a mutual problem, chief. My partner has been kidnapped and we need to make a trade."

Skunk leaned back in his chair and smiled at Hobo.

"You like to get to the point, I guess."

"I heard about your skunkass bullshit and I'll tell you one time only I ain't no goddamn Stratton. I see one knife come out it'll be the one I use to castrate you."

"You like sardines?"

Even Hobo furrowed his brows at this turnabout.

"What?"

"You like sardines?"

"What the fuck are you talking about?" Torgeson asked, searching the recesses of the insult file in his brain.

"Nothing. I just bet you like sardines."

Torgeson figured the safe course would be to glare at Skunk.

"I realize you are impatient to get on with the operational segment of our meeting, but you are in my office and I'd appreciate if you'd grant me this single digression. I think you'll find it of some help. You like to eat liver maybe?"

Torgeson admitted to himself he was curious.

"I eat liver and I eat sardines."

Skunk slapped his thigh.

"I knew it. Both are high in purine. You've got gout."

"Gout?"

"You got sore knees, don't you?"

Torgeson did not respond.

"You hide it, right? Cause you think you got arthritis? Well it's gout, friend. No, don't say anything. Just listen to me: cut out the liver and the sardines, giblets if you're fond of them, drink a lot of liquids — other than coffee, though coffee won't hurt — and you can beat this thing before it becomes chronic. Gout. At this stage it can be beat by a simple alteration in your diet . . . Now, about your partner . . . "

"You done with the medical bullshit?"

"Oh, it's gout all right."

"Yeah, it's gout, now are you done?"

"He's got gout, Hobe, what do you think of that?"

"He's a lucky man."

"You two fucking through?"

"We're through — but mind me about that diet."

"You can shove that fucking diet up your skunkfucking ass."

"I think he'll do it, Hobo. I mean, I think he'll follow the diet. You think so, I mean even though he's a little burled about it now?"

"Yes."

"Yes."

"Through?"

"Through. But no liver, no sardines, plenty of liquid."

Torgeson chuckled despite himself. "What the fuck is with you?"

"Say your partner has been kidnapped?"

Now Hobo chuckled.

"Easy does it, Hobe. Officer of the law has been kidnapped. You think we done it?"

"I know you didn't do it. I know who did it. Gerard. Gerard has him."

"Gerard? We know him, Hobo? He one of them Outlaws?"

"Don't know him."

"Sorry, chief — we don't know him."

"I don't give a rat's ass whether you know him. He wants to make a trade. For some FBI asshole you kidnapped."

"Eddie?"

"That's right, Eddie. That's what he said."

"This fella Gerard wants Eddie, Hobe. He say dead or alive?"

"What?"

"Gerard want Eddie dead or alive?"

"What the fuck are you talking about?"

"You know, you got a magnetic personality, chief, charisma. Isn't it funny how you call me chief and then I start calling you chief? Not many people can do to me like that. That's what I been thinking while we sit here."

"There's a lot of bullshit in you, boy. You kill this FBI guy?"

"Eddie?"

"Yes, goddamn fucking Eddie. You kill him?"

"Eddie passed on."

"You killed him."

"I had the misfortune of witnessing his passing, detective. He was a good man, loyal to the end. Would not talk. I think partly because I didn't know what I wanted him to say."

Torgeson suffered a slipping of his thoughts, like a dreamer who finds the objects he clings to rapidly changing.

Skunk looked at the roof of the Winchester on Fifth building. He stood and walked to the window.

"How did — "

"Shut the fuck up!" Skunk hurled at Torgeson with such ophidian savagery Torgeson did indeed shut the fuck up.

"Hobo?"

"Yes."

"Eddie was over here at the window."

"Yes."

"Like maybe when we caught him he was turning from the window."

"Yes."

"Who saw us with him?"

"Nobody."

"We were careful about that, weren't we?"

"Yes."

"When we transported him."

"Yes."

"He had his equipment, but it wasn't turned on or anything, right?"

"Right."

"So nobody could've heard anything."

"Right."

"Gerard knows we have Eddie, Detective?"

"It seems that way."

"He spoke to you?"

"He called me."

"What did he say?"

"He made the mistake of calling you my friend. And he said you had Eddie — the FBI guy."

"He said my name?"

"All three of them."

"I'll be damned. This Gerard fella was over there on that roof."

40

THE DETECTIVE AND THE BAR SLUT

I woke up in the exact mood of someone who knows immediately that he is alone, that all his money is gone, and the two are in cahoots.

When I sat up in bed a fat man slammed his fist against the right rear quadrant of my skull. I lay back down. There was a woman next to me and I could tell by her warmth she was alive.

When I woke up again she was still there.

I went to the bathroom to soak my face in cold water. On my way there the fat man hit me again.

While toweling my face in the bathroom doorway I looked the place over. It was an efficiency apartment and it smelled like several cats had spent a long weekend in it. The dirty dishes didn't fill every inch of the kitchen sink. The empty bourbon bottle was on its side under the dining table. The carpet was stained everywhere except a spot under the leg of a chair.

I walked to Carly's side of the bed and looked down at her. She was still asleep, with her mouth closed.

"God put you on earth," I told her, "to drink booze and pick up men in bars."

She didn't disagree.

Of my clothes, I recovered all but one sock. I piled them on the bathroom floor. What sense of purpose I had nearly expired during my search for a clean towel.

The apartment was in an old building, so there was a bathtub under the showerhead, and I was grateful to find it was the one place Carly kept clean. I imagined her in there swilling liquor in the afternoons.

I clung to the showerhead as long as I could, but I knew the fat man was about to hit me again, and that was the last thing I wanted. I lay down in the tub.

While I was down there Sandy Calderon came in, removed the showerhead, and stuck her own head up there. I was glad the liquid from the fountain bursting out the top of her skull wasn't blood. It was good clean hot water. But it was backing up under her skin around her eyes, and when it burst out again two jets rushed from her face; the same happened with her nose and her mouth and still the pressure mounted. I could see the crack spreading down her forehead, water spurting through like it was a dyke, before the whole face came apart and either the scene kept repeating itself or Carly woke me up soon after I had fallen asleep.

"You're lucky I got up to piss," she said, handing me a towel.

I sniffed it.

"Is this the one you used for the cat piss?"

She smiled tolerantly.

"I don't have a cat."

I must have looked as if I'd never used a towel before, for she snatched it from me and dried my body while I managed to stand there, more or less staggering in place.

"You need to go back to bed," she said, and she led me there.

"You're either a fine woman or I'm still drunk. Or dreaming."

"I think both."

"Which both?"

She had me on my back where it was easy to get a hand over my mouth.

"Be quiet," she said, "I'm going to put you to sleep."

I took it as a good sign that when I woke up again I remembered everything that happened the last time I was awake. While on top of me Carly had managed to undulate while remaining fully flush with my body without making me undulate. It was that conundrum I fell asleep to.

Carly had stayed awake, and now she was moving about with alarming efficiency in a smart gray pantsuit. I sat up in the bed, my back against the wall. She brought me coffee, put a cigarette in my mouth and lit it.

She sat on my feet.

"Move your feet."

I moved my feet.

"So you're not FBI."

"Would you believe C.I.A.?"

"No."

"How about some secret agency you never heard of, like S.P.Y. or W.H.Y.?"

"No."

Long as she'd been awake I noticed little change in the apartment, though it was beginning to seem like the array of clothing was more concentrated. The dirty dishes were still in the sink.

The only thing I could be sure of was that she'd been through my wallet.

"Did you leave me any money?"

"There wasn't any in there."

"Did you put any in?"

"Ten bucks."

"Does that mean I have to come back tonight?"

"You haven't left yet."

"If I should happen to?"

"If? I'd think a big detective like you would have a full schedule."

"What time is it?"

"After five."

"Sometimes we work nights."

"So who are you, then? What's your — "

"Involvement in this case?"

"If you like."

"I'm a friend of the not-quite deceased."

"That's it? Just a friend?"

"That's it."

"Where'd you learn to grill a suspect like that?"

"Did I do okay?"

"You were great."

"Believable?"

"Completely."

"I'll be damned."

"If he finds out you'll be dead."

"He a friend of yours?"

"Not close enough that I'd tell him."

"Have you fucked him?"

"You jealous already?"

"If that's what it takes."

"I've fucked him, sure, but I'm not his favorite."

"Who's his favorite?"

"Are you a detective again? Am I just another witness to you?"

"No, you're a swell dame, that's what you are. Who's his favorite?"

"Sandy Calderon."

"You jealous?"

"Am I a suspect now?"

"Everyone's a suspect, lady."

"You are good at it, honey, but Tommy's kind of a moron. I hope you're not going to try it on those other guys. I think they're motorcycle gangsters."

"Can I ask why you're wearing that smart gray pantsuit?"

"All my dresses were dirty."

"It doesn't suit you."

"I know, that's why I save it for laundry day."

"Are you one of those women it's impossible to insult?"

"Are you one of those men who can't be taken seriously?"

"I like talking to you. Do you think Tommy Marco might've tried to off Sandy Calderon?"

"Look, hon, I might as well tell you, I don't know anything about that incident except Tommy had the hots for Sandy and Sandy had the hots for Terry McDonough. I'm not in love with Tommy and he's not in love with me. I'm just a working girl you met in a bar. I haven't got a man right now if you want to stick around awhile and see what happens. As for this other business, you do what you want, but I can't help you."

"That was a pretty speech."

"Let me put on a freshly laundered dress and I'll make you some supper."

Carly wasn't much of a cook, but I was expecting that and was prepared to view our dinner as an entirely utilitarian affair. The steaks were overdone, yet still arrived half an hour before the hashbrowns. I finished what I could without figuring the moral angle, and balanced my plate in the sink.

"I'll have to be going now," I told Carly.

She hurried to find her purse.

41

WELL IF YOU'RE LEAVING, I'M GOING TO THE BAR

"Well if you're leaving," she said, "I'm going to the bar."

"Fine. Just don't forget to Tommy I'm a fed."

"You're a fed to me, too, baby."

"I'll be back," I said, and I meant it.

I walked back to the office feeling like a square of toilet paper stuck to a shoe. I heard Paganini again, only this time it was an exoteric taunting, the ghost of Gerard flying off the strings of a viola, playing in the silence about me. Never was I more certain that phantoms exist not in a parallel world, but in this one, unseen if they so choose, than I was on that short walk. It was Gerard's ghost, all right, but he wasn't interested in me. His passing stripped him of all emotion — that was the freedom of his afterlife. This Gerard ghost manifest in the lingering of a Paganini piece cared nothing for me, had nothing to say to me . . . I made of him one day my volition, and when I squandered it, he was still there, as perhaps my volition was, a thing apart, the constant by which I could gauge my absurdity.

When the door to Winchester on Fifth closed behind me, Paganini was gone.

"There's nothing for me here," I said out loud.

Back outside Paganini was still gone.

I walked to the Harem Club, thinking about Sandy Calderon, that false ghost. She was no ghost, just a woman with her face smashed, showerhead of my dreams. I was going to get her case reopened? And how would that help her face? She would see those men behind bars. She would find out what happened during that horrible blank stretch of time. But what of all those other horrible blank stretches of time? Who would report back from those?

My doubts were tiny fibrillating wings that couldn't flap me away from the Harem Club. Sandy Calderon wanted her case reopened and that was that. What difference did it make one way or the other? And fuck Paganini, I thought, I can handle this on my own.

But there was a row of Harleys parked outside the Club like dominoes, and when it occurred to me I could sneak up, knock the first one over and run, I knew I wasn't up to the masquerade this time. I pulled my sunglasses from the pocket of my jacket and put them on. In the reflection of a barbershop window I saw a skinny man wearing sunglasses at night.

"Coward," I said to him.

"Chickenshit motherfucker," I said.

And we were right. I was afraid to go into the bar. I did not want to end up like Gerard.

I retreated to a pay phone and called instead. Marco answered.

I asked for Carly, disguising my voice.

"Hello," she said.

"You got anything left to drink in your apartment?"

"I'll get a bottle from Tommy."

"I'll be at your place in ten minutes."

"Why don't you meet me here?"

"I'm on the other end of town."

"All right, ten minutes then."

I was afraid to end up like Gerard, and I'm alive to nourish my disgrace. I did not swell fully into the contours of my own capacity for heroism like Gerard had by the moment of his demise. Never more than then was he Gerard; he died adamantine in his Gerardness, an unalterable, unadulterated embodiment of Gerard.

Rare is the man who exists.

I do not exist.

I suppose I could have derived inspiration from Billy Verité's accomplishments, his deformation, as it were. One can only be stretched so far, right Billy? Gerard broke, but he was as Gerard as could be. Billy didn't break, but did he exist? I think not, which is not in any way to diminish his accomplishments, his deformation.

I accuse Billy of delusion. *I* am not deluded, and that's where I see the difference. I know I don't exist, and therefore the results of my heroic gestures would necessarily have rendered me as pitiable as, say, a motherless pink-torsoed baby bird.

I had my pride.

I retreated to a pay phone and called the bar.

42

DAY TWELVE

Billy hears Lola trill far off in the woods. He drops the stick he's whittling into a spear and cups his ear with his hand.

Two short trills follow.

That's it, his call. It means "come."

It doesn't mean danger. That's three longs and one short.

Ever since Lola found another footprint, along East Shore north of Bath Bay, as she was taking the shore route to her bath on Day Ten, they have been practicing their calls.

Billy runs until he finds Lola in the Central Highlands by the Lonesome Willow.

Lola is wearing boots and shorts and mud. She went hunting. She wanted meat for supper.

"I got one Billy! I got one!"

"One what?"

"A squirrel, I got a squirrel."

"Where is it?"

"It ran off that way," she says, pointing to a thorny thicket of grapevines and miscellaneous other wild undergrowth. "The knife is stuck in its back."

On his hands and knees, Billy penetrates the thicket. He finds a drop of blood on a leaf but can not find the squirrel.

"You see him?"

"No," Billy calls over his shoulder. "Go look on the other side, I'll be right out."

Lola walks around to where she thinks Billy might come out. She can't see him, but some leaves are shaking.

"I found the knife!" Billy shouts.

Something moves underneath a mossy log on Lola's side of the thicket. It's the squirrel, dragging along like a man dying in the Atacama desert.

Lola finds a stick and clubs the squirrel's head until it's dead.

At night the aroma of roasted meat hovers in the trees on the island.

Billy insists on cooking the liver, but when it comes down to it he can't eat it.

He leaves it on a flat rock near the fire.

43

DAY THIRTEEN

In the morning the squirrel liver is gone.

Early in the afternoon Billy is napping at Weather Point Lookout on the southwestern rim of the island. When he wakes up, storm clouds he'd seen lowering down off the sky over the Minnesota bluffs are nearly upon him. He trots through the woods trilling two shorts repeatedly: "Return to Base Camp, Return to Base Camp, Return to Base Camp . . . "

Lola is at Base Camp when Billy arrives. The storm is seconds behind him.

Billy's roof doesn't leak. All three walls hold up. Billy has been busy and it pays off.

Lola wishes she had a deck of cards.

A runnel of rainwater runnels into the shelter. Billy diverts it with a stick.

The rain continues into the evening and Lola and Billy sit next to each other with nothing to do.

"You think when he comes again we'll be able to leave?" Lola asks Billy.

Billy wishes Lola didn't want to leave so badly.

Billy doesn't want to leave at all.

"I don't know," he says.

"When's he coming? Is it three days?"

"Two days. Day after tomorrow."

"I hope we can leave then."

Billy doesn't respond.

"Think we'll be able to leave then?"

"No," Billy says, to be cruel.

"Why not?"

"Because it takes time to straighten these things out. You want to be arrested?"

"Well, if he kidnaps Stratton and gets the FBI guy back then right there they'll have enough evidence."

"Kidnapping takes time. You have to ransom and make the switch and then — well, first of all you don't just kidnap. You've got to plan it all out. It takes at least a week . . . "

"As if you've ever kidnapped somebody."

"I never said I did, but I know how it works. He'll probably kidnap him tomorrow at the earliest. Then he's got to come out here, so they won't make the switch until at least three days from now. Then they got to report to D.C. and D.C.'ll have to send its people. We'll be here at least another two weeks. At least."

Lola believes just about everything Billy says these days.

Billy was so demoralized by her tryst with Gerard he stopped watching her bathe and now has little faith in positive signs.

The rain continues into the night. Lola and Billy eat sandwiches and sleep in their sleeping bags under the shelter Billy made with his bare hands and an abundance of barktwine.

44

DAY FOURTEEN, OR STILL THIRTEEN

Billy wakes up in the middle of the night. The rain has stopped.
He has to piss and he can't find the flashlight.

He makes enough noise looking for it that he wakes up Lola.

"What's wrong?" she asks.

"I can't find the flashlight."

"Look for it tomorrow."

"I have to piss. Did you use it?"

"I didn't lose the fucking thing."

"Where is it?"

"Look tomorrow when it's light."

"But I know where I always put it. Right here between the
cooler and — "

"I'm trying to sleep."

First the liver, which admittedly could have been taken by
an animal, and now the flashlight. Or, first the footprints, then
the liver, and now the flashlight.

Billy walks out of the shelter and three trees downhill. He
can't see much.

When he starts pissing he closes his eyes and sighs. When he opens his eyes again he sees a light moving through the trees further down the hill, close to the West Coast. First he thinks it's a barge light, the way they sweep the night, but it's hard to mistake a man walking through woods with a flashlight for a barge for very long.

Billy doesn't know what to do. A man is walking away through the woods with what surely is their flashlight. If he doesn't act fast the man will get away. On the other hand it's dark and the other guy has the flashlight, leaving Billy at a distinct disadvantage. He'd like to notify Lola because he's afraid. Plus, if she doesn't see this with her own eyes she'll never believe it. Though maybe she would. But the flashlight is farther away even now, there might not be time. And Lola might make too much noise, in which case the man, if he were smart, would turn the flashlight off and they'd lose him.

Billy discovers what it's like to have the compulsions of circumstance rage like a river in flood past the dams of his emotions. He backs up toward the firepit, keeping the light in sight as it bobs away in the woods. He finds his best spear. Keeping to the highest ground he follows the light. He creeps with soft feet like an injun, his eyes adjusting to the dark, his spirit merging with the night beasts of the island, with all the eternally shipwrecked souls that animate the unity of darkness. It's not that Billy is unafraid; nor is fear his ally. Simply put, his fear is not in charge, it's a separate subject altogether. Necessity is the mother of his action, fear is an idle sibling.

The man with the flashlight disappears underneath Weather Point Lookout. He must have entered the tiny Pirate's Cove. Billy crawls to the edge of the point and looks over. Sure enough, a light is moving down there, sweeping out from the cove. But Billy can't see in.

He hears a voice. Are there two of them? After a while he's able to conclude that it's a single voice, an old man's voice. He's talking incoherently to himself, grumbling.

Billy wonders if it's an old farmer, stranded since the original flood back in '36.

It's like coming across a Neanderthal.

Billy spends the night on the point, braving the chill and sleeping fitfully.

45

DAY FOURTEEN

Sometime late in the morning Billy hears the old man moving about. He creeps to the edge of the cliff and waits.

The old man emerges warily, looking left and right, but not up. His pants are tattered, like he's worn the same pair since '36; his shirt is too small to be buttoned and looks to be about two years old. Billy recognizes the shirt; it's his, of course. The old man's hair and beard are the color of a pale nicotine-stained finger. The beard hangs lower than his groin. The hair appears to have been cut recently, without much consideration given over to style.

"Hey mister," Billy calls down, startling the old man, who looks up at Billy and then flees into the lake, running with high, angly steps until the water is too deep, then wading with his arms flapping, and finally disappearing about four hundred yards out. It takes a while for his head to disappear completely. Billy thinks of watching a muskrat swim.

Unlike a muskrat, the old man does not reappear ten feet from where Billy thinks he will. He doesn't reappear at all. Billy wonders whether his body will go through the locks or over the spillway. It's funny how you never know some things.

The old man had few possessions in the cove, and most of what he had had been stolen from Billy and Lola: candles, a tin of sardines, one of Lola's bras. His bed, up in a recess where a narrow ledge juts from the wall of the cove four feet above water level, consists of a long plywood plank and a couple of rank army blankets.

Billy is afraid Lola won't believe his story.

Back at Base Camp, Billy discovers otherwise.

"Why the fuck didn't you ever search the cove if you knew it was there?" Lola accuses him, as if it's his fault a loony old man shared the island with them for a while.

"I looked in it from the entrance and it didn't seem like nothing was in there."

"He could've killed us in our sleep."

"He was just a loony old man. He was harmless."

"You should've searched the cove. Security is your responsibility — that's what you said."

Billy knows Lola is right.

"Well, anyway I got your bra back."

"I don't want the filthy thing after that old pervert touched it."

Billy stands there with the bra in his hand. He kind of wants it. But Lola just said she didn't, and if he doesn't make some show of getting rid of it, she'll know he wants it and think he's just as bad a pervert as the old man.

Billy tosses the bra on the dead fire and says, "I'll burn it later."

Looking at it draped over a charred log, Billy feels ashamed.

Lola is wiping mud on her breasts.

'We have changed,' Billy wants to tell Lola, but he doesn't, and he loses the feeling he just had of being on the verge of profound discovery.

46

DAY FIFTEEN

The sun is setting on the other side of the island and Gerard has still not arrived.

Lola reels in a bullhead that's no more than five inches long.

"You keeping track of the fish today?"

"I'm not keeping the fish log anymore."

"Since when?"

"Last week."

"Why not?"

She seems peeved, which surprises Billy.

"I filled up that one ticket and didn't have no more," Billy lied.

"Oh."

The real reason Billy gave up the fish log was because he missed two days from being upset about Lola fucking Gerard. Then he decided it was stupid, like keeping track of time — except for the days, which were important since they needed to know when supplies were coming.

"I think I'll start up a new fish log tonight," Lola says.

They make their way back to Base Camp in the dark, fishless. They threw them all back because they thought Gerard would bring Chinese food again. The last one was too small anyway.

Neither Billy nor Lola are prepared to consider the possibility that Gerard won't be coming at all. When it first seemed like he wouldn't be coming today, Billy felt relieved. Now he's nervous.

"He's probably coming tomorrow," Lola says.

"Yeah, he'll probably come real early."

47

DAY SIXTEEN

Gerard doesn't come.

Billy and Lola eat a large bass for dinner. Billy hopes Lola brings up the subject of Gerard and she does.

"You think this means he's not coming?"

"No."

"Then why isn't he here?"

"Something went wrong."

"What?"

"Probably it took longer to kidnap Stratton than he thought."

"Or maybe they caught him and he's in jail — or dead. Then we're stuck here."

"No. He'll come. He's too smart not to think of a contingency plan."

"What contingency plan?"

"He'd've thought of a contingency plan, in case something went wrong someone else would bring us supplies."

"Who?"

"One of his friends, I don't know. We just have to be patient. He'll come, or someone else. He knows we can take care of things all right for a while."

"We can?"

48

DAY SEVENTEEN

Gerard doesn't come.

49

DAY EIGHTEEN

Gerard doesn't come.

While Lola cooks the fish, Billy puts on boots, jeans, and a long-sleeved shirt. For some time he paces back and forth by the fire with his hands in his pockets.

He clears his throat.

"The fish is done," Lola says.

It's bass again.

"You start. I have something to say."

"Okay."

"Lola?"

"Yes."

"Lola, Gerard hasn't come . . . "

"I know that, Billy."

"I know, but I was just starting. Lola, Gerard hasn't come and I think we have to face some facts. Now, I don't know what happened, but it's too early to assume the worst. Nevertheless, we should consider what the worst might be and prepare for it. The worst is not that we're stuck here. We can survive here easily until the cold weather comes. We've got at least two months before any real hardship visits us. So that's not the worst. The worst — "

"Speak for yourself."

"What?"

"Speak for yourself. I can't think of anything worse than two months on an island with you."

Billy marvels at the ease with which he is able these days to weather Lola's nasty little storms.

"Thank you," he says, "and it's a real pleasure being stranded here with you, too. But as I was saying. We can devise a way to get off the island before hardship visits us. It won't be easy, we'll — "

"All we have to do is build a goddamn raft."

"Oh really," Billy said with sarcasm, as he saw it, dripping like venom from his mouth. "And then what? To the east we have French Island, or past that, the mainland. To the south we have French Island, or, further west, the lock and dam. I'd like to see you go through that on a raft. I think you'd agree we'd be better off avoiding these locales, that we should at least make for Minnesota. To do so we would have to cross the main channel. That's the main channel of the Mississippi, a — "

"I know what river it is."

"Do you know how powerful it is? Do you know what it would do to a raft?"

"No, tell me."

"Carry it right into the lock and dam."

"Okay."

Lola begins to realize there's a lot she's failed to consider.

"I think you'd also agree that we must leave at night, so no one sees us and wonders who we are. At night there's less river traffic. I've been watching."

"That's real perceptive, Billy. At night there's *no* traffic."

"At night, Lola, there's barge traffic. Which means our boat would not only have to be swift enough to beat the current, it would have to make it between barges as well."

"All right, so what's your goddamn plan?"

"My plan has two components, or parts. Since we're talking about escape I'll start there. We go north, see, because the lake has very little current. So we go as far north as we can and cross up there, so even if the current takes us we'll have a lot more room to play with, two or three miles. Maybe more."

"So then go ahead and build the fucking boat."

"But we haven't come to the worst yet . . . "

"Which is?"

"The worst is if they come to get us before we get off the island."

"Who?"

"I don't know. Stratton and Torgeson. That Skunk guy. It doesn't matter — just say our enemies. What if they come?"

"Then we're fucked, so hurry up and build the fucking boat."

"It's going to take time, Lola, I've never built a boat before. And in the meantime we've got to prepare our defenses."

"Fuck the defenses, just build the boat and let's go."

"What if they come tomorrow?"

"What? You think they'll be here tomorrow?"

"Lola, we don't know if they're coming tonight, tomorrow, or never. We have to prepare our defenses *and* build a boat."

"Oh god," Lola says, "I wish Gerard would get here."

"Thanks," says Billy, who is more determined than he's ever been in his life.

50

DAY TWENTY-EIGHT

"We need a name for the north bay on the West Coast," Billy says.

"How about Fisherman Bay? Sometimes I go there and fish."

"But we already got a Fisherman's Point. How about something else."

"There's always that grumpy heron that flies away. How about Grumpy Heron Bay?"

"Yeah, that's great."

Lola wants to ask how the boat is coming along, but after the fight during dinner on Day Twenty-Five that ended with Billy threatening to refuse to build one, she had promised not to mention it for one week.

Still, she suspects Billy is spending more time planning a war that may never take place than he is trying to build them a boat.

Lola is right.

Billy has her carving three-foot spears all day long while he's off constructing what he calls the Hidden Ramparts.

The three-foot spears are for Spiky Bay, the southern bay

on the East Shore. Billy's going to spike the bay in case the enemy tries to land there.

"So we got to spike the whole coastline?" Lola asked him.

"No, just Spiky Bay. See, they'll come from the east, so we only have to worry about the East Shore."

"Then what about Drop Point Bay?"

"See, the trick to defense is allowing the enemy entry at some point. That way we know where they'll be and we'll be ready for them. We're luring them into our trap."

Hidden Ramparts is intended to be a camouflaged, impenetrable wall of logs and leafy branches strewn with thorns near the southern end of the island, stretching from the east ridge to the west. If there is time, Billy plans to dig a death pit where the Ramparts end at the west ridge; he'll leave just enough room, so when one of the invaders finds to his relief that he can just squeeze by without having to climb down to the shore and then back up, he'll find himself ten feet into the ground, hopefully with broken ankles.

"We'll have spear clusters on our side of the ramparts," Billy explained to Lola. "In case they're right on top of us and we have a pitched battle. We can spear them through the ramparts."

"They'll have guns, you idiot. They'll shoot us."

"They won't be able to see us. You'll see."

51

DAY THIRTY-TWO

"So how's the boat coming?"

"Has it been a week?"

"Yes, Billy. I waited a week like I promised."

"Okay, but first let's get through the Defense Report."

Lola rolls her eyes.

"How many spears today?"

"Ten."

"Ten?"

"What, that's not enough?"

"No, I was just wondering, I — "

"Billy, I finished spiking Spiky Bay and I caught dinner. So ten, okay?"

"Ten. Excellent. Perimeter Patrol?"

"I went to Binocular Point ten times, on the hour. I went to Weather Point Lookout three times. No sightings."

"North perimeter?"

"Check."

"No sightings?"

"No, Billy."

"Good."

"Okay, so how about the boat."

"We're not done with the Defense Report."

"What else?"

"You have to ask about my further progress."

"Further fucking progress?"

"Lola, some day this'll pay off."

"I said: *Further fucking progress.*"

"I found a shovel!"

"What?"

"I found a shovel in the Farm Ruins, under a bunch of wood."

"What were you doing fucking around there and not at the Boatworks?"

"I was seeing if there was any wood I could use and I found a shovel!"

Billy could see Lola didn't appreciate the significance of the shovel.

"I can dig the death pits for sure now."

"What about the fucking boat!"

"No progress. But I started Death Pit One. I'll show you where it is in the morning."

"What about the last week? The boat."

"It's not done."

"Billy, I asked nicely so tell me what you've done on the boat the last week."

"What you have to realize is I'm doing a lot of thinking about it. Even while I'm doing something else."

"So you've gotten nowhere."

"Not really. Remember that one night I left for a while after dinner?"

"No."

"Remember?"

"No."

"Let me see the fish log."

"What for?"

"So I can show you what day it was. I remember we had all those perch."

"Just tell me. I remember."

"I wanted to test my raft in the dark, so I went all the way to the Boatworks to test it."

"And?"

"It won't work. It leaks."

"Great."

"But I've been thinking and I think I came up with the design. That's why I was at the Ruins, to see if I could find the right wood — and some nails."

"And?"

"I'm not sure. But I'm working on it. I think it's got to be longer and narrower, with sides. In the bottom I can use the Loony Man's bed. I just got to figure the sides. I'm working on it, okay?"

"Okay."

52

DAY THIRTY-THREE

In his death pit enthusiasm, Billy digs himself into a hole he can't get out of. An eighth of a mile away, Lola suns herself at Fisherman's Point. It's ninety-two degrees at around one in the afternoon. For the first time in a month or so on the island, Lola feels like she's in paradise. What could Cancun have that she doesn't have? A beach is a beach. Water is water. Sun is sun.

Bronze men with black hair on their bodies.

Fruity drinks you can suck down one after the other and then when you try to get up to pee you fall on your ass.

A bronze man with black hair on his body picks you up and carries you off.

At night there are ceiling fans.

In the morning the bronze man is gone, back home to his hula dancers.

You lay in bed all morning, swim awhile, start drinking fruity drinks about three, watch the sun set over the ocean, watch the hula dancers, ignoring the bronze man who can't take his eyes off you even though his wife is shaking her bare hips around the fire and everybody's clapping their hands. You start swaying — you can feel the beat of the bongos in your ovaries. Everybody clears the way for your dance. The native men have never seen anything like it. The bronze man approaches. You drive him crazy the way you move. When he tries to touch your hip you move away slick like an eel. You shake your hips up to another bronze man.

In the morning he's gone.

So you go get another one.

Before long . . .

Lola hears a long trill, followed by two shorts. "Come," she thinks, but then she hears three more longs and another short. That's — what? — a long, a short, three longs, wait . . . no matter, here it comes again. This time Lola gets it: one long, two shorts, three longs, one short. That's a fucking sentence. Lola can't recall that particular secret call. Billy must be working on a longer call, the moron.

She hears it again, this time more adamant: ONE, two, THREE, one. Fucker's practically shrieking. She'd like to go wring his skinny little chicken neck — why the fuck aren't you at the Boatworks where I can't hear you practicing your goddamn bird language.

Fuck it, Lola decides. She lays on her back on the towel. She can feel the heat of the sand rise up through it. Give me one bronze man and one fruity drink and I'm in paradise. With her arm over her eyes like this she can concentrate her ears on the water, its constant movement. The trills are far, far away. When you think about it, this is the same water they got in Cancun. All the way down the Mississippi, into the Caribbean, through the Panama Canal . . .

Lola falls asleep.

Not long before sundown Lola makes her way back to Base Camp. Billy is still trilling. Let the fucker tell me he worked on the boat today, Lola thinks; he's been in the same place all goddamn day.

Lola is frying a bass when she hears Billy wail in the old language: "Lola? Come! Danger!"

It's a five-minute walk to Death Pit One where Billy is.

Lola looks down at him and thinks she sees tears in his

eyes; she laughs like she hasn't for a month.

"Oh Billy," Lola laughs, "you're wonderful."

She thinks how hilarious it would be if she left him down there for the night.

"Toss me the shovel, Lola," Billy says.

The pit is so deep, Billy's words echo.

"What's it doing up here?"

"I threw it up and I was going to climb out, but then I couldn't. The sides are too steep."

"Find any worms?" Lola asks, suppressing her laughter. "It looks like good wormy soil."

"Just throw me the shovel, I've been down here all day."

"First the Defense Report. Perimeter Patrol?"

"Lola!"

"All clear to the north. Boatworks?"

"Lola!"

"Boatworks."

"I didn't go there, I was down here."

"Fuh . . . fuh . . . " Lola says, breaking into hilarity with each attempt. "Fur . . . fur . . . " Lola has tears in her eyes now.

"Lola! Please!"

"Further . . . " Lola's belly hurts badly. "Further progress?" she blurts, and she laughs like a dozen shrieking herons.

Billy wants to weep, but perhaps the lushness of Lola's humor, the lushness of Lola in good humor, leaves no room in his pit for self-pity, and he can't prevent himself from laughing along with her.

"All right, Billy. So I hand you the shovel and then what?"

"I dig my way out."

"How?"

"I dig steps in one wall."

"What's the point of this Death Pit?"

"To . . . okay, I see your point . . . "

"I'll go get some rope."

Half an hour later Billy's arms feel like long heavy rags. He lays on his back in the dark, his legs dangling into the pit, looking up at black leaf clusters giggling in an imperceptible breeze. He smells fish frying in a pan . . .

53

DAY FORTY

Strategically, the best place on the island to build Billytown would be along the North Lip, Billy figures. The South Lip is too steep. From South Lip if you go straight south you run into the spillway and dike that extend from the lock and dam. From North Lip if you go north, which you'd have to if you want to stay on water, you go way upriver. You'd get the lake traffic and it would be a small matter for the river traffic to swing by. It's hard to put into words, but the thing is the North Lip is more *open*.

The first huts would be on the coast, but before long the settlement would extend as far as historic Base Camp. Historic Fisherman's Point would be part of the settlement. Actually, the settlement would curve on the East Shore almost to Drop Point Bay. On the West Coast, all of Grumpy Heron Bay would be incorporated and that's where the rich would have their villas, or the poor their shacks, one or the other. Drop Point Bay maybe would be the most historic place, so it would be like a reserve, even though it would make a good bay. Not every seaport has a great bay. Strategic location is every bit as important.

Besides, Billy knows, sometimes just because a city is there it becomes strategic vis-à-vis locale. A lot of people think cities grew up as a result of the hinterland. The farmers, for instance, needed a place to trade their goods so a town started up. But what a lot of people don't realize is that sometimes the city comes first, then the hinterland. That's what it will be like with Billytown. Billytown will exist because Billy Verité had the foresight to found it. The reason it's in a good place will come later.

Billy does not mention Billytown to Lola.

Lola's upset because Billy finally finished building a boat and dragged it down to South Lip yesterday afternoon where he left it moored. He planned on testing it today, but when he got to it this morning it was gone.

Lola thinks it's gone because Billy can't tie a decent knot.

The real reason is that Billy snuck out in the middle of the night and untied it.

Billy thinks about the future Billytown as a way to keep from brooding over the morality of his action. He just made Lola his prisoner, in effect. There was no way to talk her into staying on the island. If the boat worked they would've had to leave tonight. Billy could argue that fleeing would be a bad move because they have no money and they'd most certainly be caught, but the truth is he's not sure. Maybe nobody in Minnesota would be chasing them. Maybe since Stratton and Torgeson are rogue cops, they'd be searching privately, they wouldn't even have an APB out on them. Of course, he could reason that Lola could leave if she wanted and he could stay — but she *would* leave and then what if she drowned? It would be Billy's fault for not going with her when he knew it would be a lot safer with two people paddling. Worst of all, he could have escorted Lola across and then returned to the island if he wanted. That would've been the solution, obviously. But he couldn't face being on the island alone, which calls into question his concern even over her drowning. When it comes down to it, that's all there is to it. Therein lies Billy's culpability and he knows it.

Perhaps Billytown will justify his wrongdoing. Attaching a name to a place usually does the trick.

54

DAY FORTY-ONE

Billy runs through the woods trilling for Lola, one long and one short, so that it actually sounds like he's calling "Lo-La." Since the Death Pit fiasco they have refined their trilling system.

"What's wrong, Billy?" Lola asks at Base Camp, where they meet up.

"The binoculars are gone."

"Really?" Lola says, but to Billy her voice sounds peculiar, like she maybe doesn't even get why that's a problem.

"They aren't there. I looked all over. Who had them last?"

"I don't know, did you check Binocular Point?"

"Of course. I was just there. The binoculars are gone. I never take them from there."

"They aren't hanging on the Binocular Tree?"

"No. I said they're not there."

"Well I don't know then."

"Didn't you check the point yesterday? Wasn't it your day for Perimeter Patrol?"

"So what. Are you accusing me of stealing the binoculars?"

"No, but were they there?"

"I don't remember."

"You don't remember?"

"No."

"Last night during the Defense Report you reported checking the point every hour. Were you lying?"

"No. I checked every hour. Jesus, Billy."

"Well, were the binoculars there or not?"

"Yes."

"Then you remember."

"Yes."

"Then why'd you say you didn't?"

"What is this, the fifth degree? I don't know what happened to the binoculars. I left them on the tree yesterday."

"Well, they're gone."

"I gathered that."

The truth is Lola broke them in a fit of temper. She was mad about the boat.

She feels guilty.

55

DAY FORTY-TWO

What if the enemy comes by night?

First of all, it's unlikely because the lake is so shallow. Navigation could be a logistical nightmare. Plus you'd have to figure that the enemy would realize that the element of surprise gained by night assault would be countervailed by the fact that they wouldn't be able to see what they were doing, while the islanders themselves would have the tremendous advantage of being familiar with the terrain.

But what if?

There's only one answer: Ujiji. Base Camp is unfortifiable, so Billy and Lola have to start sleeping in Ujiji, Billy's round-fort, which he envisions as the place where they'll make their last stand, if necessary.

Ujiji is Billy's masterpiece, a fort ten feet high, almost perfectly circular, with a diameter of twenty feet. It's not finished yet, but when it is, a platform will circle the inside of the fort, a sort of catwalk six feet high. Already, the fort is impregnable, situated in the densest woods. For the enemy to sneak up on

Ujiji at night they would have to, if they landed in Drop Point Bay, navigate quietly and safely Billy's system of false trails that form a delta on the northeast quadrant of the island and all lead eventually to Death Pit One. If the enemy ignored the trails and headed south into the Central Highlands, they would find themselves in Forbidden Sector I on the west, or Forbidden Sector II on the east. The only safe passage is the unmarked Safe Trail, which Lola and Billy have committed to memory. First of all, the two sectors have a combined four death pits, one in Sector I and three in Sector II. Each sector has five branch traps, branches that will swing with deadly force once the trip thread (fishing line) is disturbed. At least six of the ten could kill a man. Each sector has two spearthrust traps, two overheads and two sideswingers — the latter being essentially branch traps involving a number of spears. In addition, each sector has between five and ten rock traps. Billy isn't sure how many because several times he's thought he's heard something heavy fall in the Forbidden Sectors. Where the land drops to the coast there are innumerable hidden spikes to discourage hikers from taking the shore route. If they should happen to survive a safari through the gauntlet they would come upon the Hidden Ramparts, Billy's barbed, wooded wall. Perhaps it could be climbed, but probably not without waking Billy and Lola. Or maybe not — but more likely it wouldn't be climbed. The enemy would search the ramparts for a breach, coming finally to Death Pit Seven on the west or a sheer spiky drop on the east at Binocular Point. Ujiji would not be reached.

That's what.

56

DAY FORTY-FIVE

Billy finds his rattlesnake. Going through the Farm Ruins he finally lifts the right piece of rotted wood. A five-foot and fat timber rattler looking untampered with by isolation is curled and sluggish, though its rattling suggests a degree of irritation.

Billy has the courage to subdue the snake by pressing down on it behind the head with a stick, then grab it firmly and carry it all the way to the nearest death pit (one). Before throwing it in he imagines it being quick enough to turn and bite him as soon as he lets go, so he gets on his knees, suspends it the length of his arm, and releases.

Tomorrow he'll see if it'll eat fish.

57

DAY FORTY-SIX

The rattlesnake eats a small perch.

58

DAY FORTY-SEVEN

Billy goes over the battle plan with Lola.

"Let's say the enemy lands at Drop Point Bay. That would be best, and that's what we expect. Then we have a decision to make. If their numbers are large, we try to take a few out with the catapults and then we retreat on the Retreat Path, which as you know is designed to lead them onto the False Trail System and at least one of them into Death Pit One. In their search for us they should find the trick shoe and that should lead them to the Central Highlands and the Forbidden Sectors. Chances are, that will wipe them all out. Meanwhile, we will have reached the Hidden Ramparts, dashed along to the south end of Seaweed Bay and — oh yeah, leave that spear cluster alone, there's plenty south of the ramparts. We go along South Lip to Pirate's Cove and use the secret tunnel to reach South Highlands. We follow the trail to Ujiji. The tunnel into Ujiji we may need later for escape or sneak attack, so we'll skip it. At that point nobody should be hot on our heels. Once you're safe in Ujiji, I'll make for the Ramparts to keep watch. Remember the secret calls?"

"One coo per enemy."

"Right. And what then is the signal for enemy wounded?"

"One whoop."

"Enemy dead?"

"Two whoops."

"Good. And we'll use the same trill system."

"What about the spear cluster on the secret tunnel/trail system?"

"We'll have to decide as we go. We don't want to waste them, but at the same time we can't let them fall into the hands of the enemy. The one in the Cove we'll definitely leave there because they won't find it."

"What if they land somewhere else? What if they land south of the Ramparts?"

"Good question. First thing is we make sure we know how many of them there are so we can keep track. Then we let them see us while they're still in the boat and we have a head start. We let them see us running along the East Shore, but up on the ridge. Then we sneak along the Ramparts and down to the West Coast and into the Cove. I'll keep watch from the tunnel. They probably won't even see Ujiji before they take off to search north of the Ramparts. They'll be certain we fled north. When it's safe I'll come out and check to make sure, come get you, take you to Ujiji, and then I'll check the Ramparts. The important thing to remember, Lola, is that we'll have plenty of time because we'll know exactly where we're going. From, say, the Boatworks to Binocular Point to Seaweed Bay and into Pirate's Cove takes me between seven and eight minutes — I've timed it. They won't know where they're going, so everything will take longer. They don't know the terrain. Plus they'll be going slow looking for us. But I'm not going to lie to you, Lola. No plan is perfect. A lot of this we've got to play by ear. We have to expect the unexpected, but we can't because it's unpredictable."

"Billy?"

"Yes, Lola."

"I don't mean to be . . . I don't . . . I'm not just saying this, but my honest opinion is that it's a great plan and all but I don't think the catapults are going to work. I don't think there's a good chance you'll hit anybody. And even if you do it's only mudballs."

"With rocks in them."

"Even with rocks in them."

Billy thinks about this. It hurts a little, but he can see she's trying to be nice about it, and a good commander does have to be objective. He pictures a boat arriving, the barktwine cut, a mudball being slung into the air. He's tested the range; minor adjustments can be made. If he shoots all twelve at the same time . . . The image of a mudball slamming into Stratton's forehead as he stands on the prow of his ship — the rock coming as such a surprise — is so glorious Billy can't entirely give it up. Yet he can see Lola is right.

"All right, that's true, but it may give us an immediate psychological advantage. They certainly won't be expecting it. So we won't make it a big part of the plan, but if we can shoot them off safely, we will. Okay?"

"Okay."

"I think it's hard to underestimate the psychological aspect of warfare. Or overestimate it. We don't know how they'll react to anything. They probably think they're coming to catch us hiding out and that's it. They won't be expecting any defense. So as soon as things go wrong they'll probably be pretty shaken up — "

"Or pretty pissed."

"Yeah, but what if Torgeson, for example, is one of the enemy and he falls into Death Pit One with that rattler? Don't you think he'll be pretty scared? Especially if he gets bit. And then if Stratton hears him scream and sees what happened, I think they might even lose their nerve and try to flee."

"Great, and then they come back later better prepared."

Billy gets a look in his eye Lola's never seen before. It's a very compelling look, the look of a man who's seeing something, and though Lola may not know this is going through her mind in a code she's yet to decipher, it's also the look of a man who *can* see what he's seeing. It's a Gerard look and Billy's got it.

"What is it, Billy?"

"That is, unless . . . unless they can't leave."

"What?"

Billy has green lightning in his eyes.

"Are you ready to take this all the way?"

"What do you mean?"

"I mean we, or I, sneak back to their boat and sink it — we sink their boat and they're stuck."

"Oh no, Billy . . . "

Lola feels a bolt of terror seize her body.

Billy sucks it into his eyes.

"Yes."

"No, why not just sneak back and steal their boat?"

"They have radios — we wouldn't get more than a nautical mile away."

"But they have radios anyway."

"What do you mean?"

"They can radio for help — or a new boat."

"They won't. They're rogue cops. They can't radio for help. Plus they'd be too embarrassed. But if we were getting away . . . no, they still wouldn't use radios. But they could see where we went and they could radio Skunk's people on shore to watch for us. We'd get caught for sure. No, the thing to do, Lola, is fight them to the end, on our territory."

"What do you mean 'the end'?"

Billy draws his forefinger along his throat.

That night the crickets have Ujiji surrounded. Billy permits a tiny fire. They have their sleeping bags close to the fire. They're both leaning on their elbows, smoking cigarettes, their heads just a few inches apart. During pauses in their lilting conversation they watch the flames and feel a blankness arc toward the backs of their skulls and curl up. Fire is impossible to figure out, even when you're not thinking about it, and that's the mood they share this night inside the fort called Ujiji; they are suffused with the spirit of conundrum; the night is heavy with foreboding, buoyant with wonder. The stars seem to flicker and for a moment Billy imagines it's the stars making the cricket noises. Lola hears the crickets in a circle and feels them closing in on her, and feels them protecting her, closing in, protecting . . .

"You know what Gerard told me once?" Billy asks, keeping his eyes on the fire, or parts of it, or where it was, where it might be again . . .

"Hm?"

"He told me when the explorers came to the New World they'd keep a cricket on the ship in a little cage and when it started singing they knew they were near land. The cricket knew before they did, before they could see the land. That way they never crashed at night."

"What do you think they fed it?"

"Grass probably."

"You think they had extra crickets in case some died on the way over?"

"I don't know."

"Billy?"

"Hm."

"Don't you think if that noise we hear sometimes at night is fox pups we'd've seen a fox by now?"

"I don't know. They're supposed to be pretty smart."

"Well, we heard it the other night, right?"

"Yeah."

"Well, how long does it take them to grow up?"

Billy has to think about that.

He can't come up with an answer before his train of thought drowns in the fire/a fire/fire . . .

Lola has forgotten the question.

"Billy?"

"Hm."

"You really think the enemy will come?"

"Yes."

"Before the boat's ready?"

"I don't know."

"Billy?"

"Hm?"

"Remember the binoculars?"

"Yes."

"I broke them."

Billy doesn't say anything. Some of the fire runs along a log and disappears.

"Because I was mad about the boat. I smashed them against the tree."

"The Binocular Tree?"

"Yes."

Sometimes a log will just be sitting there and suddenly fire will come out of it.

"Lola?"

"Yeah?"

"I snuck out at night and let the boat loose."

"I know."

The smoke from the fire rose out of Ujiji and up through the trees to somewhere in the sky over the island. In the darkness it could not be seen from any shore.

59

SOMETIMES ALL PEOPLE REALLY WANT IS TO TALK

"Oatmeal again," was the first thing Stratton said ungagged. He stated it flatly; then he said, "I don't mind." A few seconds later he said, "I like oatmeal."

The worst part about holding Stratton hostage was having to shovel food into his mouth. To Gerard it was a loathsome nexus of two unnaturals, faggotry and babysitting. But as he had Stratton bound to a chair in his maintenance closet he was forced to go through with it this one last time before the scheduled hostage exchange.

"Well, don't think you deserve it."

A puzzled look rappelled its way out of Stratton's apathy. "Why not?"

Weary of Stratton's acquiescence — since his capture he had yet to struggle or even squirm — Gerard asked, "Why have you been such a bad man?"

Stratton seemed to consider the question seriously, with equanimity.

"I don't know what you mean," he said.

Gerard smiled without malice.

The truth was, he missed the company of man.

"Well, Detective, I don't know everything, nor all the details of what I do know, but to start with you're a crooked cop who provides protection for drug rackets for a percentage of the take."

"You know that?"

"Everybody knows."

"Well, that seems pretty harmless, I — "

"I'm not done. You also harrass innocent people, use your authority to get women into bed, have had a hand in several murders, one of which was nearly mine and could still be — "

"What innocent people do I harrass?"

"Billy Verité."

"He's innocent? He's a weasel, a worm, an informant, the worst kind of scum . . . "

"He's not an informant. Not anymore, if he once was."

"Oh, he was."

There was a silence that neither wanted.

"But you bring up some interesting points," Stratton said, "I mean, some of it's true."

"And so?"

"And so what?"

"So what if I decide to kill you right now? Can you come up with a good argument against it? Some of the people who died because you let a hit man run loose — knowing exactly who he was going to kill — some of them were my friends."

"Like?"

"Barlow, Spleen."

"Yeah. Say, did Spleen kill Sherri Holloway, do you know the truth about that?"

"He didn't."

"You're sure?"

"Positive."

"So you know about all that."

"Yes. And my question is why shouldn't I kill you. I wonder if you could come up with an argument against it."

"I thought you were going to trade me for the FBI guy."

"I was, but to tell you the truth, I think the FBI guy is dead. So they'll try some kind of trick. Then I'll be faced with the immediate decision whether to kill you or not. This way I can think it through."

"So you're serious. You might really kill me. Right here, tonight."

"Right."

"How would you do it?"

Gerard looked around. "I've got a gun. I guess I'd hit you with it hard once to knock you out, then keep hitting you on the skull till you were dead. Does it matter to you?"

"I'd rather not suffer very much."

Gerard laughed.

"I'd rather not make you suffer much."

"So do I really get a chance to talk my way out of it? You really'll listen and think about maybe not doing it?"

"Sure."

"Well, to start with, about your friends — "

"Don't lie about anything either, all right? Like telling me you're sorry about killing them. There hasn't been time. No lies."

"Okay. I guess you're right, anyway — I'm not sorry. But — and this is the truth — I'm not happy about it either."

"Why'd you do it?"

"Do what?"

"Participate in the death of my friends."

"I don't know. I guess it was all part of the way it went. I never thought their death was key. In fact, I wanted Spleen alive so I could nail him for the Holloway thing. I couldn't stop Buck. He was a pro. He even beat me up once."

"I didn't know about that. That makes it worse."

"Worse? How so?"

"You made the deliberate choice not to apprehend him. Otherwise, if you really went after him one of you'd be dead. So you didn't just let things slide, you had an actual confrontation with a killer and let him go."

"Worse yet, I made a deal with him. After he beat me up. That was when I got your name on the list. Cause you were fucking my partner's wife and I figured he'd appreciate it."

Gerard chuckled.

"You *want* me to kill you?"

"No."

"Well I'm closer now than I was a minute ago."

"Yeah, but this is just the factual stuff, I haven't started trying to talk you out of it yet."

"After that I can't see how you could."

"If you kill me, won't you be as bad as me?"

"You were going to have me killed because of who I was fucking. You think that's as bad as killing you because of that?"

Stratton took a moment to make sense of what Gerard said. Something was blocking him, something he wanted to say that was eclipsed by what Gerard said. The field of his interior vision went pure white.

"Say that again."

"You want the rest of this oatmeal?"

"No."

"I said you wanted me killed because I was fucking your partner's ex-girlfriend — not even his wife at the time, as if even then it would be okay — who was also your ex. That's different from killing you for nearly getting me killed."

"Oh. Okay, I see what you mean. That's true. Killing me wouldn't be as bad."

"There's another aspect to this, too. Isn't your partner after me now? Don't you think he wants to kill me? Aren't you going to help him?"

"You beat him up."

"He attacked me. Unlawfully. I haven't broken any laws."

"You assaulted a cop."

"A rogue cop, who attacked me."

He had Stratton there.

"All right. My partner was wrong."

"But you're still in it with him. That makes you my enemy."

"Yeah, but how do I get out of it? It's all going already. You know what I mean? It's — how do I stop it? Cause to tell you the truth my heart's not in it anymore. I'm changing. I can feel it . . ."

Gerard found himself charmed by Stratton's meek objectivity. For a moment he tried to imagine what Stratton's hands would be doing if they were free to move.

"I don't just do things anymore, like automatic. I can't stop thinking about it. The other night, last night? The night before? When you got me . . . "

"The night before."

"I was out for a walk and that's what I was thinking about . . . "

"What?"

"All this stuff. How I'm changing. I mean, just the fact that I was thinking about it. I don't know what to think. Because I never did before. So you know what I thought was I can't be like I was, because now I wasn't that way or I wouldn't be thinking about it, but the problem is I don't have any idea what to do next. You know what I mean?"

"I'm not sure," Gerard said, thinking 'Just kill the bastard and get it over with, for his own good.'

"It's like fucking a woman. It's no good once you think about it. That's why you get tired of fucking your wife. But now I think about it with every chick. I don't just get off on her like before. I'm already bored cause I can see the next day before it happens."

"You're world-weary."

"What's that?"

"You're tired of life."

"So what do I do?"

"If you live."

"That's what I mean. Suppose this wasn't happening, nothing was happening. What should I do about being world-weary?"

"I'm learning the viola."

"What's that?"

"It's like a violin, only bigger. A fiddle."

"Are you world-weary?"

"No."

"Were you before you started learning the viola?"

"No. I've never been world-weary. There's too much I want to do before I die."

"How old are you?"

"Forty-eight."

"What else do you want to do?"

"Learn Spanish. Meet the right woman, maybe have kids. Start up my own machine shop. There's a lot of things I want to read . . ."

Stratton felt the bilious uprising of a familiar contempt. He remembered what it was like to interrogate a retarded kid caught in the act of breaking a shop window and not in the least understanding what he'd done wrong. He remembered his frustration — he'd caught the retard going from window to window downtown, smashing them with a length of pipe. Somehow in the course of routine questioning it came across to Stratton that the kid didn't even think he'd done anything wrong. He got mad, so he broke windows. And as far as he was concerned that was all right; which was too much to take, even from a retard. He tried explaining to the kid why it was wrong and couldn't put it into words. Maybe that was the most frustrating part, having to explain something that was so obvious it couldn't be explained. His mind acquired the stark image of neon circuitry gone haywire. He kept saying to himself, 'What are you, retarded?' And answering, 'Yes.' And he found that insufficient. Finally he hit the kid; Torgeson had to restrain him. So for a second he thought Gerard was like that retard, and then he felt the urge to struggle against the ropes that bound him to the chair, and then he thought he himself was like the retard, and he did struggle briefly before subsiding into a tearful funk.

Gerard felt a little uncomfortable at the sight of Stratton's tears. He figured it might be a good time to make a point.

"You afraid to die?"

Stratton had to think that through.

"I don't know, I can't even feel it. I think I'm too depressed."

"Because you don't want anything?"

"I don't want to learn an instrument. I don't want to learn Spanish. I don't know what I want. I want to want something, though."

"So you need time to let something happen."

"Maybe."

"Yet, if I don't kill you, you're going to go after me and Billy Verité and Lola."

"Where are they? If you kill me could you at least tell me where they are first?"

"Then I'll *have* to kill you."

"That's right — then don't tell me."

"My point is, why not — if I were to let you go — why not quit, or at least become a good cop?"

Stratton needed to blow his nose. Gerard could already see snot creeping about his nostrils.

"I don't want that, either," Stratton said. "I don't want to go on like I've been, but I can't just stop if I don't have a reason. It's all gone too far."

"You can't even see how stopping Torgeson, stopping Skunk, would begin to make up for what you've already done?"

"I couldn't just all of a sudden go against my partner."

"So it's all right if he kills me."

"I didn't say that."

"But if I let you go you won't stop him."

"I could try."

Gerard couldn't help laughing.

"That's the first attempt you've made to talk me out of killing you. But you don't mean it, do you? Be honest."

"I guess not."

"So I have to kill you, right?"

"No."

"No?"

"I'm not saying that."

"So, are you saying I should let you go?"

"Yes."

"So you can help kill me."

"No."

Gerard let Stratton assume the initiative.

"I don't want to kill you."

"But can you see my point? I have you captured, right here before me. And if I let you go, you'll feel forced by circumstances to help someone kill me. Why would I let you go?"

"You could keep me here and not kill me."

Gerard reached for a roll of paper towels. There was one left. He wiped Stratton's nose roughly and tossed the towel to the floor.

"Thanks."

"How long would I keep you? Until what happens? Isn't the only way out of this for me to kill you one by one?"

"What about the FBI guy?"

"He's already dead."

Stratton looked off toward a private corridor where all the images he knew he needed to conjure were absent. He would not have felt differently if he knew these images were mocking him elsewhere. Gerard could tell by his look that he knew nothing about Eddie.

"Let me ask you something," Gerard said. "Do you think, right now, that I'm going to kill you?"

"Yes."

"How does it feel?"

Stratton looked down that corridor to see if he could feel anything.

"It feels like it's not real. Like I believe it but I can't really imagine it."

"So you aren't scared?"

"It feels like even ten minutes from now is a long way away."

"It's not. It's ten minutes away."

"So you're going to kill me in ten minutes?"

"Did I say that?"

"I thought that's what you meant."

"You brought up the ten minutes."

"Oh."

The ropes kept Stratton from slumping to the floor.

"I was hoping you'd be frightened, begging for your life, so I could get across to you how your victims feel, and then maybe you'd go straight, and I wouldn't have to kill you . . . but the more we talk the more I'm convinced I *have* to kill you."

Stratton was watching Gerard's lips move. When they closed, and stayed still, he responded like an automaton.

"What."

"Forget it. Killing you maybe really would be a favor."

"I — ," Stratton said weakly; he was sobbing, quietly and with his head hanging down. He was more discouraged at the lack of desire, the dismal feeling of being rootless in the center of a vast calm, than he was about the fact that he was soon going to die. So he cried. And the corridor had nothing in it, no doors, no lights, no air — it wasn't even endless. He lacked even the hint of imagery that could mutate into the recent disappearance of a metaphor, the sense even that a vague shape once lurked somewhere, the notion that anything in any realm or division or spectrum of space could ever possibly move, so that he might at the very least be able to think to himself, 'I've come unhinged,' which in this man whose focus of torment was lack of desire, had become without his knowing it — though one does suspect a sense somewhere in his mind that he was missing the specific knowledge of an enormous ungraspable verity — his only desire.

The conversation was over. Gerard knew that. Stratton couldn't talk his way out of his predicament. There remained, therefore, only Gerard's will to execute. His tactic had backfired. By bringing up the possibility of killing Stratton, he'd offered Stratton the chance to talk him into it. It was confusing at first, but then Gerard realized that what it came down to was Eddie. He was the variable. Had he been able to convince himself that Eddie was a goner, Gerard would never have kidnapped Stratton. But now that the situation had acquired the taint of immediacy, he was forced to reckon with the convergence of his logic and his gut feeling, and at that nexus lay the corpse of Eddie the FBI guy. Ipso facto, Torgeson would not be able to make the exchange; Gerard could gain nothing, in fact stood to lose a great deal, up to and including his life, and therefore having Stratton made no sense unless it were so he could reduce the number of his enemy by one, a good idea, especially considering that in contacting Torgeson he had most certainly succeeded in tipping off Skunk that he had witnessed Eddie's abduction, and so increased the number of his enemies by whatever the current membership of B.A.D. totaled. In fact, during the little time he spent thinking it through, more or less watching Stratton vanish from in front of him, he realized that had he been able to convince himself earlier that Eddie was dead he would definitely have removed Billy and Lola from the island, and fled with them to a large city far, far away. What was keeping him from doing that now? Stratton, the man weeping further and further away from him, a man so far gone he paid no heed to the snot running all the way down into and beyond his open lips. Automatically, Gerard looked at the cardboard cylinder he had recently bared. And he smiled as he stood to go to the bathroom for a towel from the dispenser, smiled because he knew all along he would never kill Stratton, knew all along exactly who he was, and he knew he could have done this no other way, for he could never have talked himself into abandoning Eddie, could not have brought himself to conclude that Eddie was dead without acting on the slim chance he was alive; and most of all he was smiling because he knew he was about to leave the urgency and danger of his life behind, immediately, and that meant he wouldn't have to kill Stratton.

He walked into the bathroom, turned on the light, noticed the feet in the first stall, turned toward the towel dispenser, realized he was in danger, and turned back around just in time to see Hobo in the act of bringing a lead pipe down on his head so hard it killed him instantly.

60

ZENO'S PARADOX APPLIED TO GOD AND TORTURE

Or I could admit that I refuse to divulge the tortures Skunk Lane Forhension employed in his attempt to get Gerard to say where he'd hid Billy and Lola. I could say that Moses Maimonides long ago decided that since it's impossible to determine the nature of God, what you should do is figure out what He isn't, kind of hem Him in. God isn't bad. Right there you've cut the field of speculation in half. I've thought about God and I've thought about Gerard's death, and I regard Gerard's death as more difficult to bear than both what God isn't and what He is. Does God lie? Does God accept the torture of Gerard? If no and no, then no God. If God, better a little lie than the torture of a good man. So God-like I lie if I lie — and besides, what has man not done to man? Would such an investigation — before God — bring me closer to what happened to Gerard? Or to God, for that matter? Skunk Lane Forhension did not take Gerard up in an airplane and toss him, still living, into the sky over the ocean. Forhension did not hang Gerard upside down and beat the bottom of his feet with a stick. He didn't bury Gerard up to his neck in the desert, put honey on his face to attract ants and leave him there in the sun (with his eyelids either taped up or torn off). He didn't starve Gerard to death. There was certainly no form of public humiliation, no pillory, no parading him before crowds with a confessional sign draped over his shoulders. Forhension didn't stand Gerard in front of a firing squad only to have the executioners fire blanks. He didn't stick burning needles under Gerard's fingernails, or in his eyes. He didn't drive a nail into Gerard's skull. He didn't resort to sleep deprivation, nor use any cold water tactics — he didn't even use nudity in any way. He didn't order one of his lackeys to sodomize Gerard, didn't cut his balls off (slowly or one by ripped scrotum one), didn't cut his penis off and stick it in his mouth. Forhension didn't break any of Gerard's bones. He didn't put his face in a cage with a starving rat. He didn't tie Gerard down and let water drip onto his forehead drop by drop until it bored a hole through his skull. He didn't perform dental work without an anesthetic (much as Gerard actually needed the work done). He didn't slice off Gerard's ears or his nose. He didn't use any kind of slicing tactics followed by dousing with bleach. He did nothing with acid or gasoline. He did not set Gerard on fire. He didn't stretch Gerard's body until it broke. He employed no machinery whatsoever — he did not use the strappado, for instance, nor did he electrocute him. No, none of these tortures, these that we can contemplate so much more easily than we can the nature of God, was used on Gerard. If Hobo knocked Gerard out and when Gerard revived he was tortured by Skunk Lane Forhension, we can not determine what exactly happened, what form of torture Skunk chose, not without calling into question the existence of God, Whom we need all the more desperately if Gerard was indeed tortured. We can only know what wasn't done, and, after that, that Gerard didn't talk.

61

THE DETECTIVE IN HIS RETIREMENT

All is bleak and bare, a desert landscape.

Kiss me, my sweet.

Fill my navel up with bourbon, we'll figure out what to do with it later.

You are my camel lover. I feed you liquor and it's never too much, for you may have to, someday, cross an infinite span of time without it, an Empty Quarter, or fifth.

The nomad's home is his camel.

I love you, baby.

And if I don't, we can work that out, here in this room, with the heat way up and the window open or the air conditioning on and the window open, and we'll want together nothing more than to lose track of the different places our heads woke up at in this your little oasis apartment.

Carly wasn't at her place in ten minutes that night, it was more like fifteen. But to my great relief she came alone. And all night long no one broke down the door. It must have been in the morning I decided I loved her, or that I may as well. She couldn't get enough of love or liquor, and if that meant she had on occasion fallen asleep on me, it also meant she awoke with a smile, no matter how I woke her, or with what. Not that I can clearly remember that particular night, it being in no wise different from any other I shared with Carly. If the sex came first it wasn't by much, nor the other way around, and we both felt the two went well together. And if, ultimately, her emphasis was on booze and mine was on fucking, maybe that was all we could expect from equilibrium. Ah, Carly, the two of us: we were insatiable.

That first morning I loved Carly I woke up knowing I was a different man. I wasn't the mourning loner, I wasn't the avenging detective. I was sitting up with my back against the wall, the blanket drawn decorously to my navel. Carly had her back to me, yet was so resolute in her hunger her ass was, in her mumbly sleep, climbing me about the thigh. And I was thinking about what I had to do that day, thinking about how I intended to meet the D.A., one Janet Flagra, to discuss the Sandy Calderon case. I was trying to piece together the movements that would be required to get me to her office, all the while taking in the odors left by our persistent coupling, which saturated the apartment, and while I was doing so Carly wriggled her ass in her sleep, as if trying to situate it perfectly, and I gave it a little slap, and it leaped at me — yet I could tell by her breathing she was still asleep, so I said out loud, "If it's all the same to you," meaning anybody, really, "I think I'll just stay here in bed with my baby."

I found the bourbon beside the bed, let some of it down my throat, put a few of my fingers inside Carly, and she rolled onto her back and I slid my penis in from the side.

The first thing I thought with any coherence after that was 'I bet Gerard would have loved this woman.' And when she kissed me she could taste bourbon, and she wanted some, and we got it without disengaging, so she was happy and I was happy and somebody's bells outside told us it was noon.

Isn't that pretty?

That's how it was. I never got out of bed that day, not even to eat, not even when Carly did. I know for sure she went to get some food.

"Can I get you anything?" she asked.

It was late afternoon.

"There's a book I want from the library. You got a card?"

She did.

"Write it down," she said.

That's the way Carly was. Nothing was difficult for her and whatever she did for me seemed generated from an illimitable vacuity, as if her love diffused into a substance no less banal than air.

I read about a paragraph while she cooked supper. The line I couldn't get past was, "The peasant is historyless." Carly was a lot like that sentence. You could look at her until she meant nothing, but you could never stop looking at her after that. I tried to think about the peasant and his historylessness because I knew that in some way the source of my grievances — none of which I could any longer name — was lodged in my desire to be that historyless peasant. But I got stuck on two notions: first, that desire was a lot like a hailstone; second, that Gerard was that peasant. I got this image of Gerard behind a plow, and I labeled the image: The Last Peasant. And just as when you take a razor blade to a hard-boiled egg and can't prove it didn't hurt, I can never be convinced Gerard in his peasant overalls was not in that room as much as me and Carly. Maybe even more than Carly. And I know that had I had it in me to get off that bed and leave that place, Gerard would've either stayed behind or come with me. Concomitantly, if I'd said to Carly, let's go, she would have, and if I told her to stay, she would have. Gerard's ghost at least had a palpably free will. Maybe the thing to say is what's real and what's not real matters less than our current involvement with the one or the other. Gerard, my friend, what did you see? Speak, peasant! Were you there when Carly and I proclaimed our sterility at the same time? We laughed less from the coincidence, the romance of it, than from relief. One chance in a million our union could ever be accused of procreating and we'd have thrown up all the defenses: condom, spermicide, diaphragm, cigarettes and pills, interruptus — at the very least. But we've emerged free and clear through the time of attrition — the sewers, the defenestrations, the suction, the hangers, the doorsteps, the kitchen knives — and cried no more.

So we had a good night, I'm sure, Carly and I. And the next morning I located in my penumbral bourboned vision somewhere between those same dishes only more and the plaster flaking into the bathroom sink from our firmament the last of my dutiful nature, and I called Sandy Calderon.

"It's me," I allowed.

"You. What happened? I talked to Flagra yesterday. She's expecting you."

"Sandy?"

"Yes."

"The peasant is historyless."

"What?"

"The city is intellect."

"Quit fucking with me — what's going on?"

I quit fucking with her.

"Did you talk to Tommy Marco?"

"I did."

"And?"

"My spiritual postulates are satisfied."

"Are you drunk?"

"A little, from last night."

"Have you gotten anywhere or not?"

"Yes I have."

I said. And I hung up.

62

THE DOCILITY OF PIGEONS (DAY FIFTY-SEVEN)

"Wow," Lola said.

Billy was talking about pigeons, his essential theme involving how he brought a country trick into a city and what happened to it once it got there.

"See it don't matter how you kill them if you're going to kill them, right? Every farmer shoots pigeons cause you get too many they eat the crop. So one day I went to my cousin's step-farm and — "

"What? What's a stepfarm?"

"What?"

"You said your cousin's stepfarm."

"No, my stepcousin's farm."

"You said stepfarm."

"No I didn't."

"Yes. You said step — no, cousin's stepfarm."

"Okay. Anyway, I went there and he had these pigeons captured and he showed me how to snap them so their heads come off in your hand."

"I wish I had one so you could show me."

"I know."

They looked from their perch near the Catapult Fort out over the lake. A cormorant flew like black revenge low over the choppy blue.

"It's easy, though. The main thing is the wrist, but you also got to keep in mind you have to hold onto the head real tight. You got these two fingers closed on its neck and its beak pressed into your palm — and you throw it real hard, snapping, see — and hold the head. And it comes right off. The body hits the ground and you open your hand and there's the head, right in your palm."

"I couldn't stand the blood. Don't you get blood spurting through your fingers?"

"No. They got hardly any blood."

"Maybe I could do it, then."

"You could. I know you could. But the thing is, Lola, it was all right out on the farm — "

"Stepfarm."

"Stop it."

"Okay."

"Out on the farm it's natural. But — and I didn't feel bad. Because out in the country it's natural. But when we did it at the record store guy's house it felt bad because in the city it's not natural anymore."

"Why'd you do it?"

"He caught me stealing and called the cops on me."

"That seems fair."

"But I was just a kid."

"How old?"

"Thirteen."

"He could've just warned you."

"That's what I figured."

"So you killed one of his birds?"

"All of them."

"Wow."

"Me and my stepcousin went up there to his roof one night when we knew he and his wife was gone — we spied on them every weekend for a month. Every Saturday night they went out to the North Star till bar time. We went about midnight and snapped all their necks, every single one of them. There was over thirty. Racers. We just left them there, too. Thirty heads, thirty bodies."

"Did he ever find out you did it?"

"No. I mean, he may have suspected me but he could never prove it. Me and Timmy made a blood pact never to tell nobody."

"Timmy's your cousin? From the stepfarm?"

"He's Spleen's cousin."

"You were related to Spleen?"

"No."

They were silent awhile, and maybe one of them wondered where that cormorant was now.

"I wish we had them binoculars," Billy said. "I don't mean to make you feel bad, but every time I see a sailboat over there I can't help thinking it's Gerard."

Lola squinted at the point of French Island, just two miles away, not far at all considering the sea in between. A boat was moving out from the slough, just coming in fuller view off the point.

Lola felt like a baby squirrel, still hairless, was rubbing its sleepy back against the nether reaches of her belly. She couldn't believe what she was seeing, but she was sure of it. She had good eyes.

"Billy," she said tentatively.

The boat yawed broadside to the sun.

"Billy, that's him. That's Gerard. That's his sail. I remember. Billy — he's coming!"

Billy leaped to his feet; he shaded his eyes even though the sun was off above his right shoulder. He didn't remember the sail. What he remembered was the blue stripe that followed the sheer. The boat he was looking at appeared to have that stripe.

"You're right, Lola — it's him!"

Lola stood and they embraced. This would be it, of course. They both knew Lola would leave with Gerard, and maybe Billy would decide to as well; but the main thing, inside both of them, was relief that Gerard was still alive.

"What should we do?" Lola asked.

The question puzzled Billy. He didn't want to be sarcastic.

"Wait for him, I guess. He's against the wind so it'll probably be over an hour. Probably two hours."

Billy didn't fully understand how sailboats worked.

"I know," Billy said. "Let's make a joke. Let's get some of our water and bring it down to Drop Point. You know, offer him a drink."

"Yeah, so we can show him how we had to live here while he was fucking off in the city."

"Right."

63

(MEANWHILE ON THE BOAT)

Meanwhile, in the hold of Gerard's sailboat Torgeson worried about his partner, who stared out an oval window at the passing changeless waters. The water was riled and fervent, yet no one part of it, from where Stratton sat, was any different from any other. And the fish rumored to thrive in there were no more likely than teams of seraphim.

"You up to this, Ace?" Torgeson asked.

"What's there to be up to?"

"If they're on one of these islands we'll have to hunt them down, maybe even eliminate them while resisting arrest."

"We're talking about Billy Verité, right?"

"And Lola."

"How hard can that be?"

"You're not yourself, that's all?"

"What's my self?"

Hobo, laying opposite the two cops, lifted his arm from his eyes and looked over.

"I never seen a cop so full of shit," he said.

Torgeson, who agreed, reflected on the years of friendship it took to build the tolerance to withstand his partner's pathetic decline. He failed to find justification for his loyalty.

"He's still a cop, pal. And you're still a hood. Don't forget that."

"Fuck you," Hobo said lazily, replacing his arm.

Two decades of freelance corruption had done nothing to erode Torgeson's instincts, and he was getting a bad feeling about this excursion. Something was not right. Skunk Lane Forhension figured out that Lola and Billy were on an island, that Gerard — who knew the fucker had a sailboat? — took them there. It made sense in a simple way. Skunk checked Gerard's post office box until something provided a clue: a flyer from the Sail Club. So Gerard had a sailboat. Skunk went to the club, asked around until he found out which boat was Gerard's, checked the boat, and found a note: "salt.cit.and." That was it. Skunk looked in a dictionary and found citronella. From that, Torgeson was supposed to believe, and more or less did, that Skunk guessed Gerard was running supplies to Billy and Lola in his boat. The logical choice of islands, he decided after some study, was Red Oak Ridge: plenty of cover, probably abandoned structures from before the flood, plenty of high ground. So it all made sense, yet Torgeson had the feeling that something was off, like maybe he was supposed to be on his way to his own execution. Hobo was clearly a dangerous man, but the other guy, the pilot — Goldberg — was hard to figure. Torgeson had never seen him before they met up at the Sail Club just before setting off. Skunk introduced him as Goldberg, that was all. A slight man with glasses, a look of perpetual amusement on his face. Just a little guy, but like Skunk he moved among dangerous men with apparent fearlessness. Torgeson never understood people like that and the urge to beat him up was difficult to suppress. When they reached the island, Goldberg would be the one to watch.

Stratton turned from the window and looked about the cabin. He tapped Torgeson with the back of his hand. He wanted to convey something with his eyes that he couldn't be sure existed. He knew the impatience that resided permanently in Torgeson's eyes and smiled at it with avuncular detachment.

All Torgeson knew was that Stratton's gestures were saying: Watch this.

And he watched as Stratton unholstered his pistol and crouched up to Hobo and pressed the barrel against his temple.

Stratton fired before Hobo reacted. The bullet made it through both sides of Hobo's skull and lodged into the hull. Blood, brain matter, and skull bits decorated the cabin.

"That doesn't change anything," Stratton said, still in his executioner's crouch.

"No," said Torgeson.

From his seat at the rudder Goldberg looked through the companionway with what amounted to suspicious equanimity, given that he had heard an unmistakable retort and looked in time to see the bloodmist of Hobo's exploded head. He couldn't see Torgeson, but he wondered when Stratton would wipe his face. They were about two hundred yards from the island and two people on it were jumping up and down, waving their arms.

Goldberg decided he ought to say something.

"Let's stay focused on our objective, boys," he said.

64

WELCOMING THE ENEMY

Veering off Bath Trail down toward Drop Point, they heard
what sounded like a gunshot.

"That sounded close," Lola said.

She slopped water out of the jug she carried.

"Sound carries," Billy said. "Probably hunters over on Bryce
Prairie."

"In summer?"

"There's always some hunting. Besides, maybe it's fall now."

And then Billy saw the water through the trees and felt
himself again in a paradise of perpetual wonder, a marvel no
less marvelous for the way the lake tilted vertical as if sucked
onto a canvas, and the boat dropped to the bottom, near to
shore.

"He's almost here!" they shouted together, and ran down
to Drop Point where they jumped about like mongoloid idiots
trained to spend their joy on sporadic saccharine moments.

Lola was the first to notice Gerard was wearing sunglasses.

Billy was the first to realize that meant it wasn't Gerard.

Lola recognized Torgeson first — as soon as he emerged through the companionway to see what Goldberg was pointing to, which was them, Billy and Lola.

"Oh my god — it's Torgeson!" Lola shouted.

"And Stratton," Billy said, for Stratton followed. "To the catapults!"

They dropped the jugs and ran up the slope. The enemy was just fifty yards offshore.

As they had often rehearsed it, Lola watered the mudballs and Billy pulled the machete from the vinesling. Only this time it was for real. When he saw that the man with the glasses was going to ram the boat full speed onto shore — something Gerard would never have done — Billy decided to time it so that the second the boat stopped he'd cut the vines that held the catapults taut.

Half the catapults could not withstand their own force. Since Billy'd found no coconuts on the island, he'd fashioned cups from salvaged bits of wood, which, in the end, rained down about Stratton, Torgeson, and Goldberg along with mudballs.

Lola wanted to run immediately, but Billy had to wait to see the result. They were only spectacular within a limited context. The boat stopped with its nose ashore; Billy cut loose all twelve catapults in four strokes; first Stratton, then Torgeson leaped into the shallows holding their pistols; then Goldberg, carrying a Sten strapped to his shoulder, ran to the bow so he could jump directly on to land and keep his feet dry; and just as he was about to disembark, the sky rained mud and wood. Only one mudball hit the boat; the rest splashed around it or thudded into the sand, while the wood trailed down like explosion debris in a line from the catapults to the boat, betraying Billy and Lola's precise location to Goldberg, who fired a stuttering burst in their direction.

"These guys mean business," Billy remarked.

Lola could only whimper fearfully, and cling to Billy as he ran her along the Retreat Path. Exactly according to Billy's designs, he and Lola reached the spine of the northern Central Highlands just as the enemy climbed Drop Point Bluff, the fifteen-foot scarp above the bay, which would've appeared to them to be the route to take if they wanted to cut off a northward retreat; and because they eschewed the gentler slope Billy and Lola were out of sight on the west side of the highlands before they could be picked off. They would've appeared to be making a desperate dash northwest when they disappeared, but they made an abrupt turn and were now moving with enhanced stealth on an arc around the Ruins, coming back up to Central Highlands, back where the Safe Trail began to snake between the two Forbidden Sectors.

There Billy stopped. He looked back and saw no one, no movement through the trees. He heard no clumsy crashing through undergrowth. Maybe his plan was working. Maybe the enemy — three of them, he'd have to remember that — was creeping along the false trails.

"Hold my hand through here," he told Lola. He could see she was frightened.

The good thing about that was it made her obedient. They didn't have time for internal squabbling.

Billy knew the Safe Trail like the map on his palm. Like an Indian he stepped lightly, moved deftly, quickly, without having to think. Lola wasn't bad, either, though fear threw her breathing off and she was emitting a series of asthmatic grunts.

When they reached the spear cluster at the Clearance Zone past the Forbidden Sectors, Billy felt enough at ease to chuckle over the image he couldn't shake from his mind of the enemy combing the woods, one of them suggesting they fan out. He just knew one of them would end up in Death Pit One.

There were only five spears in this cluster because Billy knew he'd want to take these along to Ujiji, or hide them on the way. He'd only planted them here as a precaution, in case the enemy was right on top of them and gaining fast.

He collected the spears and they moved along the Ramparts, avoiding Death Pit Seven, descended the steep massif, and made the south tip of Seaweed Bay, where another spear cluster was hidden.

"We'll leave those," Billy said. "I don't think they'll see them."

They were hidden under a pile of rancid beached seaweed that crawled with ambitious semiaquatic life.

Having reached South Lip, they were definitely safe for the moment, though it was too bad he had no way of monitoring the enemy's progress.

Leading Lola toward Pirate's Cove, Billy wondered if his present combination of nerves, excitement, and fear was the way everyone felt in battle. He thought of Vietnam and how he'd read the Americans never knew what the enemy was up to. But he was more like the Vietcong here on his home turf, and the invaders had a lot of surprises in store for them.

At the mouth of the Cove, Lola experienced the sort of crisis to be expected from an ordinary person delivered into the unfamiliar terrain of extreme danger. She refused to enter the dark, muddy cleft.

When Billy went in Lola stood fast, pulling her hand from his.

"Lola, come on, there's no time to lose."

Lola couldn't express herself. Neither 'I don't want to die' nor 'I can't go on,' said quite enough.

So she stood and shook her head, her wide eyes dry.

"Lola, they're not in here. They're out there, where you are," Billy cajoled her — but she was unmoved.

"And if you stay out there, they'll get you."

But Lola wasn't thinking straight. Maybe they'd find her and she'd cry and they'd take her home and put her to bed and it would all be over.

Billy felt like every movie he'd ever seen in which the woman hesitated and got the man killed would pass before his eyes. Now he knew why the man never simply said, 'Fuck it, let her die.' You just can't do that.

He closed in on Lola. Her eyes moved rapidly back and forth.

Billy slapped her and said, "We don't have time for this, now get the fuck in there."

Before she could set upon him, were she so inclined, Billy got behind her and pushed her into the Cove.

Lola felt along the mud walls with her hands — only once muttering, "Okay, okay, I'm sorry," too softly for Billy to hear — until she reached the tunnel.

"Should we take the spears?" she asked.

"No, just these," Billy said, and Lola scrabbled up through the tunnel to the South Highlands.

"To Ujiji?" Lola asked Billy once he'd emerged.

"To Ujiji," he said, "just like we planned."

65

MONITORING THE ENEMY

"Fan out," Goldberg hissed.

He used his gun to indicate to Stratton he should swing a little south of where the fugitives had disappeared beyond the rise.

"You follow the trail," he told Torgeson, sending him straight ahead.

It was amazing how easily the rogues submitted to his authority, even Torgeson, who had forgotten how far he'd drifted out of his element.

Goldberg himself would cover the upper rim of the island. From his experience he figured Billy and Lola probably had some kind of dugout near the shore, a place where they felt safe and from which they couldn't escape.

Stratton trudged along swatting at the mosquitoes that were rapidly gaining in number in a cloud that swallowed his head, occasionally swinging in front of him and ebbing back. He felt his old edge returning; he could remember the singular purity his hatred attained when he refused to wait for a reason to channel it toward one pathetic object — it was a simple matter to divert the pulsings of self-pity that accompanied his each tormented step into a greater determination to ensure that Billy Verité's suffering exceeded his own. It was a shabby kind of transcendence, and Stratton had been missing it.

Torgeson's thoughts were more business-like. His initial aversion to the webby undergrowth he easily dismissed in the same way he dismissed, say, a fence that got between him and a suspect in flight. You climb the damn thing and get on with making the bastard pay for making you do it. For Torgeson it wasn't personal until he stepped on the loose sticks that camouflaged Death Pit One.

He knew immediately that his ankles weren't broken, but they were both sprained and Billy Verité had to die. Of course, there was first the matter of getting out of the pit, which became all the more urgent when his eyes had adjusted enough to the dark to notice he shared his pit with a rattlesnake that lay belly-up, apparently dead.

"Stratton!" he yelled, hoping he hadn't landed in a den. He looked behind to see if the ground was clear, then backed against the clay wall. Sometimes they live under ledges. He looked above his head for one of those. The walls went straight up to the sky.

"Stratton!" he called again.

As far as he could tell there were no more snakes in the pit, but it was possible another was laying alongside the first. Every time he looked up at the sky he lost some of his pit vision. He and the snake or snakes shared roughly thiry-six square feet of ground space.

"Torgeson?"

It was Goldberg and his voice sounded close.

"Down here."

Goldberg's shady head appeared against the sky. He extended his hand to Torgeson, who barely reached it when he stood on his toes. Torgeson was amazed by the strength in Goldberg's skinny arm.

Stratton ran up just as Goldberg pulled Torgeson out of the pit.

"Fucking bugs!" he said. "What happened?"

"Death pit," Goldberg said.

Stratton looked down into the hole.

"There's a snake down there — rattler," Torgeson said. "It was dead."

Stratton got down on his belly for a better look.

"I don't see any snake."

"Forget the snake," Goldberg said, and Stratton hustled back to his feet.

"What're we dealing with here?" Goldberg asked.

"Just a little scumbag and a bimbo," Stratton said.

"Well," said Torgeson, testing one foot and then the other, "the little scumbag made a booby trap."

"My point," said Goldberg.

"You think he's got help?" Stratton asked.

"You tell me."

"Could've been Gerard," Torgeson said, "but he's dead now. They're alone, if that's what you're worried about."

"What about arms?"

"If he had a gun he'd've shot at us already."

"Is that what you think?" Goldberg asked, turning to Stratton.

"Of course."

"All right, but keep your weapons at the ready. We're going to have to search this place one end to the other. We'll backtrack to the north, then work our way south. You," he said, indicating Torgeson by pointing his Sten gun at him. "Can you walk?"

"Not without thinking what I'm gonna do to that little bastard when I catch him."

UJIJI

Billy had Lola safely inside Ujiji. People are really going to remember the name now, Billy thought, though he still couldn't quite remember where he'd heard it himself.

Lola slumped against the wall of the fort and slid down until she could no more. Billy raised the driftwood hatch over the hidden cooler and pulled out a jug of water. He wet his hand and patted his face.

Lola smiled.

"Thanks, Billy," she said — and she meant it.

There was no time for romance.

"You wait here — I'll go and guard the Ramparts."

Lola clutched Billy's arm.

"Be careful," she said.

Billy nodded and slipped down into the tunnel. Outside the fort, in his haste to reach the Ramparts, he nearly found himself down in Death Pit Six, just managing to contort the potentially fatal step to the side of it and engineer sufficient momentum to flaglate on a weaving angle away from the hazard.

He was not demoralized. If it was so easy for him to nearly fall into the very pit he built, imagine how easy it would be for the invaders. He imagined, as he hiked to the Ramparts, that Stratton and Torgeson and the guy with the glasses could already be dead, done in by his guerrilla devices.

He parted a patch of grape leaves to look through the wall. So far no one was around. Were they dead? How long should he wait?

Billy sifted through the spears in one of the two Hidden Ramparts spear clusters until he found one that appealed to him. Probably they used to be a great deal heavier, when men were stronger; but his had a nice heft to it, and was sharp enough, he guessed, to puncture a man through light clothing.

He parted the leaves and again saw no one.

He wondered what it would be like to get shot.

67

GUERRILLA WAR

The bug spray sealed it. Whoever this Goldberg was, he was in charge on this island.

"I always hated the way this shit smells," Stratton said. Nonetheless, he was grateful. It worked.

"Let's move," Goldberg said, putting the aerosol canister back in his pocket.

On the way to the North Lip, they came upon Base Camp. Torgeson kicked Billy's shelter to the ground.

"Fucker won't be needing that," Torgeson said, suppressing the pain shooting up his legs by encouraging his spirit of vengeance.

At North Lip, they split up, Stratton walking the West Coast ridge, Torgeson the East Shore ridge, and Goldberg the spine.

"Shoot to kill," Goldberg offered for inspiration. Yet he did not expect the two cops to survive. A death pit was an alarming thing, and not even the one who succumbed to it seemed to realize they were up against a clever enemy. As he walked the rough centerline of the island he made sure to allow Stratton and Torgeson a good fifteen- to twenty-yard lead.

Stratton had the best route. The heat of the midafternoon sun was tempered by the wet breeze. He unbuttoned his shirt and let his belly warm. Much of the way he could avoid the tortured undergrowth and all the spider webs. The slope down to Grumpy Heron Bay was gentle and grassy and the view across the lake and the river to the Minnesota bluffs was spectacular. He did not remember while he hiked his conversation with Gerard; but he had often thought, since that night, of his lack of desire — and now here he had stumbled upon something to live for, the natural beauty of the earth. With some of Skunk's drug money and his wife's savings he could get together enough cash for a down payment on a nice house overlooking the river. As the coast curved outward between bays and the terrain grew increasingly brambly and dense, so Stratton's spirit etherized and his vision flooded a downy blue, and, so, nimbly did he overskip the webby brush.

And, of course, for Torgeson every step was the shabbiest of petty torments. He was not a man for great thought-systems, nor was he insecure enough to find it necessary to arrange his worldview into squadrons he could deploy in argument, but he did walk the land convinced he was, next to Billy Verité, a sort of übermensch. Yet for now Billy had got the best of him, and it was nothing short of heroic the way he pressed on, suppressing his frustration and the sense of hopelessness he felt as a man lured from his element and quickly wounded; it was as well via heroic instinct that he gripped his revolver as a means of deriving comfort through the correspondence between its elemental functionalism and his own torrid determination.

Ironically, Goldberg was the first to encounter a Forbidden Sector hazard. Despite the fact that the Forbidden Sectors were parallel rectangles separated only by the narrow Safe Trail, to the outsider they would've appeared, after all traps were accounted for, to be one large, square sector. On the ridge sides of the rectangles there was room enough to avoid the hazards up to the halfway points, where fields of spikes designed to funnel ridge walkers into the sectors made walking difficult. Allowing

Stratton and Torgeson, up from their respective shores, to walk well ahead, Goldberg yet walked straight through one of Billy's tripwires.

A rock larger than Goldberg's head thudded to the ground two feet behind him.

"Heads up!" Goldberg called. "He's got tripwires set! Watch your feet!"

Goldberg did not know fear, but he was glad the rock missed his head. He knew his enemy now: a clever little weasel who didn't quite know how to rig a trap. It would be interesting to see what came next; for instance Death Pit Two, which any idiot could spot from ten yards away. There's a fluid sort of imagery to virgin wilds — how could Torgeson not have spotted the orderly square of twigs and leaves?

Just past Death Pit Two was Death Pit Three and not ten feet away a stretch of fishing line. Goldberg followed the line until he saw how disturbing it would release a bent branch affixed to which was a spiked palette. With a long stick, Goldberg slapped the wire. He would've been run through. The force of the branch was such that the palette stuck to a thin maple tree, from which fell another large rock.

"Careful men! Traps everywhere!" Goldberg shouted, causing Torgeson to look away just as he was stepping gingerly onto a six inch spike planted firmly in the earth. The spike wasn't sharp enough to penetrate his shoe, but his ankle twisted and he fell forward, landing on yet another spike, which was sharp enough to gouge a divot from his neck. Stratton heard Torgeson's yelp and its abbreviation and ran precipitously into the heart of Forbidden Sector I, leaping over the underbrush and dodging trees until a branch trap slammed his stomach, knocking the wind out of him. Unbeknownst to either, Torgeson rose before Stratton, stumbling instinctively back the way he came, but woundedly wayward enough to plunge off the ridge, falling fifteen feet and impaling himself onto yet another spike, which managed to bore through his pelvic shield and emerge through the skin of his back.

From where he waited for the cataclysmic spurt to subside, standing still with his back to a black locust tree, Goldberg was lucky enough to see Stratton get the wind knocked out of him and still turn in time to see Torgeson stumble up into and then off his plane of vision.

Now Stratton was down and Torgeson was wailing like a conscript awakening to horrific truths in the dark between trenches.

Goldberg waited patiently for Stratton to catch his breath. He knew how long it would take. He knew how to knock the wind out of a man with two fingers.

"If you can make it this far," Goldberg said when Stratton finally got to his feet, "I'll lead you out of here."

They could hear Torgeson moaning and whimpering.

Stratton made it to the black locust tree without thinking about the future.

"What happened to Lew?"

"Let's go see. Stick close to me."

The island sloped from the Central Highlands down to the Hidden Ramparts and up again to the South Highlands. Hidden behind the grapeleaf cluster, Billy Verité could see Stratton and the man with glasses moving through the woods. He could hear Torgeson's death wailings. He didn't know what to do next. He had that sick feeling a man gets when the odds against him are so overwhelming he knows he must deny a portion of them. Billy wanted to deny the gun portion. He imagined his guerrilla traps decimating the enemy, leaving at most one armed man whom he would spear through the Ramparts. It sounded like Torgeson was out of commission, but if both Stratton and the man with glasses made it through the Forbidden Sectors he'd have to count on one of them landing in Death Pit Six or Seven, and after they had already passed Two and Three, that seemed too doubtful a proposition.

Billy knew he needed to improvise.

With spears.

Unless he could get to Torgeson's gun.

And where might that be?

Somewhere over by where the enemy was headed.

He wished Lola had risen to the occasion. But she was back in Ujiji virtually shut down, a fleshy organism in a state of pause. He pictured her crouched down covering her ears, her eyes slammed shut, dumb as a opossum. He felt a pang of pity and then went "Whoop!" He'd forgotten to call out the enemy wounded signal.

That ought to cheer her up, Billy thought.

He lost sight of the enemy through the trees.

Now I don't even know where they are, he whined to himself.

But then he heard a gunshot from the vicinity of the suffering Torgeson, who wailed no more.

So the enemy was down by the East Shore, picking their way along Spiky Bay. If they split up, maybe Billy could spear one of them, grab his gun, and go shoot the other. The only other choice was to retrieve Lola and sneak back to the boat and flee. He wondered why he'd ever thought of sinking the boat. He crept along the Ramparts toward the East Shore, toward the enemy. His imagination was vivid enough to picture him and Lola sailing north away from the island, watching the future sight of Billytown recede and fade in the distance and the dusk. He could not abide that scenario.

The clever thing about the Ramparts was the way Billy had made use of the natural environment. A thick barricade of leafy, latticed branches, a few logs, and as many thorn bushes as he could find, the Ramparts followed a line of trees which were incorporated into the fortification. It's true that "hidden" was a mite misnomeric, since an impenetrable wall of vegetation winding across the island could not be invisible, yet at first glance it looked like some heady natural phenomenon, a hanging garden of Babylon arisen wild from the earth — it was only deliberate rational explication on the part of the brain that denied this wonder — ranging from nine to fourteen feet in height, nearly a quarter of a mile long — that exposed its trickery.

Billy made it to the Binocular Tree, where he heard voices plotting below. The enemy had survived the spikes of Spiky Bay and was huddled on the shore, conspiring beneath Binocular Point.

"Look," Billy heard, "if this had been a serious op he'd have had a cyanide capsule on him. And believe me he'd have taken it. He knew the risks."

"I don't think he did. I know I didn't."

"Well, do you want to stand here and argue about it or do you want to try to get this over with by nightfall?"

Billy couldn't make out the response.

"I think we're past the spikes. What I want you to do is go up to the ridge and march straight to the west shoreline. I'll swing along the shore and meet you there. The way to do this is go from tree to tree. First look up and make sure you don't see any big rocks up there. Then scan the ground carefully, look for anything irregular — fishing line or piles of twigs. Then if it looks like it's clear move to that tree and examine the next tree. Go slow and you'll be all right."

Billy heard Stratton begin scrabbling up toward the Binocular Tree. It would be the easiest thing in the world to let him get close and then spear him in the face. But the man with the glasses would hear and Billy would lose the element of surprise. And overhearing the enemy's planning session reminded Billy of his one advantage: this was his territory; he had to exploit that advantage to the fullest. If he could eliminate Stratton without the man with the glasses being the wiser, he could use the turf advantage and the surprise business to get the drop on him. A Sten gun loses its superiority when it's facing the wrong way.

But first there was Stratton, his hands gripping trunks of little trees and clumps of brush, pulling himself up the scarp. There wasn't much time to think. In fact, what thinking had already been done eliminated the possibility of creeping away to drygulch the copper elsewhere. Besides, he didn't know which side of the Ramparts Stratton would choose to navigate.

Stratton was very close. Like that same opossum mentioned earlier, Billy dared a look around the tree just as Stratton, dumber even than that opossum, set his gun down to pull himself up. Billy, having been given so little thus far in life, knew a gift when he saw one. He reached back with the spear like the most natural of javelinists and precisely when Stratton's face appeared above the lip of the point thrust his spear into Stratton's mouth, open in surprise and one of the very worst kinds of horror. The moment Stratton ate the spear was profound, a nexus of opposing rushes of time harboring more explosive potential (unrealized, of course) than any theorized nuclear blast. If man is certain of one thing, it is that the design of civilization, however wrongheaded it may be, has in the process of creating a multiplicity of brand new fears, at least eliminated a great number of old ones, such as being speared in the face — and, the fear being gone, its abstraction, Stratton's split-second remembrance of a lost memory of sheer terror, which terror provided him more than anything with the assurance that none of his modern ills were for nought, that very abstraction aimed spearlike as well at the very nerve center of his intellect, collapsing his superstructure of being in the moment before his death, so that he died at the moment of acutest awareness of meaninglessness coupled with regret, at the same time that Billy Verité, cast permanently into delusion by the same civilizational ills, or the inability to adapt or cope, and seeking to emerge in a bright yet dimly imagined cartoonish beyond, enlivened by the current of Stratton's horror as if what was sucked out of Stratton vampirically suffused Billy, rushed back in time to inhabit an elemental being that proliferated before civilization's first bizarre steps were conceived, perhaps even before monkeys discovered the power of combining stick and brain, when it was still possible to feel the crushing bones (in this case, teeth and skull) of a corporeal enemy without an exhilaration of ego, without bloodlust or recoil, without hope or relief or a sense of triumph or loss, without pity or the gladhanding warmth of stewardship, without tense recollections of imagined formulae, without, in short, a care in the world and as well without the absence thereof. Stratton was the first man to reach the end of time, and Billy was the first to make it partway back.

After experiencing a moment like that there's no reason to go on living, so in a sense Stratton bowed out gracefully while Billy persisted with an idiocy similar to that of any insect that has been dismembered by a child. Yet that was a grander idiocy than most men ever know and did not deprive him of the right to his cunning.

Stratton crashed to the greenery below, a dead man with a spear posthumously destroying his face in the crazed geometry of an ungainly descent.

Billy grabbed the gun and slipped round the Binocular Tree to the north side of the Ramparts. The man with the glasses would be coming back this way.

"Quick Lola! To the boat!" Billy cried.

He whooped twice, as loud as he could, and then whooped two more times. Hopefully, Lola would hear the whoops, but not the part about the boat.

He stood behind the east extent of the Ramparts waiting for the man with glasses to appear. Stratton's gun was a heavy, unfamiliar object, and he knew he'd have to be very close before he could be sure to hit the last enemy.

But the man with the glasses never showed. Either he hadn't heard anything, or he was too crafty to fall for Billy's simple tricks. Probably he was running scared, just now coming to realize what he was up against. Or he'd found Ujiji and was holding Lola hostage.

Billy suppressed just enough panic to move with stealth through the woods of South Highlands toward Ujiji. The gun was so heavy he had to switch hands. He wished he'd have thought of an all clear signal, an are you safe/yes I'm safe call. Instead, he had to walk all the way to Ujiji and whisper through the walls. He'd been too careful about covering all the cracks.

"Lola?" he hissed.

"What?" she replied, too loud.

"You okay?" Billy whispered.

"Yes."

"Let me in."

Billy held the gun at the ready as the gate swung open. The barrel dipped toward the ground.

No one was inside holding a gun on Lola.

Billy locked the gate.

"I got Stratton and Torgeson. There's only the other guy left and he's got a Sten gun."

"Really?"

"Yeah, that's what he shot at — "

"You really killed them? They're dead?"

"Yeah. Torgeson got his in Forbidden Sector II and I speared Stratton in the face. This is his gun."

Lola looked at the gun, her face registering the amazement of someone whose parachute failed to open yet had fortune enough to land on a giant sponge.

Billy climbed to the lookout catwalk and marched Ujiji's perimeter. There was no sign of the man with glasses. He climbed down and went to the gate.

"You're leaving again?"

"Got to," Billy said.

"But he's out there. And he has a Sten gun."

Lola didn't know what a Sten gun was, even after one had shot at her.

"We can't just wait here for him to find us."

"Why not? When he comes we can escape out the tunnel."

"Too risky — he might be expecting that."

"Then go out through the tunnel so I know he's not coming in that way right now."

Lola had a point. Billy had to risk going into the tunnel.

Fear isn't such a bad thing, Billy realized, if you can learn from it. The thought of worm-wriggling straight into the nose of a Sten was frightening enough to give him tunnel sweats and subsequently cause him to doubt the efficacy of his system of branch supports, and, further, to realize with a jolt of panic that there was no room to turn around if he wanted to; but when his head popped up clear in the forest and no Sten guns about, he realized it was just as likely that the tunnel system would spell doom for the man with glasses as it would for him.

It was obvious from his lecture to Stratton that the guy knew his guerrilla warfare. Billy figured, then, the guy would find the entrance to the tunnel in Pirate's Cove and carefully investigate. Yes, he'd find the spear cluster and he'd realize it was an important strategic locale. The only way he could investigate the tunnel would be to crawl through it. Otherwise, he'd never know where it led. He'd probably guess it led to Billy and Lola's hideout — and he'd be right, give or take a tunnel, only he wouldn't realize that Billy would be propped against a hackberry tree, holding Stratton's gun with both hands, pointing it at where the man with glasses would have to emerge.

Billy sat against the tree, smelling victory on the quieting crepuscular breeze. He had never been clairvoyant before, and he found that it made him strangely calm. But that made sense in a way, since most of the forces of unrest derive power from uncertainty. He wondered if he'd feel as calm if it was his own doom he foretold.

First Billy knew the silence of the wild island was alive; he knew the land — not opposed to the air — was as alive as he. Then he heard the blue jays again, the birds who sing the first warnings in utopia, who flee the degradation and return to warn again. He lost his thoughts in their song, as if his winged self had risen to the leafy yonder to carry their voices to and fro.

Who knows but that a half an hour did not pass by before Billy sensed disturbance underground. This was Billy's island now, as much as it was any bird's, any insect's, any mysterious fox pups' that haunted by barks the night.

He held the pistol cocked, pointing at the back of the skull that wasn't quite there yet.

The twighatch rustled, shifted, slid, paused, and finally flipped. Two hands appeared, one of which did not release the Sten gun. When the head came up Billy fired and blew the top of its skull right off.

Without exulting, Billy stood and looked over the body slumped in the hole. Two feet ahead the largest solid portion of skull was propped against a husk of bark. The glasses, unharmed, had landed on top of it, but no eyes under the hair looked up at the sky.

68

THE MEANING OF UJIJI

Leaning back into the hackberry tree, the braindregs of his triumph desquamating from the leaves about, Billy heard a motor spinning closer like the implacable resumption of the latest epoch.

That would be Skunk, he figured, and about fifty commandos. And he knew then, or thought he knew, that the true residence of victory is in posterity, that what's important is not the waning years of an old soldier but how he fought his way onto the pages of history. Like the Zulus, he thought, and finally remembered the meaning of Ujiji. It was at Ujiji where the Zulus, armed only with spears, defeated the British, an impossible victory by natives over a modern army.

"Shaka Zulu," Billy said aloud.

The motor fell silent off Binocular Point. They'd come swarming up the scarp like Redcoats.

"Let them come," Billy said.

Sure the Zulus were eventually wiped out, but what everyone remembers is Ujiji.

Billy Verité too would die like a hero. They weren't going to have to find him cowering under some planks by the Farm Ruins.

"Let them come," he said again.

Dozens of frantic blue jays answered.

For a moment Billy felt his courage was palpable, that it could calm the blue jays. "Let them take Ujiji," he told the birds. He would hide here in the woods until they were all in the fort with Lola and then waltz in like Churchill in Khartoum.

Better yet, he'd take the tunnel, tunnel up right in the middle of what would be Skunk's command central, get the drop on him, and he and Lola could make their getaway in Skunk's boat. If only Lola was smart enough to figure Billy's next move, maybe create some kind of diversion when Billy was ready to spring into action. If she was really smart she'd actually be sitting on the trap door and Skunk wouldn't even know the tunnel was there.

Billy heard a gunshot, followed by the insane plummeting shriek of an expiring blue jay. He was head first in the Ujiji tunnel before he knew it.

Plenty of historical figures, come to think of it, didn't die, at least not right away. Some of them disappeared and were never heard from again. Like Zorro. There was nothing cowardly about him. There was nothing cowardly about disappearing and becoming a legend. Marlon Brando in *One-Eyed Jacks:* Ah shamed ya, Luisa. He ran. But Billy wasn't running yet — he still had Skunk Lane Forhension to deal with, an even more formidable force than Dad Longworth.

How far to Ujiji? Billy knew from experience that as soon as he thought he was halfway, he was about one third, and the next time he thought it was half it was one third left to go. A few nights ago he had lain awake trying to put a name to the mathematical qualities of illusion, but he ended up waking in the morning without having slept.

He thought of Lola. They could go way upriver, to the next lock and dam, maybe find another island. They would be alone and free and Lola would be overcome with gratitude. After making love they would lay together in the dark and talk about taking a Greyhound to Oregon. But in the black of the tunnel

Billy remembered Lola moaning in the tent with Gerard. He remembered a thousand insults. Sure, they would get to the island — and then what?

Of course all this depended on Lola having the brains to help him get the drop on Skunk. And what were the chances of that? This whole episode was like the tunnel he was in. Once you're in you can't turn back, once you're out you can run like a madman in any direction. The chances of he and Lola making it upriver alive were about as good as the Zulus coming back and taking over England, but if they did make it Billy Verité would know what to do.

Just as Billy thought he must be reaching the halfway point the tunnel began to slope upward. He thought he could hear voices. He crawled up to the trapdoor and tried to hear what they were saying. No light at all was filtering through the door, which meant it was possible Lola was sitting on it. He applied slight pressure with his palm and the door flew up, light blinded him, and hands much bigger than Lola's had him by the wrists.

69

THE CONFERENCE AT UJIJI

Ujiji was a little circle and Red Oak Ridge Island was a bigger circle and the water around was a moat and it didn't surprise Billy Verité who ran things in the enormity of the even bigger circle about. He went limp in the inchoate atrophy of his daring, two mute ursine visigoths lifting him from the tunnel, then nudging him toward Skunk with their fat elbows, ignoring the clumsy metallic fecklessness of the gun that was still in his hands. Behind him Lola started gibbering hysterics, "I didn't do it, he made me, I never wanted to be here, I tried to warn them but he had a gun — "

"Clamp a paw over her face," Skunk ordered the beast who detained her.

Billy looked at Skunk without fear.

"Are you Lee Harvey Oswald?" he asked.

"No Billy," Skunk said with something that could have been mistaken for tenderness, "I just look like him. Tell me, did you get Goldberg?"

"The man with the glasses?"

Skunk nodded.

"I shot the top of his head off."

A loud curt whimper escaped the ventriloquism of Lola's predicament.

"Bring her over here," Skunk said. "Keep your hand over her face."

Lola knew she was going to be executed, shot in the head with the tiny gun Skunk kept using to scratch the back of his neck. And now that she knew the precise scenario of her last moments, now that she could see it and see that she couldn't lie or snivel or fuck her way out of it, she witnessed the unbearable crumbling of the byzantium of her deceits, felt a pain like hunger vacuuming her guts. She would die and never see Billy again.

"Lola," Skunk told her, "I'm going to tell you this one time: The sight of a woman in tears moves me in such a way as I want nothing but to shoot her, so you stop whimpering immediately. You are not going to die by my hand. If I were Billy Verité I'd probably shoot you, but I figure he won't either, so that's enough now."

"I ain't gonna shoot her," Billy said.

"You're a headstrong boy, Billy. No, you weren't gonna shoot anybody. You were just planning on taking me hostage, stealing my boat — as if I didn't have enough reason to skin your ugly hide. But Billy, a man what can't think on his feet is no better than a coon up a tree staring at a flashlight. Get my point? We got a new situation here — a war was fought here today and we got dead soldiers to account for. Some of these men had families, and what these families are going to want to know is who killed two crooked cops out here on Red Oak Ridge, who rid the police department and the city of two drug-dealing, witness-killing, bribe-taking, extortionist, racketeering, rogue and dirty cops. Do we expect anybody to believe that you did that, Billy Verité? I think not. So you let me worry about the mess you made, and meanwhile you will remain here, in exile, within reach and no closer. These are the conditions of the peace: you get an island. You are Napoleon and this is Elba — not to overstate the historical significance of the event. Though in its own small way this is a Lepanto, a Gallipoli, throw in a few more bimbos and maybe even a rape of the Sabine women. Very few men are called upon these days to engage in even these kind of fitful, futile heroics. Seen in that light you should be right proud, albeit never forgetting how lucky you are to be left alive and how easily that could change. You will thrive on this island, Billy. You're a clever boy, you're in good health . . . in fact, your lone malady is your ugliness, and that, too, makes you more fit for a life of exile.

"As for you, Anna Magnani," he said, turning to Lola and handing her his pearl-handled derringer, "like all liquor-addled trollops," her arm somnambulating toward Skunk to receive it, "the last thing you lose is your aim . . . and now you're both armed — see, I can't control everything even if I try — but when he lets you go I'd as soon not have any shots fired till we're clear of the fort."

But as soon as the gravid mitts of the giant simpleton released her, Lola dropped the pistola and rushed to embrace Billy, who kept a firm grip on Stratton's service revolver.

"Billy," Lola gushed in a simper.

"Somebody get her off me," Billy said dispassionately, and when no one did, he accomplished it himself, shoving Lola so hard she stumbled back into the walls of the fort, where her legs gave way and she fell into an approximate lotus position.

I guess that settles that, Billy said to himself, wondering where the decision came from and how it so quickly acquired its resolve. He felt pretty good.

"Take this dame with you," he said, to test the feeling.

Lola gaped silently at Billy the way she once surrendered before the ominous indecipherability of a spiny prehistoric fish, as if in diminishment before the mockery of unfathomable secrets. She shook her head and looked around. Several big men better looking than Billy Verité were staring at her. So what, she decided, even Helen of Troy probably would've fucked one of those fat pharaohs if she hadn't been rescued.

"If you're coming, let's go," Skunk said. "An outfit like this can never have too many of your kind." And he led his men out through the gates of Ujiji.

Lola stood and followed with her head down, the slow and heavy steps of terminal defeat surrounding her with the claustrophobia of simple noises. At the rudimentary locust branch door she turned to look one last time at Billy Verité.

"Ugly fucker," she said.

EPILOGUE

So that's all over except for me, hanging around like a sharpie.

Here's a dramatic way to put it: I walk the empty street at night making wisecracks to myself.

It would be fair to say that I've learned to relentlessly inhabit my doppelgänger. It's the only way to tolerate the ambiguities I demand and I demand a lot of them, for in focusing on the foreground I've blurred the backdrop, and I never know if the curtain is up or down. As the ghost becomes less ghostlike, the exoteric becomes the haunter. That's the way I see it when I'm holding the vertically grinning skull of Sandy Calderon in my hand, pointing at the ghostliest of holes and saying, "Her nose was once there, and then it was there . . . "

And that's the way I see it when I look out the window of Skunk's office at the roof of the Winchester on Fifth building and can't see hide nor shell of Gerard. Lola is as fleshy as ever in a fine tight skirt and a nice crisp shirt that's unbuttoned to show there's a lot there, yet still leaves room for some guesswork. She's getting better at lipstick, too. You could say she looms hyper-real, standing silently beside the large and hairy Skunk-minion she calls her own. She'll never get away from that one. A lot of Lola and no Gerard. Very little Carly. She led me into the office and shut the door behind her retreat, all wisp and efficiency. It was Carly who said Skunk wanted to see me.

"Should I thank him for setting us up?" I asked.

"He knows you're grateful."

Skunk is dapper behind his new nickname — Mayor. He knows very well how to say "Sit down." When I do he wastes no time getting to the point.

"You're a hypochondriac," he says, and he sees I'm looking at the poster taped to his window of a man wearing glasses and a red beret, looking like an Aryan Guevara who knows figures.

"He was a great man," Skunk says, and then he tells me to go on about my own affairs and not bother anyone.

"I'm not inclined to," I say, getting up to leave without gratitude.

Maybe what I'll do is go on out to Billytown and make a new life for myself. No reports issue from there, but I imagine hearing vague rumors about a port of call, and fledgling enterprises, and a resurgence of the drama once thought inherent in commerce. The lonelier the city gets, the livelier these rumors . . .

The way to get to Billytown is to go on out to the rough bars on French Island, hang out for a while, keep your mouth shut, make yourself invisible. You'll hear the tail end of wild rumors and most locals will tell you none of it's true. But eventually, if you're patient, you'll find a man at the back table of a tavern, a man who reeks of the river, and by the look in his eye you'll know he knows something. He won't say a word, so you'll know it's true. And for the right price he'll take you there.

ACKNOWLEDGMENTS

I received what's called a Michener/Copernicus Award for this novel — twelve grand in small, unmarked bills, delivered in twelve monthly payments to prevent me from investing unwisely — and I'm thankful to the Michener Foundation and the University of Iowa, especially now as I write because I have another six months of this literary swag coming. However, as is generally the case with awards, this came long after the book was finished and so did nothing to lift me from the circumstance of wretched dependence I was in while writing it. It seems more important, therefore, to thank, with the help of an exhaustive list, those who provided me aid when I needed it:

Financial Aid: Sasikala Perumal ($500), Adam Snyder ($30), John Harsch ($50), Whitney Terrell ($300), Steve Carlson ($100), Lauren Rauk ($10), Michael Welch ($260), Bill & Marty Pemberton($170), Jack and Ellie Harsch ($150), Jim Lafky ($20), Steve Hardin ($10), Dan Marcou ($2), Trent Stewart ($3)

Food and Drink: Marc Wehrs, Michael Welch, Dave Moburg, Jim Lafky, Warren Liu, Ondine Bue, Vicki Bott, Jim Niessner, Larry Snyder, Dick Mial, Lauren Rauk, Tom Mutz, Leah Mutz, Sherri Sikora, Ethan Mutz, Larry Laiken, Bill Pemberton, Lisa Chen, Dolores Bravo, Jason Snyder, Joe Concra, Ruth Wetzel, Umeko Foster, Ray Lankford, Jim Donnelly, Scott Coffel, Sara Veglahn, David Van Foss-en, Mary Baumann

Clothing: Robert D. Bott, Dave Moburg, Shirley Bott, Vicki Bott, John Wiebke, Sandy Snyder, Pat Gilchrist, Jill Fisher, Bob 'Capo' Fisher

Advice: Mort Morehouse, Rita Morehouse, Rita Oldenburg, David Vardeman, Michael Moore, Warren Frazier, Todd Kimm, Citlali Foster, Jim Brown, Prasenjit Gupta, David Lee Miller

ABOUT THE AUTHOR

Rick Harsch lives in La Crosse, Wisconsin where he is working on the novel that will complete, with *The Driftless Zone* and *Billy Verité*, his "La Crosse trilogy." He was recently the recipient of the James Michener/Copernicus Award for this novel.

◆

ABOUT THIS BOOK

The text for this book was composed by Steerforth Press using a digital version of Sabon, a type face designed by Jan Tschichold and first cut and cast at the Stempel Foundry in 1964. All Steerforth books are printed on acid free papers and this book was bound with traditional smythe sewing by Quebecor Printing Book Press Inc. of Brattleboro, Vermont.